Jane wat[...]

She had exp[...] [...]he
saddle and h[...] [...]s a
charming m[...] [...]his
staying with Lady Farringdon at this time was
fortunate.

Walking back into the house, Jane recalled the
slightly dazed look in his eyes when he'd first
seen Amanda. There was no doubting that he
had been much taken with her. It was too soon
to be making plans yet, of course. But it was
fortunate. Very fortunate indeed.

Anne Herries lives in Cambridge but spends part of the winter in Spain, where she and her husband stay in a pretty resort nestled amid the hills that run from Malaga to Gibraltar. *Miraflores* means 'See the flowers', and there are lots of beautiful flowers to see. Gazing over a sparkling blue ocean, watching the sunbeams dance like silver confetti on the restless waves, Anne loves to dream up her stories of laughter, tears and romantic lovers. She is the author of over thirty published novels, thirteen of them for Harlequin Mills & Boon. Writing has been a dream come true—a dream she enjoys sharing with her readers through their welcome letters.

AN IDEAL MATCH

Anne Herries

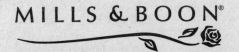

MILLS & BOON®

First published in Great Britain 1998
Harlequin Mills & Boon Limited,
Eton House, 18-24 Paradise Road, Richmond, Surrey TW9 1SR

© Linda Sole 1998

ISBN 0 263 81155 7

Set in Times Roman 10½ on 11 pt.
04-9809-90297 C1

Printed and bound in Great Britain
by Caledonian International Book Manufacturing Ltd, Glasgow

Chapter One

It was a beautiful morning in June, sun streaming through the leaded lights of the parlour window, softening the slight shabbiness of old furniture and playing over the glass lustres on the mantelpiece to shower the room with a rainbow of colour. The woman sitting by the window had a wistful expression in her eyes as she looked out on a garden filled with roses and fragrant flowers, their perfume wafting on the gentle breeze towards her.

Jane Osbourne sighed, conscious of a faint ennui, which she was struggling to throw off. She had no right to feel bored, there was always so much to occupy her—but she longed for some excitement, something that would take her away from domestic problems.

She was too familiar with her home to notice any fraying of curtains or wear on the arms of the comfortable sofa, nor would she have been particularly concerned if she had. Her mind had for the past hour been wrestling with more important things—like the loss of some five hens to a fox the previous night and the general running of the family estate, which had been in her charge for several years now.

'Oh, bother!' she muttered to herself and stood up, determined to shake off this unaccountable mood of self-indulgence. Her life was hers to order as she wished, and

it was quite her own fault if she was sitting at home mop-
ing when she might just as easily be out visiting friends.
'This really will not do!'

She glanced up as someone knocked at the door.

'Captain Carter has called, miss,' said Jane's little parlour maid, hesitating in the doorway, a faint flush in her
cheeks. 'And this letter was delivered for you a moment
ago.'

'Thank you, Bessie.'

Jane took the letter from the silver salver. She noticed
the girl's flush and suspected the reason for it. Captain
Carter still thought himself the dashing young officer who
had, many years previously, been the toast of every
London society hostess, but was now one of Jane's trio
of devoted but highly unsuitable suitors, and incapable of
greeting any female without quizzing her. He had been a
kind friend to her father, visiting Mr Osbourne most days
during his long and distressing illness, and a good neighbour to her.

Jane liked him, despite his unfortunate habit of asking
her to marry him at least once a month.

'Ask the Captain to…' She gave a cry of distress as
she opened the letter and found it had come from a
London solicitor whose name she did not recognize. 'No,
stay, Bessie. Please ask Captain Carter to call again tomorrow if he will. Tell him I am indisposed for the moment.'

'Is something wrong, miss?' Bessie ventured to ask,
knowing her mistress well enough not to fear being
thought impertinent. Miss Jane was one of the best, kindest ladies ever born, and if anyone ever asked Bessie
would swear to it. Not that it was likely, she being only
a servant and beneath the notice of some. Indeed, in most
households she would not have been permitted to speak
unless spoken to. But Miss Jane never showed anything
but respect and an unfailing courtesy towards her people—just as she did the old flirt waiting in the main par-

lour. If it had been up to Bessie she would have shown certain folk the door long ago, but Miss Jane was a real lady. 'Not bad news, I hope, miss?'

'Yes. I fear it is,' Jane said as she read on quickly. 'An old friend of my mother's has died—and her ward is coming to visit with us. Good gracious! It seems we must expect her within a few days. Pray tell Mrs Bracks the best guest chamber will need airing—' She broke off as they both heard something and the girl moved aside to allow a young man to enter the parlour.

He was dressed in the height of fashion: his boots had a superb gloss, his hair was impeccably cut, his pantaloons fitted to his shapely thighs like a second skin, his coat had been fashioned at the hands of a master—and his cravat was a work of art. All this was not lost on Jane, who stared at him in surprise and some disquiet.

'John…' she cried, starting to her feet. 'What are you doing home? Is something wrong?'

'I'll explain later,' he said, avoiding her eyes. His manner was sheepish and she guessed what might be behind his unexpected arrival. 'It was just a prank, Jane, but old Phillips made such a fuss that…'

'Thank you, Bessie, you may go.' Jane waited until the door closed behind the girl before giving her brother a searching look. 'You haven't been sent down?' She read the answer in his guilty face. 'Oh, John! Why?'

Jane did not believe she was being overly prejudiced in his favour to think him an exceptionally handsome man. His dark hair suited him cut in the style long favoured by Mr Brummel, and his shoulders were wide enough for fashion without excessive padding. Blessed with considerable charm and intelligence, he was very dear to her, but there was no doubting that he could on occasion be a very troublesome young man. Especially when he had been drinking with his friends, who were apt to be wild when in their cups.

'We'd had a little too much wine,' he confessed, a look

of shame in his dark brown eyes. 'There were three of
us—and I drew the short straw. I had to run old Phillips's
unmentionables up the flagpole for a wager. All the fellows turned out to see and it caused a bit of a rumpus.'

'No wonder he was cross.' Jane shook her head at him,
trying her best not to laugh but not succeeding. 'It was a
foolish thing to do, my dear—but hardly enough to get
you sent down. Indeed, I think you have been harshly
treated.'

'Well, that's what we thought.' Her brother sighed and
ruffled his hair artistically. 'Apparently, it was the last
straw. And, truth to tell, we *had* been cutting a few larks
all term—so he decided to make an example of us. We've
all been sent home.'

'I suppose it was bound to happen,' she said, accepting
the fact because there was no point in making a fuss over
something that couldn't be helped. 'As it happens, it may
be more fortunate than you suppose. Now that you're here
you will be able to help run the estate. It seems that I am
to have a more pressing duty…'

John Osbourne relaxed and breathed a deep sigh of relief; he had been giving himself some stick as he rode
home, imagining an unpleasant scene. He was an amiable
young man who always preferred to take the easy line if
possible, and, being as fond of his sister as she was of
him, would have hated to be in her bad books.

Jane had indeed been almost like a mother to him since
their dearest mama had died of a fever ten years earlier.
In the intervening years, Jane had been a tireless helpmeet
to their grieving father, giving up her one decent chance
of marriage to nurse Mr Osbourne when his health began
to decline. John knew he owed her a great deal.

It was nearly a year now since brother and sister had
stood together, united in grief at Mr Osbourne's graveside.
If it had not been for Jane, John would have been forced
to take on the burden of the estate long ago, thus forfeiting
several years of freedom. He had used those years to sow

his wild oats, and now felt ready to be a support to his
sister.

'You're a complete sport, Janey,' he said. 'Most sisters
would have cut up rough or read me a lecture.'

'It would be useless,' she replied, sending him a look
of mild reproof mingled with affection. 'Father wanted
you to have a good education, but I never thought you
were suited to an academic life. The army might have
been more to your liking.'

'I've let Father down.' John looked ashamed. 'And
you…'

'Not at all,' she replied in a bracing tone. 'I am not in
the least put out by your coming home sooner than we
expected. I have been in the fidgets lately, but now it is
all changed. I warn you, I shall rely on you to help me
out once Amanda arrives.'

'Amanda?' He looked at her in surprise, as well he
might, never having heard of the girl previously. 'Who is
Amanda?'

Jane paused for thought, turning to glance at herself for
a moment in the heavily carved, gilt-framed wall mirror.
She was perhaps dressed a little less fashionably than her
brother but had a natural air of elegance, which more than
made up for anything her gown lacked. Her luxuriant dark
hair was swept up in a shining coronet, which gave her a
regal look. She had a clear skin, fine features and eyes
that were more green than hazel just at that moment—but
she looked tired to her brother's way of thinking. Too
much of her youth had been squandered on the care of an
invalid and the duties of a not inconsiderable estate.

'Do you remember Miss Mary Roberts?' Jane asked.
'She used to come and stay when we were younger. She
was Mama's best friend. I liked her very much but I
hadn't heard from her for almost two years. Now I've
learned, a little late in the day, that she died three months
back—and apparently her will, which they were unable to
find for some time, nominated me to take over her role

as the guardian of a young girl. Amanda is—or was—her great-niece, and Mary's ward since her parents were drowned in a shipwreck some years ago. I believe they were on their way home from India, where they had spent some time as missionaries. Amanda is, of course, still too young to handle her own affairs and it seems—for some reason known best to herself—Mary Roberts decided I was the fittest person to have charge of her.'

'She had no right to do that!' John exclaimed, indignant on her behalf. 'To lumber you with the charge of a girl you don't know, without even consulting you— it is the outside of enough! You should refuse to accept.'

'Mary Roberts was very rich,' Jane said, wisely ignoring her brother's outburst. 'She has left a handsome bequest to me—and the remainder of her fortune in trust for Amanda. She will have a generous income of her own so I shall not be burdened in that way.'

'That is something,' John admitted. 'But you will nevertheless be obliged to put yourself out for the girl. How old is she?'

'Not yet eighteen. I shall have to think of taking her to London at some time in the future, but she is a little young to be introduced into Society for the moment. We often entertain our friends here at the Lodge, so it will serve as a means of overcoming any shyness she may at first suffer.' Jane gave her brother a smile of great sweetness. 'I think I shall enjoy having the child to stay. It will give me a new interest. You will be kind to her, won't you, dearest?'

'For your sake, of course.' He bent to drop a kiss on the top of her head. 'I saw one of the Troublesome Trio as I came through—do they still plague you with their attentions?'

Jane nodded, her mouth quirking as she tried to suppress her mirth. 'I fear they do, the poor dears! I have tried, again and again, to convince them all that I have no thought of marriage but they all seem to imagine that I cannot survive without one of them to take care of me…that I am really eager to be married.'

Her eyes lit with amusement, but she did her best to suppress it. It really was too bad of her to laugh, when they were all so kind.

'To one of them? I should hope not indeed!' John did not try to hide his disgust. 'If you wanted a husband, which you probably don't—being no longer a green girl and settled in your ways—I'm sure you could do better than the Trio.'

Jane smiled at his indignation and all too accurate description of herself, then shook her head. At six and twenty she was very much on the shelf. Any chance of making a good marriage—the kind that would be agreeable to her—had passed her by. The fact that she had been ardently pursued by her three unsuitable admirers for several months was a source of continuing amusement to her, though she had no illusions concerning their various reasons for wanting to marry her.

The Reverend Bertie Burrows, plump, flatulent and an endless bore in the pulpit each Sunday, was enamoured of the excellent dinners she gave regularly for her friends and neighbours. Having endured the tasteless efforts of his housekeeper in the draughty dining room at the Vicarage, Jane couldn't blame him for coveting a permanent place at her table.

Captain Carter had retired from a lifetime's service in his regiment; a bit of a dasher with both the ladies and his hunter, he rode better than most men in the county and had an eye for a pretty ankle. Of the three Jane liked him best. Unfortunately, he was an unlucky gambler and needed a wife with a fortune of her own to restore his crumbling estate.

Sir Charles Pendlebury was comfortably off, but, having seen his third wife recently buried and with a brood of six noisy children all under the age of fourteen, was desperate to marry again.

Jane had never for one moment considered marrying any of them, but felt a certain sympathy towards them, was grateful for their friendship, which had saved her from a great deal of boredom these past months, and resolutely gentle in rebuffing their advances.

'I've no intention of marrying,' she told her brother now. 'For the moment I am content here. We have always got on well, I think, and when you marry I shall take a house in Bath and visit you twice a year.'

'You will not!' John denied hotly. 'This is your home as much as mine and you shall never leave it—unless you marry a man you love.'

'How fierce you are, dearest John,' said his amused sister. 'I am not likely to fall in love at my age, and do not wish for a marriage of convenience. No, I am quite content with my life for the time being—and I do not think you are ready to take a wife just yet?'

'Not for years,' he declared stoutly. 'All I want is to learn the business of the estate and make you proud of me.'

'Then you shall start today. Ask Ned to have our horses saddled and we'll ride over to the home farm and talk to Peter Meadows. He has a problem with the roof of his barn.'

'I'll see to the horses at once,' John said, and walked to the door. Pausing there, he looked back at her. 'Thank you for not making me feel more stupid than I already do, Janey.'

'We shall forget the incident,' she said, slipping her letter into the top drawer of the bureau. 'I'm glad to have you home, John.'

He was convinced of her sincerity and left without further ado. She sighed as he closed the door behind him. The letter from Mary Roberts's solicitor had caused her far more concern than her brother being sent down from university. She would do her best for the unfortunate girl, of course, and was prepared to be sympathetic. Amanda would naturally be grieving for her great-aunt, who had cared for her since the tragic death of her parents; they would all have to do their best to raise her spirits when she arrived.

She wasn't expected for a few days. Time enough for Jane to get used to the idea of having a young girl in her charge…

It was such a lovely afternoon, the air soft and warm, drowsing to the sound of bees droning, tiny birds trilling their impatient song from the branches of scrubby gorse bushes or flitting from one patch of wild flowers to another.

Jane was enjoying her ride across the wide sweep of the moor, which was dotted with large boulders here and there and cut through by a shallow, tumbling stream. She had earlier been for a wild gallop to settle her mare, who had been frisky after a couple of days spent in the stable, and now she was cantering gently, making her way home in time for tea.

The sharp crack of a pistol shot somewhere nearby made her mare prick its ears and snort uneasily. The shot had not been close enough to cause Dainty Miss to bolt but had come from somewhere ahead. Jane spurred the horse on and, as she passed the cluster of boulders which had obscured her view, was shocked to see a man lying on the ground.

Dismounting hastily, she hurried to the man's side and knelt beside him on the rough ground, peering anxiously into his face, which she could not help noticing was exceptionally handsome. His hair was as black as a raven's wing, and when he opened his eyes and stared up at her— which he did, to her relief, almost at once—she saw they were a very clear ice blue.

'Damn and blast him!' the stranger muttered as he sat up, then glared at her suspiciously. 'Who the blazes are you?'

'Jane Osbourne...' she said, not in the least disturbed by his less than polite greeting. In the circumstances his choice of words was really quite mild. 'I was riding and heard a shot...'

He touched the side of his head. She was horrified to see blood on his fingers. Until that moment she had not truly realized how close he had come to being killed, and it gave her quite a turn.

'That rogue winged me,' he muttered, apparently more indignant than distressed. 'Damn his eyes!'

'Someone actually shot at you? Good gracious! I had thought it must have been an accident. Someone after a hare, perhaps. Did you see who it was?'

'Some wretched highwayman,' he muttered. 'Had the effrontery to ask for my purse and when I told him what he might do...'

'I had not heard there was a highwayman in the area.' She frowned as he struggled rather unsteadily to his feet, catching at her arm for a moment to steady himself. 'Are you badly hurt, sir?'

'Shaken rather than hurt,' he said, his eyes narrowing as he looked at her. She sensed that his pride was more damaged than his head. 'I dare say the rogue meant only to scare me—but he'll pay for it if we ever meet again.'

'We must hope you won't.' Jane shivered, feeling goosebumps all over as she thought of what might have happened. 'I suppose your horse was frightened off by the shot?' She glanced round for some sign of it but could see none.

'I was on foot.' He glared at her once more, an air of defiance about him now. 'I'm an amateur botanist and was looking for wild flowers...an odd pastime for a man, you may feel?'

Jane did but was too polite to say so. It struck her that he was extremely well turned out, and looked more suited to the hallowed precincts of a gentleman's club than the studious life of a botanist, amateur or otherwise.

There was perhaps something a little mysterious here.

'My home is not far across there...a mile or so.' She pointed out the direction with her whip. 'My mare will carry us both for that short distance—and I should like, if you will permit me, to tend your wound and give you a little brandy for the shock.' She gave him a winning smile as he hesitated. 'I confess I should be glad of your company if there are such wicked rogues on the moor.'

'I am very willing to see you safely home, ma'am,' he said as she had known he must, because he was a gentleman. And no gentleman could refuse to escort a lady when she might be in danger. 'But I shall not burden your horse with my weight. Why do we not walk together since your home is so near?'

'An excellent suggestion,' she agreed readily, falling in with his wishes out of a desire to see him safely attended. To ride off and leave a man who had come within inches of losing his life was something Jane could never do, but she could tell that he was used to having his own way and guessed he would respond more easily to persuasion than bullying.

'What did you say your name was?'

'Jane Osbourne.'

'Maximilian,' he said after a moment's hesitation and offered his hand. It was cool to the touch and felt strong, firm, as she took it. 'I believe I was rather abrupt earlier; please forgive me. I am honoured to meet you, Miss Osbourne. I am staying with the Farringdons at Ormond House and your name was mentioned the other evening. I believe you are dining with us soon?'

'Yes, indeed,' she replied. 'I had not heard there were visitors at Ormond. How long do you stay, sir?'

'My visit is of indeterminate length,' he said, looking thoughtful. 'But I believe I shall stay for another week or two. I have business at home but...yes, I believe I may stay a little longer.'

'Then your mission today was successful?' He seemed

puzzled so she said, 'You were looking for wild flowers—
did you find what you wanted?'

'Ah, yes…' Did she detect the merest glimmer of humour in those eyes? She suspected him of not being quite
truthful with her. 'Yes, I believe my mission was successful.'

'I saw some fritillaries growing by the stream back
there,' she said, with a little toss of her head to indicate
the track behind them. 'They were quite delightful…such
dainty things.'

'A little late in the season, I think?' He raised his brows
at her, and she laughed at being caught out. 'Yes, strange
as it may seem, I do know a little of these things, Miss
Osbourne. My sister was a keen botanist from childhood
and I must confess my interest springs mostly from hers.
I was hoping to present her with a rare orchid pressed
between pages of notepaper.'

'You must be fond of her,' Jane said, still not completely convinced that a flower was his reason for wandering alone on the moors. There was something about
this man that intrigued and puzzled her. Yet as a guest of
the Farringdons he must be respectable and his manners
were those of a gentleman—once he had recovered from
his initial shock, that was. However, being shot at and
wounded—or at least grazed—by what could have been
a fatal ball was surely excuse enough for one small show
of temper and she was inclined to forgive him.

'Lady Farringdon and I have a comfortable relationship.' There was a challenge in his eyes now and Jane
blushed like any schoolroom miss. 'Don't tell me she has
never mentioned my name to you? I am deeply mortified.
Perhaps she may have spoken of me as Max?'

'Lord Massingham!' Jane gave a cry of embarrassment
as she suddenly realized who he must be. 'My wits must
have gone begging. Of course. Lady Farringdon has spoken of you several times. Please do forgive me.'

'For what?' he asked with a lift of his mobile brows.

'I do not flatter myself that the mere mention of my name should command your instant attention. I have it on good authority that you have a great many matters to take up your time—that you are in fact a very capable young lady.'

'Hardly young…but if you mean that I run the estate…' She wrinkled her forehead. 'While my father was alive I consulted him and afterwards… I have neighbours and friends. Besides, my brother has now come home from Cambridge so much of the burden will be lifted from my shoulders.'

'Your brother has finished his education?'

'A little sooner than was expected.' Jane smiled at him, completely unaware of how charming she looked with the roses in her cheeks and her hair a little wind-blown where it had escaped from beneath her hat. 'Mortified as I am to say it, I'm afraid exception was taken to an incident with a pair of unmentionables.'

'I see. Your brother is a young man of spirit.' Lord Massingham looked amused. 'The careless days of youth…'

'It was high spirits, nothing more,' Jane said, 'but an example was made and perhaps it was just as well. John was never suited to the life. Some education was necessary, of course, but my brother is intelligent and I hardly think it advantageous for him to read Latin and Greek beyond a certain standard, which he has done since the age of nine. We shared the same tutor, and it was a game between us to see who could best the other. Naturally John has gone far beyond me now. Which is only right and proper, don't you think? It would not do for a female to be too bookish, would it?'

There was a flicker of appreciation in Massingham's eyes as he looked at her. 'You are indeed a remarkable woman, Miss Osbourne. I see my informant did not lie.'

'Now you *are* flattering me. I am not particularly

clever, sir, but I see things in a clear light and do not care to make a fuss without good reason.'

'How very wise,' he agreed, the corner of his mouth twitching slightly. 'Just the sort of woman one wishes for as a comfortable companion but so seldom finds—except in advanced years.'

She suspected him of laughing at her, but decided not to take umbrage. After his first outburst he had proved himself a reasonable companion, and, though she suspected something deeper than he chose to reveal about his reasons for being alone on the moor, she was determined that she would keep him in an agreeable frame of mind until she had attended to his wound and administered what other comforts she could induce him to accept before seeing him on his way. Even thinking him a stranger she must have shown him every consideration, but now that she knew he was the brother of one of her most hospitable neighbours she was even more anxious to be of help.

They walked leisurely in the warm sunshine, talking of this and that, almost as though they had met at a social affair. Jane discovered she was enjoying herself excessively. Especially when, after some minutes had passed, she began to discover that they had several shared acquaintances.

'Yes,' Max said as she mentioned a lady she had met recently. 'Sir Hugo's wife—now you mention it, Miss Osbourne, I did notice a certain tendency to gossip.'

'Fie on you, sir!' she cried, her eyes brimming with mischief. 'I said no such thing—only that she had kept me talking so long that I was almost late for my appointment with your sister.'

'You forget I have met the lady,' he replied, a definite twitch developing at the corner of his well-shaped mouth. 'It is too late for deception, Miss Osbourne. I know you found her as boring as I did…'

'Oh dear,' she said, mortified. 'Did it show that much?

I must watch my tongue in future or I may give offence where none was intended.'

'I have a talent for detecting these things,' he said. 'But I doubt that many would have been as quick to discover your secret—which, you may depend upon it, is safe with me.'

Jane was amused. She was lucky in having a great many friends whose company she enjoyed, but few of them could match this man for wit and temperament. She had not relished a conversation as much as this for a long time.

'Here is the Lodge,' she said as her home came into view. 'Please come in and let me bathe your head, sir— and perhaps a glass of brandy for medicinal purposes?'

'If your brandy is drinkable I shall take a glass for its own sake,' he said, 'and if it will make you happy to play the ministering angel...' He shrugged. 'I believe I have suffered little harm—the ball merely grazed my scalp. I shall no doubt have a thundering headache for some hours but nothing worse.'

'Does your head ache?' She looked at him in concern. He had given no sign of being in pain, but was perhaps not of the disposition to show any weakness. Her father had been very much of that ilk, making light of what had been a most debilitating illness. 'Perhaps a tisane instead of the brandy?'

'Now you go too far,' he said, with a look of disgust. 'The brandy and bandage and I shall be on my...'

They had entered the front hall together to be confronted by a mountain of luggage; trunks, boxes and miscellaneous clutter had almost completely blocked the entrance. So much of it that Jane was quite taken aback and could only stare in dismay.

'It seems you have company...' He gave her a quizzical look. 'Were you expecting someone?'

'Yes—but not for another three days.' Jane glanced up

as footsteps came clattering down the stairs. 'John—when did Amanda arrive?'

'Just a few minutes ago,' he said, and grinned at her. 'You're in for a surprise, Janey. Lord! You could have knocked me down with a feather when I saw her.'

'What do you mean? No, pray do not tell me,' Jane corrected herself hastily. Her brother was not always the most tactful of men. 'Say hello to Lord Massingham— he's Lady Farringdon's brother.'

'Yes, of course. We've already met once previously, but I don't suppose you remember me, sir?' John offered his hand, his manner a mixture of friendship and the deference owed to a man some ten or fifteen years his senior. 'It was at Newmarket and I was with some friends who were neighbours of yours.'

'I remember you distinctly,' Max said. 'You gave me some very good advice on the winner of the next race.'

'Good Lord! Did I really?' John asked, astonished. 'I couldn't have taken it myself; I went away without a guinea to my name.'

'I on the other hand was a winner,' Max assured him. 'At ten to one. I wagered my companion that the horse would lose and it did. I came off with a hundred guineas.'

'You're bamming me,' John cried, and laughed good-humouredly. 'Thank goodness for that! I should have been wretched if I'd tipped the winner and not backed it myself.'

'That would have been the outside of enough,' Max agreed with him, a touch of humour in his eyes. 'Andrew was quite convinced you had it right and backed it for twenty guineas as well as taking me on.'

'Poor fellow. He must have wished me to blazes.'

'Oh, no, he took it well enough and…' Massingham's words trailed away as he glanced up at the girl on the stairs. She was poised there artlessly, her hand resting lightly on the rail, a vision of youth and beauty in a gown of palest buttercup-yellow, her hair the colour of spun silk, tumbling about her face in delicious disarray. Her eyes were a deep blue, her mouth a perfect cupid's bow that needed no artifice to give it a rosy tint, and her complexion had that unmatchable combination of cream and rose which made English women so outstanding. 'Good grief!'

Jane was struck by his expression at that moment but not surprised. She was amazed at how lovely Amanda was and thought that if she had been a man she too might have fallen instantly in love with her.

'Amanda, my dear.' She went forward, smiling warmly as the girl ran down the last few stairs. 'How fortunate that you could come to us sooner than planned.'

'John assured me you would say that,' Amanda said, her manner bright and confident. 'I was apologizing for being such a nuisance but he told me you were a sport and would make nothing of it. I had been in London with friends and when we got back it was all such a rush, because they were going down to Bath and wanted to make sure I was safely on my way before they left.'

'You had been in London?' Jane was puzzled and a little shocked, though careful not to show it. 'Did you not know of Mary Roberts's death?'

'Well, yes…but that was nearly three months ago. Besides, Mary told me strictly I wasn't to wear mourning for her—and I was invited to stay with my friends until everything was settled. Since they were going to London I thought… Perhaps I ought not to…but it was so awful after she… I dare say you think it uncaring of me?' The last few sentences came out in a tumble as she flushed uncomfortably.

Jane saw the shadows come to her eyes, and remembered the girl's unhappy history. 'No, of course I shall not. It was sensible of Mary to forbid mourning. Black is so unbecoming and dull for young girls.'

'Very,' murmured Max from behind her. 'Especially when that girl is a beauty. Please, Miss Osbourne, won't you introduce me? I should very much like to make the acquaintance of your delightful guest.'

The sparkle had returned to Amanda's eyes at hearing herself called a beauty and she dimpled as the introductions were made. Jane made a mental note to thank Lord Massingham for his assistance one day: it was far better to see this child happy, and she had no wish to censure her. Guided by prudence, she had told her neighbours only that Amanda was coming to stay, which was just as well since otherwise some of them might have been shocked by her appearance. She ought properly to have worn black for at least six months, but it would not have suited her and if she was merely following Mary's own wishes there was no more to be said on the matter.

'Oh, your head is bleeding,' Amanda cried as she noticed a trickle at the corner of Lord Massingham's temple. 'Did you have an accident, sir?'

'Merely a silly fall from my horse,' he returned, with a warning glance at Jane. 'Nothing to fret over. Miss Osbourne is going to patch me up—and then perhaps we can all take tea together?'

Jane hid her smile. He was talking very differently now. Tea indeed! Yet it was hardly surprising he should change his mind when you considered how lovely Amanda was. She was quite certain that, before too many months had passed, there would be a score of young men beating a path to her door on the chance of impressing a girl who was both a beauty and an heiress.

And it was going to be very different having her as a guest than the frightened and miserable child Jane had pictured. Very different indeed!

Chapter Two

'Tea in the garden!' Amanda cried and clapped her hands in delight. 'Of all things I love to eat alfresco. I think I shall be very happy living here with you and Jane.'

John could not help noticing the way her hair glittered like spun gold in the sunlight. He smiled as he set one of the garden chairs for her so that she was partially shaded by the branches of an ancient apple tree, and would not damage her perfect complexion. What a very beautiful girl she was. He had never seen anyone he thought more lovely.

'Did you often take tea in the garden at home?'

'Oh, no, not often—not since I was a child.' Shadows clouded her face for a moment. 'Aunt Mary was too frail to sit outdoors much. She had been ill for months before she died, you know.'

'So you were not in the habit of entertaining?'

'My great-aunt's friends came quite often—and then there was Molly Wainwright, of course. Molly is my very best friend—or she was until I met you and Jane.' Amanda dimpled charmingly.

'It was the Wainwrights who took you to London, I believe?'

'Oh, yes!' Her eyes lit up once more. 'We had such

fun—visiting the gardens at Vauxhall and the theatres.
And there were such wonderful shops.'

'Did you attend any of the *ton* parties?'

Amanda shook her head, a wistful expression in her
expressive eyes. 'I'm afraid my dearest Molly doesn't
move in the first circles…' She saw his frown and hastened to add, 'Oh, she's perfectly respectable. Pray do not
imagine that I have been mixing with low company. My
great-aunt would never have permitted that—but Molly's
husband was only the second son of a country squire and
his portion would never run to a proper season in town.
They stay with Molly's sister for two or three weeks and
then take a house in Bath for a month—but they live
quietly and do not entertain on a large scale. Just a few
dinners and tea parties for their friends.'

John gathered from her tone that she longed for a more
exciting life, but before he could say anything more he
saw his sister and Lord Massingham leave the house and
begin to walk across the lawns towards them. Jane was
laughing at something her companion was saying, all the
faint signs of tiredness her brother had noticed a day or
so earlier seemingly banished.

'Haven't you started your tea yet?' asked Jane. 'You
shouldn't have waited for us, John. I'm sure Amanda must
be hungry after her journey.'

'Oh, yes, I am,' Amanda cried. 'Amazingly so. I always
am, you know, especially on such a lovely day. You
mustn't scold John on my account, though. We have been
having a comfortable coze.'

'Ah, Bessie is bringing a fresh tray of tea—and I believe I see a jug of Mrs Bracks's delicious lemonade.'
Jane smiled at her maid. 'Thank you. I am very ready for
a cup of tea. Now, what will you have, Amanda?'

The next few minutes of Jane's time were taken up with
dispensing drinks, dainty sandwiches and meltingly delicious cakes, but the conversation flowed about her, mixing
with the buzz of bees in the lavender beds and the sweet

trilling of a garden thrush. It was lively chatter, ranging
from the latest *on dits* to the joys of being in the country
on such a beautiful day.

'You must bring Miss Roberts to visit us at Ormond,'
Max said as Jane handed him a cup of tea with sliced
lemon. 'If the weather continues fine we could take a picnic out to the Abbey ruins. If everyone would like that?'

'A picnic?' Amanda's eyes glowed with excitement.
'Pray do let us go, Jane! Tell me, sir—are the ruins
haunted?'

'I'm perfectly certain they must be,' he replied, a faint
lift to the corners of his mouth. 'They are situated within
the grounds of my brother-in-law's estate and were burned
to the ground by King Henry the Eighth—or one of his
henchman, more like. Some of the monks died resisting
eviction from their home. I dare say it would be possible
to see at least two or three of the poor wretches walking
the ruins at midnight.' He laughed as Jane pulled a dis-
approving face at him. 'I fear, however, they will not be
so obliging as to put in an appearance at our picnic.'

'So I should hope,' cried Jane. 'You will give us nightmares, sir. Amanda will lie awake all night with the
frights.'

'Oh, lordy! I am not so pudding-hearted as that,'
Amanda instantly denied. 'It gives one such delicious
shivers down the spine to visit haunted ruins, and is the
greatest good fun. My great-aunt's house was supposed
to have a ghost—a lady in white—but I was never fortunate enough to catch sight of her.'

'I am very thankful that mine has none,' said Jane.

'What a spoilsport you are, Miss Osbourne,' reproached
Lord Massingham, with an amused twist of his lips. 'Now
at my home, Miss Roberts, I could offer you at least two
spectres. We have a grey lady and a headless Cavalier…at
least, he is said to carry his head under his arm and moan
a great deal. Which he might well in the circumstances,
don't you think?'

'Have you seen him?' Amanda was clearly enthralled, eyes glowing like pale sapphires, lips parted in breathless anticipation.

'Since he comes to warn the head of the house of approaching death I am happy to affirm that I have not—though once, when I was a boy, I did have a brief glimpse of the grey lady.'

'No! Did you?' Amanda squeaked with excitement. 'What did she do?'

'She walked through a wall,' he replied, the merest flicker of humour in his eyes. 'I have since discovered that there was once a door in that particular spot, though it was later bricked up.'

'How I should have loved to see her!'

'You are very brave,' Jane remarked with a smile. 'I think I should have screamed—or fainted.'

'You would not be so hen-hearted,' her brother retorted. 'You would be far more likely to ask what she wanted and whether she had lost her way.'

'I fear you are right. I am sadly practical.'

Jane said this in such a dismal tone that her guests very reprehensibly erupted into laughter.

'You are all of you most ill-mannered,' she reproved them with an admonishing wag of her finger. 'I shall be awake all night with the frights—or worse still dreaming of headless Cavaliers!'

'It would be a brave ghost to disturb your sleep,' John teased. 'Come off it, Janey! You're doing it rather too brown. You love a good ghost story as well as the next. I've not forgotten a certain Christmas before poor Mama died.'

Amanda instantly demanded to be told the story, which was of how brother and sister had conspired to play a prank on an uncle they both held in great affection.

'Poor Danty was so certain there was no such thing as a ghost.' John laughed as he concluded his tale. 'But—

by Jove!—by the time Madam here had finished scaring the life out of him he had changed his tune.'

'You rattled the chains,' Jane reminded him in mock severity. 'I only hid in the closet and moaned a little...'

'And drifted down the long gallery wearing a white sheet over your head just as he was on his way up from supper.'

'If he had not drunk quite so much brandy he would have known it was me.' Jane blushed as her guests laughed. 'I was only thirteen at the time, you wretch. And Danty's house had all those wonderful secret passages we discovered.'

'Of which he had no knowledge. I dare swear he still thinks he saw a ghost to this day.'

'They say there is a secret passage leading from Ormond House to the ruins,' Lord Massingham said, 'but if there is neither my sister nor her husband have ever found it. Personally, I doubt it—since the house was built after the Abbey was burned.'

'What could be the purpose of such a passage?' Jane asked. 'It must surely be just a rumour. Hardly a great house in the county does not have such stories attached to it and most are pure invention.'

'Unless it was built for the business of smuggling,' said John, looking thoughtful. 'We are not so very far from the coast...'

'Lord Farringdon is a magistrate,' Jane reminded him. 'I am very sure he would have nothing to do with such things.'

'But his grandfather might have done so,' Max said, a gleam in his eyes. 'I believe the sixth Marquis was a bit of a gambler—and other things besides which I dare not mention before ladies...'

Seeing the wickedness in his eyes, both Jane and Amanda instantly demanded to be told. He launched into a long, improbable tale that was clearly nonsense and designed to amuse. Since he was an excellent story-teller, the next half an hour passed very pleasantly.

It was past five o'clock before he recalled that his sister had guests for dinner and hastened away, Jane having prevailed on him to accept the loan of a horse from her stables.

'If you walk you will most certainly be late—and I have a very good gelding that is more than up to your weight, sir.'

'You are generous, ma'am.' He saluted her hand with a brief kiss. 'You will be hearing from me shortly—and now I must go!'

Jane watched as he rode away. She had expected him to be at home in the saddle and he did not disappoint her. He was a charming man and the circumstance of his staying with Lady Farringdon at this time was fortunate.

Walking back into the house, Jane recalled the slightly dazed look in his eyes when he'd first seen Amanda. There was no doubting that he had been much taken with her. It was too soon to be making plans yet, of course. But it was fortunate. Very fortunate indeed.

Jane went along the hall to Amanda's room after she had changed for dinner. She knocked and was immediately invited to enter, finding Bessie putting the finishing touches to the girl's toilette by running a green ribbon through her hair. Amanda looked more beautiful than ever, if that was possible, and Jane observed her pretty manners when she thanked Bessie for her services.

'Are you ready, dear?' Jane nodded to the maid. 'Thank you, Bessie. You may go.'

Amanda stood up and glanced at her own reflection.

'We had this gown made in London. I hope you think it suitable?'

'Very suitable,' Jane replied with an approving nod. It was a draped muslin caught in at a high waist with a wide green sash that matched the ribbon in her hair. 'You must show me your wardrobe tomorrow so that I can judge what you may need for the next few months.'

'My great-aunt allowed me to choose my own dresses, but since we seldom went anywhere I did not bother with much—that's why Molly insisted that I had some dresses made in town. I wasn't sure what I would need…but I thought this must be unexceptional.'

'We dine often with friends,' Jane said. 'You will need several pretty evening gowns. And a ballgown for the dance at Ormond House. Since Lord Farringdon married two years ago he has formed the habit of giving a summer ball. Last year I was unable to attend, because of my father—but we shall certainly do so this year.'

'Shall I be invited?' Amanda looked wistful, a little uncertain.

'Of course. Lady Farringdon is too kind to exclude you. Besides, I should not attend without you. Had you gone into blacks it might have been awkward—but I've decided that we need tell no one how long it is since Mary died. If you are asked you should merely say it was some months ago, which is perfectly true.'

Amanda bit her lip. 'Was I very wrong not to have ordered black gowns? Only Aunt Mary was so particular that I shouldn't—and Molly said it was time I put grieving behind me. I wore black for twelve months when…Mama and Papa…'

'And that was only three years ago, was it not?' Jane laid a sympathetic hand on her arm, forestalling the tears that had gathered in the girl's eyes. 'Then you certainly shall not be forced to it again, my love. I agree with Mrs Wainwright. You are young to have known so much sorrow. I am determined that you shall be happy with us.'

The tears vanished and almost at once the sparkle returned to Amanda's eyes. It seemed that it was not her nature to be downcast for long, which was something Jane admired and liked.

'I already feel so much at home,' she assured Jane.

'You've given me this lovely room—and you have such charming friends. I do so like Lord Massingham! He is such a tease.'

'Yes. Yes, he does have a remarkable sense of humour. I confess I rather like him myself.' Jane smiled at something he had said during their walk home. His sense of humour was very much in tune with her own, which was something she had not often found in a man.

'I do hope we can have a picnic at the ruins. It would be so agreeable.'

Jane smiled at the excitement in Amanda's eyes. The girl was very easy to please, and having her here would make her own life so much more interesting.

'Yes, it would,' she said. 'Shall we go down now? I believe dinner may be ready—and the one thing we must not do is to keep Cook waiting.'

'It was fortunate that Miss Osbourne happened along when she did.' Lady Farringdon looked at her brother anxiously. 'If she had not come just at that moment you might not have been so fortunate, Max.'

'I doubt he would have had another go at me, Catherine.' He frowned as he saw her worried look. 'He missed. It's over. Stop looking at me as if you thought I was about to drop dead at your feet. You are making a great deal too much fuss over this.'

'How can I not?' she asked. 'It isn't the first time, is it? There was that urn…' She shuddered with unease. 'If Andrew had not been there, I do not know what might have happened.'

'I might have been injured,' Max agreed. 'But that was an accident, Catherine. And this was probably someone shooting at a hare. Miss Osbourne thought so and I agree with her.'

'Jane does not know as much as I do, Max. Please do not try to make light of this.' She caught her breath on a sob. 'I am so very fond of you.'

'And I of you, my dear sister—but please, no fuss. I must deal with this in my own way.'

'Very well, I shall not say another word on the subject.'

'I only wish that were true.' Max gave her a rueful smile. 'I was careless, I admit it. But I shall be on my guard from now on. And I shall take steps to protect myself.'

'Oh, yes, please do,' she said, moving towards him. 'You are sometimes quite impossible, Max—but I should not want to lose you.'

'Dear Catherine,' he said, a smile in his eyes. 'Please excuse me now. I want a word with Farringdon about something.'

'Something neither of you will tell me, I suppose?' She pulled a face at him. 'Well, then, keep your secrets if you must. I am sure I do not care.'

Max smiled as she flounced off in high dudgeon. She was quite right, he had no intention of telling either her or her husband what was on his mind. The least said for the moment the better—but he rather thought Miss Osbourne had some suspicion of what he had been about.

She was, to say the least, a rather unusual young woman.

Jane was not at all surprised when Bessie announced that Lord Massingham had called the following morning. Indeed, she would have wondered at it if he had not paid a courtesy call to return the horse she had lent him. When he walked into her parlour, bearing gifts of flowers and soft fruits from his sister's garden, Jane was sitting with her friend Mrs Margaret Graham and made the introductions at once.

'Lord Massingham,' she said, a becoming flush in her cheeks. 'This is my dearest friend—Margaret Graham.'

Mrs Graham's status was obvious, being five months gone with her second child and in the full bloom of her very interesting condition.

'Madam, I am honoured to make your acquaintance.' Max bowed charmingly over her hand. 'I fear I intrude on your private conversation?'

'Oh, no,' Maggie Graham denied, blushing delightfully as his eyes conveyed both warmth and approval. 'We have been together for more than an hour. I was about to take my leave. My house is barely ten minutes from here and we are forever in and out of each other's home.'

'I'm sure you need not go on Lord Massingham's account,' Jane said. 'Are you certain you won't stay for nuncheon, Maggie?'

'I came only for a moment and must return before Mr Graham begins to think me lost. And Sarah has just started with her first tooth. Poor Nurse has more than enough to do with comforting her.' Maggie rose a little awkwardly. They kissed and Jane went to the parlour door with her. 'No, no, Jane. Stay with your guest. Bessie will see me out.'

'If you're sure.' Jane kissed her again. 'I'll come and visit with you soon—and bring Amanda.'

She returned to her former seat by the window. Massingham was standing by the spinet, glancing at some sheets of music, his back turned to her so that for a moment she was at liberty to admire his very fine shoulders.

'Mozart… Handel… Haydn… "Greensleeves…" Your tastes are varied, Miss Osbourne. I see some of my own favourite ballads. Do you play all these pieces?'

'For my own amusement, and very ill. I am not greatly accomplished—but I believe Amanda to be talented in that direction. Are you fond of music, sir?'

'I find it soothing,' he said. 'Catherine used to play for me when she was at home.'

'You do not play yourself?' He shook his head. 'Perhaps you sing?'

'With my sister sometimes. We shared many interests—as I have previously mentioned.'

'You must miss her now that she is married?'

'I was pleased to see her happily settled with Farringdon—but yes, sometimes, I miss her.'

There was a faint wistfulness about his mouth, which made Jane decide that she liked him more and more.

'Lady Farringdon is fortunate in having an affectionate brother—as I am myself.'

'John is not with you this morning?'

'He went riding with Amanda. We thought it best she should be acquainted with her surroundings. The moors are a little daunting if you have not been used to them, and there are pretty rides elsewhere if you know where to look.' She lifted her clear eyes to meet his. 'I trust you have taken no harm from that shocking incident yesterday, sir?'

'None at all, thank you.'

'Have you reported the attack?'

'No—and I beg you will not think of doing so.'

'Should we not warn others of a possible danger? Do you not think it our duty?'

Massingham gave her a searching look. 'I think you already know I was not the victim of a highwayman, don't you?'

'I suspected it,' Jane confessed. 'I think…someone tried to murder you, did they not?'

'It was an attempt to wound, perhaps to frighten me. I'm not sure murder was intended.'

She was shocked despite her earlier suspicions. 'Why should anyone wish to harm you?'

'I can think of no sensible reason.' His eyes seemed fixed to a spot just beyond her shoulder. 'I must have done something—won a wager too many or…who knows?'

'Surely it cannot be anything so trivial?'

'I wish I knew. I have felt for some time I had an enemy.' He shrugged carelessly. 'Perhaps it *was* just someone shooting for sport…an accident. It is no matter. Let us speak of something less distasteful. I have spoken to Catherine and she is delighted with the idea of a picnic at the ruins. I have come this morning on purpose to arrange it—for tomorrow, if that will suit you?'

'I can see no reason why not,' Jane replied, wondering why the suggestion of an outing she had been on several times should seem so delightful. 'Amanda talked of little else last evening. Poor child...I fear she has had an unhappy time of it these past three years. Her parents were drowned returning from their mission in India, you know—and Mary Roberts was ill for months before she died.'

'It must indeed have been hard for Miss Roberts. So many bereavements in so short a time; she has done well to recover her spirits, but I believe she has a sunny disposition.'

The sincere tone of his voice pleased Jane. It was obvious that he had both feeling and compassion towards Amanda, and who knew what other, deeper, more intimate feelings he might be harbouring towards the beautiful girl?

'I intend to see that she enjoys herself from now on.'

'Yes. We must find ways of amusing her. I am certain Catherine will enjoy getting to know her. We shall begin with the picnic and see how we go on.' His smile for Jane was full of warmth and understanding. Her heart quickened and she thought what a really charming man he was. 'And now I must go. I have errands that will not wait. Pray tell Mr Osbourne that I was sorry to have missed him—and Miss Roberts, of course.'

'Certainly. They will be sorry not to have seen you.'

Jane rose and accompanied him to the door.

She was thoughtful after he had left, more certain than ever that he was interested in Amanda. He would make the girl an ideal husband. He was perhaps fifteen years her senior, maybe more—but not too old. Oh, certainly not too old. At about four and thirty, Lord Massingham was in his prime. Attractive—no, exceptionally hand-

some! Charming. Good-natured. Intelligent. Cultured...
Jane listed his virtues in her mind.

There was no doubt he was an ideal match for her ward.
No doubt at all.

She had never thought herself the matchmaking type.
Indeed, she had been far too busy to give such thoughts
an airing for years, but John was home now. She could—
and must!—gradually relinquish the care of the estate into
her brother's hands, which would leave her with very little
to occupy her mind.

Jane frowned slightly as she wondered what she would
find to do once her brother had the reins firmly in his
hands. She had talked of retiring to Bath but knew in her
heart that she would be bored within six months.

What she really needed was a home of her own, of
course. Preferably a large country house that would ex-
ercise all her talents to keep it running perfectly. Could
she possibly consider one of the Trio as a husband? Good
grief, no! She was appalled that she had even thought of
it. She wasn't reduced to such desperate straits yet. She
had Amanda to settle first and then it would be time to
think of her own affairs.

'What a pity we missed him,' Amanda cried, a look of
disappointment in her eyes, when she was told Lord
Massingham had called while she was out. 'Did he mention the picnic?'

'We have been invited for tomorrow,' Jane said, and
the girl's smile returned even more radiantly than before.
'So, tell me, my dear—did you and John have a good
ride?'

'Why, yes,' she replied, dimpling prettily. 'It was good
fun—and your mare is such a darling. But I can't keep
borrowing her. It isn't fair to you. You will wish to ride
her yourself.'

'We must see about getting you a mount of your own,'
agreed Jane. 'What did you do at home?'

'Aunt Mary had given up her stables, apart from the coach horses, of course. I borrowed a horse from Mr Wainwright's stables when I wanted to ride.'

'Then it's high time you had something of your own.' Jane tucked her arm through the younger girl's. 'And now we should go through your wardrobe. I have a very good seamstress in town. If we send her your measurements she will make you a few gowns, which will see you through until we can visit ourselves.'

'Shall we go up to London?'

'You would find it thin of company at the moment. Nevertheless, we may go up for a short visit before the winter, when as you know the roads can be shockingly bad. Just for some shopping. Your come-out proper cannot be until next spring. Down here we may do much as we like, but in town we should be sure to meet someone who knew your great-aunt. And it would be unfortunate if your being there were to upset any of her friends.'

'I dare say they would not bother,' Amanda said. 'But it doesn't matter. Why should I want to go to London when I'm enjoying myself so much here? John is such good company—and Lord Massingham makes me laugh.'

Jane looked at her with approval. She was a good-natured girl, easy to please. Being her guardian was going to be so much less trouble than she had anticipated.

Later that afternoon, in the garden, watching Captain Carter and Sir Charles Pendlebury competing with each other for the privilege of bringing Amanda a glass of lemonade, Jane had cause to review her earlier conclusions. The news of the girl's fortune had spread even faster than she had expected.

'Your tea, Captain.'

Jane handed him a fragile porcelain cup as he came to sit in the chair beside her, having been forced to give way and let Sir Charles take the one next to Amanda.

'Thank you, m'dear.' He smiled at her, his eyes flicking

towards Amanda once more. 'Pretty little gel, that. How old did you say she was?'

'Not yet eighteen.' Jane shook her head at him in mock reproof. 'Much too young for you, sir.'

'Indeed, yes. By Jove, yes,' he agreed ruefully. 'Might have attempted the chase once, don't you know—but haven't got the bellows for it these days.' He patted his substantial chest. 'Besides, I'm devoted to you. When are you going to take pity on me, m'dear?'

'You don't need my pity or anyone else's,' Jane replied, shaking her head at him. 'You are always welcome here as a friend—but you know I don't wish to marry.'

'You should. Don't want to turn into a crabby spinster. What are you going to do when that brother of yours decides to take a wife?'

'That won't be for ages yet.'

'Don't know about that.' Captain Carter glanced at John, who had somehow managed to steal Amanda from under Sir Charles's nose and was now pushing her gently to and fro on the swing which hung from the branches of a tree. 'Seems mighty taken with that gel—not that you can blame him. Pretty thing and a fortune to boot.'

'I'm not sure there is so very much money,' lied Jane, hoping to dampen his enthusiasm. Having experienced his determined pursuit herself, she did not want Amanda to suffer the same fate. 'Besides, I'm sure she and John are simply good friends. My brother has no thoughts of marriage for years. He told me so himself.'

'Ah, well…' Captain Carter sighed deeply, apparently giving up for the moment. 'Tell me, m'dear—has that damned fox been at your chickens again?'

Their conversation turned towards things of a domestic nature. Jane listened with half an ear as she watched her brother laughing in the sunshine with Amanda. It would not be surprising if John were to fall a little in love with her—what man could resist such an innocent beauty? But she was sure there was no real cause for concern.

Amanda had shown a decided preference for Lord Massingham's company. Much as she admired and loved her brother, Jane could not think that Amanda would find him more attractive than Lord Massingham. No, no! Given the choice, any woman must favour the older man. There was no true contest.

Jane smiled contentedly. Her brother and ward were like two children squabbling and playing. A match between them was unlikely. Unsuitable. It would be far better to give her ward a little push towards Lord Massingham. Nothing too obvious. Indeed, on reflection, she realized she need do nothing at all. If they were in each other's company often enough the inevitable was bound to happen.

Chapter Three

'We are so lucky to have another fine day,' Lady Farringdon said to Jane. 'When Max suggested the picnic I was certain the weather would change—but no. The gods have been truly kind to us.'

They were sitting on cushions placed for them by Lady Farringdon's servants on a raised bank looking down at the ruins. The sun was shining and there was scarcely a cloud in the sky nor even a cool breeze to spoil the perfection of the tranquil scene.

'Yes, indeed,' Jane agreed, adjusting her silk parasol. 'It is most fortunate. Amanda would have been so disappointed had it rained. And your brother arranged it all just to please her, which was amazingly kind of him.'

'Oh, he is always thoughtful,' his sister said. 'And no one would grudge that child anything. Such a pretty girl. Max told me, but I was sure he had exaggerated. However, I must admit I have hardly ever seen a more lovely girl—and so unspoilt.' Lady Farringdon wrinkled her smooth brow. 'Speaking of my brother—where do you suppose he has disappeared to?'

The compliment to Amanda was all the more impressive having come from a recognized beauty. Catherine Massingham had been the most sought-after prize of her own season, turning down several very flattering offers before accepting Lord Farringdon's. Pleased with her ladyship's remarks, Jane did not at first detect the note of anxiety in her voice.

'Max can be so foolhardy at times!'

'I beg your pardon?' Jane was startled into awareness. 'What did you say?'

'My stubborn brother. He is not with the others—see, there is your brother and Amanda. Depend upon it, Max has wandered off alone again. How vexing of him!'

Jane glanced towards the ruins which consisted of several crumbling stone walls, an outer stairway leading to an unsafe tower and little else. Having seen them before, she had chosen to sit with her hostess, leaving the others to explore by themselves.

'Where is Max?' Lady Farringdon asked, looking anxious as they came to join her and Jane. 'I thought he was with you?'

'Oh, he was,' John assured her. 'He wandered off a few moments ago towards the woods. Said he was looking for a rare flower—for your collection, I think.'

'That is so like him. I wish he would not!'

Jane realized she was really worried. 'I shall go and look for him,' she said, getting up and brushing the creases from her skirt. 'I'll tell him we're waiting for our nuncheon.'

'Would you?' Lady Farringdon hesitated. 'I'm not sure—but there can be no harm in it. Only, of all things Max hates a fuss…'

'He can hardly object to being reminded of the time,' Jane said reasonably. 'Do not worry, I shall not tell him you were anxious.'

Their eyes met in a look of shared understanding.

Jane was thoughtful as she set off in the direction of the woods. It was obvious that Lady Farringdon's anxiety had nothing to do with being impatient for her meal. She must know of the attack on Lord Massingham on the moors the previous day—did she fear it might happen again? Lord Massingham had pretended not to know why someone had fired that shot at him—but Jane thought he might have been hiding the truth for reasons of his own.

If he suspected the identity of the would-be assassin, why did he persist in inviting another attack? And she believed that might be why he had gone off alone again.

It was cooler in the woods, the dense foliage cutting out most of the sunlight. Jane shivered, but not from cold. She had an odd feeling…of menace…as though someone was watching her, spying on her! She glanced round nervously, wondering if she had imagined those sounds—or was there someone near her? Her mouth went dry with fear and she caught her breath. She was sure she could hear heavy breathing, as though someone was nervous. A sharp cracking sound behind her made her jump. Someone must have trodden on a twig.

'Lord Massingham!' she called. 'Are you there?'

For a moment there was silence, then she heard the rustle of branches catching as someone pushed their way through the dense bushes ahead. It was a little frightening until she saw the tall, powerful figure coming towards her.

'Lord Massingham!' she cried, relief sweeping over her. At least he was safe. And now he was here she was no longer afraid.

'Jane!' She saw he had a thick branch in his hand; by the way he held it she guessed it had been snatched up as a means of defence. 'What on earth are you doing here?'

His brows knitted in a frown of annoyance. She knew at once that he was displeased by what he saw as interference.

'I came to tell you we are ready to have our picnic.'

'Did you indeed? Damn it!' He glared at her. 'I suppose Catherine put you up to it?'

'She…we wondered where you were.'

'I might have known she could not be trusted not to interfere.'

'What do you mean?'

Max glanced over his shoulder, gave her a warning look, took a firm hold on her arm and guided her back the way she had come. Only after they had left the woods did he stop to look at her.

'I suppose I must trust you. If only to prevent this happening again.'

Jane knew he was angry with her for following him. She took a deep breath, giving him a steady look.

'You are trying to provoke whoever shot at you into making another attack—but why?'

His eyes narrowed to thoughtful slits. 'Are you always so astute, Miss Osbourne—or have I given myself away?'

'I guessed you were lying when I found you on the moors—and then you admitted you had not been accosted by a highwayman. When you went off alone today I realized you must be trying to provoke...whoever it is.'

'My cousin Richard...or so I believe.'

'Your cousin!' Jane was shocked. He did know his attacker: it was a member of his own family. This was terrible! 'Surely not?'

'Richard is my heir,' he replied. 'The only person likely to benefit from my death. My estate is entailed, you see. So it can only be him. There is no reason for anyone else to want me dead.'

Was he trying to convince himself?

'But you will marry...have sons...'

'Perhaps...' The blue eyes were icy, forbidding. She did not dare to continue. 'Richard came to me over the matter of a gambling debt two months ago. I refused to pay. I had previously warned him that I would do so the next time he asked. The accidents began soon after my refusal.'

'Accidents?' Jane was horrified. 'You mean there has been more than one?'

'A stone urn almost fell on me at Massingham, and someone tampered with my sporting guns. If I had tried to fire them they could have exploded in my face. Fortunately, I am served by faithful friends who watch over me. I was thrust out of the way of the urn and my guns are checked regularly.'

Jane had gone very pale. She stared at him, her eyes widening with horror. It was all so much worse than she had imagined.

'This is terrible,' she said. 'But if you believe your life is in danger—why are you taking so many risks?'

His brow furrowed and for a moment she thought he would refuse to answer her, but then he nodded, seeming to accept that she was genuinely concerned.

'I cannot spend my life hiding behind friends. If I have an enemy I must draw him out—catch him in the act. Otherwise, he will eventually find a way of accomplishing my death. If he really wishes to kill me—and of that I am still in some doubt.'

'But he has tried three times! How can you doubt his intentions?'

'At Massingham there is always someone nearby,' Max said, frowning. 'I think what happened there was a warning. Richard may have hoped to push me into giving him the money he needs. I cannot yet bring myself to believe that he really wishes me dead.'

'If that was indeed his intention, he could not hope to succeed. What a fool he must be if he imagines such threats would sway you! Such behaviour is more likely to turn you the other way.'

Her indignant tone made him laugh, lightening the tension. 'I see that you understand me only too well, Miss Osbourne.'

'But you should not take risks, sir. Surely there is something else you can do?'

'I have no proof that Richard was behind any of this,' he reminded her. 'Perhaps the urn was an accident, the guns faulty…'

'And the shot that might have killed you on the moors? Can you explain that away?'

'I confess that I cannot…' He frowned at her. 'Nor the fact that someone was following me this morning. Yes, I was aware of it. You were very foolish to come in search of me, Miss Osbourne. Had I been attacked you might have been a witness—and then your life would not have been safe. He might have claimed two lives instead of one—and that would have been unforgivable.'

Jane stopped to stare at him. She too was sure that someone else had been in the woods. But was it the would-be murderer or merely an innocent woodsman on his lawful business? Had Max's sister not called out to them at that moment she would have given her opinion, but his attention was caught by Lady Farringdon's scolding.

'Ah, there you are!' she cried, a look of relief on her face. 'You have kept us waiting, Max. We are all anxious to begin our picnic.'

'Forgive me,' he begged, giving her a winning smile as he flopped down beside her on a cushion. 'I am indeed a thoughtless wretch. Please, let us eat at once. I am starving.'

'The fresh air does make one hungry,' Amanda said, turning her brilliant gaze on him. 'You should have stayed with us, Lord Massingham. It is so exciting. John thinks he may have found the secret passage you mentioned— the one that leads from the ruins to the house and must have been built by smugglers.'

'No!' Lady Farringdon gave a little cry of dismay. 'Do not say so, I pray you. I shall never sleep easy in my bed again. The very idea of it gives me the shivers.'

'What a fibster you are,' Max teased. 'When we spent hours searching for the passages at Massingham—and found them.' He smiled fondly at her. 'You were not afraid to explore them with me then, Catherine.'

'Because they led only from one part of the house to

the other. I should not like to think that someone could enter the house at night…unknown to any of us.'

'You need not worry about that,' John assured her cheerfully. 'If the passage exists, it's so well hidden that no one could know it was there. I should not have thought of looking behind the brambles if Amanda had not insisted.'

'You must show me later,' Max said, his interest aroused now. 'It would be interesting to discover if such a passage really does exist. I should like to explore it.'

'I wish you will not!' his sister cried. 'Please leave it hidden.'

'Just as you like,' he replied, but Jane saw the look that passed between him and John.

'You were saying that you thought you might make your dance a masked ball this year,' she said, to divert her hostess from something that obviously bothered her. 'Are we all to dress up in costume?'

'I thought it might be amusing.' Lady Farringdon turned to her at once. 'What do you think? And you, Amanda—should you care for a costume ball?'

'Do you mean we could wear whatever we liked—dress up like famous people from history?' She laughed and clapped her hands with delight as her hostess nodded. 'How amusing that would be! I think I should like it above all things.'

'Then that settles it,' Lady Farringdon said, amused at her transparent pleasure. 'What a lovely day it is, to be sure.'

The conversation was successfully turned from secret passages and all that their existence might signify. Jane thought it unlikely her brother had found anything of real importance. If it were that easy it would surely have been discovered long ago.

'I must go back to Massingham next week,' Max said, catching her attention. 'But I was thinking…'

'Oh, must you?' his sister said. 'I was hoping you would stay for much longer, Max.'

'I have business that will not wait…' He looked at her thoughtfully. 'Why don't you come back with me, Catherine…you and Farringdon and Miss Osbourne, John and Amanda? Massingham is that much nearer to London. We could engage the services of a seamstress, send for all the materials you will need to make your costumes for the ball, and save you all a great deal of bother… Besides, I should be grateful for your company.'

'Come with you…?' Lady Farringdon looked at him consideringly. 'Farringdon couldn't leave Ormond at the moment, but I dare say he would not object to my going. We have no social engagements for a week or so…not after our own dinner this weekend.'

'Then come,' he said, and laid his hand over hers. His eyes were warm with affection, his manner persuasive. 'It will be like old times, having you there—and I have promised to amuse Miss Roberts. I hear that you need a horse, Miss Roberts. It would please me to mount you from my stables and to find you something suitable of your own. I can engage for it that you will not be bored at Massingham. Never a day passes but what one or other of my friends arrives to keep me company.'

The expression on Amanda's face answered his question, but she sent a shy, questioning look towards Jane, waiting for her to answer.

'Should you like that, Amanda?'

'Oh, yes, please—if you think we should go.'

Jane was uncertain. Amanda had only just arrived in Cornwall, and she herself would have preferred time to get to know her ward, but she could see the girl was longing for her to accept the invitation.

'What do you think, John?'

'Stay at Massingham? I should just think so! I've heard it's a show place—good shooting and fishing too, I dare say.'

'The lakes are well stocked with carp and there are trout in the streams,' Max agreed. 'We do have plenty of game on the estate, though at the moment we could only offer rabbits or woodcock. Of course, if you care to join a shooting party in September...'

'By Jove! Do you mean it?' John was fully aware of the honour being shown him. Massingham moved in circles that John, as an insignificant country gentleman, would not normally have expected to enter. 'It's exceptionally generous of you, sir.'

Lord Massingham looked at John's sister, his brows lifting questioningly. 'So, what do you say, Miss Osbourne? Will you come—just for two or three weeks?'

Every eye was upon her. Jane could not refuse, nor in truth did she wish to. Lord Massingham's estate in Surrey was famed both for its size and magnificence. And being so much closer to London it would make the matter of refurbishing Amanda's wardrobe that much easier; they might even spend a few days in town before returning to the country.

'You are very kind to invite us, sir. We shall be delighted to accept.'

'Good. I anticipate an amusing time ahead.' Max flashed a triumphant glance at Lady Farringdon. 'I have already decided on my own costume, but I shall not tell anyone what I have in mind.'

'Oh, no, you must not,' Amanda instantly agreed. 'It will be far more exciting if we all keep our costumes a secret.'

'It is all very well for you,' John grumbled. 'But if you do not help me I shall not know what to choose.'

'Poor dear John!' Amanda teased. 'Well, perhaps I shall help *you* but we must keep it a secret from everyone else.'

'And you, Miss Osbourne—have you thought what you will come as?' Lord Massingham enquired, a wicked teasing smile flitting about his mouth. 'Or is it to be a secret?'

There was something in his eyes at that moment which

caused Jane's heart to race wildly. For a moment she felt
almost giddy, breathless. She breathed deeply, arching her
brows at him, aware that he was going out of his way to
charm her.

'I am not given to hasty judgements, sir. I shall give
the matter some careful thought.'

'How wise.' Those blue eyes were laughing at her!
'You put us all to shame, Miss Osbourne. We shall expect
something out of the ordinary now.'

'Do not expect too much.' She gave him a reproving
look to cover her momentary confusion. She could almost
think he was flirting with her. But that was impossible.
No, no, he was merely trying to gain her approval in order
to court her ward. 'Something simple is all I aspire to.'

'No, no, you do not deceive me,' he replied. 'I can see
beneath that meek face you show to the world, Miss
Osbourne. I am convinced that you will manage to out-
shine us all.'

'No, indeed, I am very sure I shall not.'

'Do not tease Jane,' his sister instructed, frowning at
him. She was a little surprised at his manner, having never
known him to show much interest in any woman.
However, the girl was very beautiful so perhaps it was
not all that surprising after all. 'This is a very good idea
of yours, Max. It may serve more than one purpose.'

'Perhaps.' For a moment the bleak look in his eyes
made Jane shiver. What was going through his mind?
'Who knows? For myself I think only that we shall be a
merry company.'

The picnic was spread out on a table before them. There
were all manner of pies, tarts, fruits, cheeses and cutlets.
Jane reached for a piece of cold chicken pie and bit into
its delicious moistness. She sensed some deep purpose
beneath his lordship's smiling banter. Had he a particular
scheme in mind? Did he hope to discover the identity of
his would-be murderer by returning to his home? She

guessed that something had happened to make him change
his plans but could not think what that might be.

Unless… Yes, that might be it, she reasoned. If these
attacks had been made in the hope of inheriting his
fortune, the arrival of a beautiful young woman at
Massingham could well bring things to a head…
especially if it seemed that his lordship was thinking of
marriage.

Max went for a late stroll in the gardens at Ormond; it
was a habit he had learned as a young man, when the
tragedy of his father's untimely death had weighed
heavily on his shoulders, and something he did when he
had a problem.

At the moment, he had two—one vastly more pleasur-
able than the other. A smile touched his mouth as he recalled a certain look in a woman's eyes. How beautiful
she had looked at that moment, and what a lively and
amusing companion she would be. He was enjoying himself immensely crossing swords with her—or he would be
if that other thing were not pressing so heavily on his
mind.

It had been hard enough to accept that anyone was trying to kill him, but now the doubts and suspicions had
begun to creep in and he did not like them. He did not
like them at all. It soured everything…even this new feeling. A feeling he thought might very well be love, since
he had never experienced anything quite like it before.

'Damn you!' he muttered aloud. 'Whoever you are.
Why don't you confront me like a man and have done
with it?'

He was not a particularly patient man. Max accepted
his own faults for what they were. In this case, however,
he had no choice but to play a waiting game.

Jane woke suddenly. For a moment she lay shivering,
wondering what had disturbed her. Had she eaten too

much supper at Lady Farringdon's the previous evening?

It had been a pleasant dinner party, attended by most of the local gentry. Jane had found herself sitting down to dinner between Sir Charles Pendlebury and her host. Lord Massingham had been at the far end of the table and, though she had exchanged amused glances with him from time to time, she had not passed more than a dozen words with him the whole evening, perhaps because whenever he had tried to approach her he had been jealously ousted by one of her admirers. In the end Max had given up and devoted himself to playing a noisy game of dominoes with Amanda and John.

Jane got out of bed and wandered over to the window as she recalled her dream. It had been of a large, empty house…and a headless cavalier. Now what in the world had made her dream such a thing?

She perched on a small seat in the window recess, puzzling over her nightmare, then, remembering the talk of ghosts in her garden a week or so earlier, she understood. Lord Massingham had spoken of such a spectre at his home—a ghost that appeared only to warn the master of the house of approaching death.

How foolish of her! How silly to have let it play on her mind. But of course just before sleeping she had been thinking of the coming visit to Massingham—and of the threat to its owner's life.

A shudder ran through her. It was too awful to be contemplated! She had known Lord Massingham only a short time but the thought that he might be murdered filled her with horror. She was unaccountably tearful at the idea that someone might wish to harm him in any way.

What foolishness was this? Jane reached for a handkerchief and blew her nose hard. Tears! For a piece of nonsense! She must not let herself give in to her irrational fears.

Nothing was certain. Even Max himself was not sure

his life was being threatened. Besides, she could do nothing to prevent it. Nor was it her concern. She naturally felt distress at the thought of a friend in danger, but she must not allow her emotions to become disordered. That would be the height of foolishness.

After all, she hardly knew him. He did seem to be an ideal match for Amanda…at least, it had appeared that way at the start. It still did! Jane dismissed the very odd thoughts that had crept unbidden into her mind.

Lord Massingham, not Max! She must not think of him as Max.

Lord Massingham had been instantly attracted to Amanda, and she to him. It was a very suitable match. Any other foolish notions that had occurred to her were quite out of the question.

Jane settled back into her bed, determinedly closing her eyes. She was six and twenty, no longer a green girl. Her ambitions now—like her duty—must be all for the lovely girl fortune had placed in her charge. It was her duty to see Amanda married to a good man—and she had every intention of doing just that.

'So you are all going to Massingham for two weeks,' Maggie Graham said as they sat together in Jane's parlour the following morning. 'I'm so pleased for you, my dear. It is ages since you went away and it will do you the world of good. You had been looking a little tired but you seem better now. There is a sparkle in your eyes such as I have not seen since your dear father died.'

'I must admit I do feel better. I still miss dear Papa, but he is with Mama now. Besides, I could not have wished him to continue in pain. And, of course, there is less for me to worry over now that John is home,' Jane said. 'Not only that, Sir Charles told me that his gamekeeper shot the rogue fox that has been killing all our chickens. So we may all rest easier.'

'I saw Sir Charles leaving as I walked up the garden

path,' Maggie said, and frowned. 'You won't marry him, will you, Jane? I have never liked him and I really could not bear it if you were his wife.'

'No, I shan't marry him—nor any of the Trio.' Jane smiled as Maggie looked relieved. 'I think I might almost prefer to take up a post as a housekeeper…'

'Surely not!' Her friend looked startled. 'You have not thought of it, Jane?'

'Oh, I have thought of it,' Jane contradicted her. 'Do not look so worried, Maggie. I know it would not do. John would never allow it—and it would hurt him to know that I had considered the idea for one moment. But I shall have to leave the Lodge one day, you know.'

'John isn't thinking of marrying yet—is he?'

'Not to my knowledge,' Jane replied. 'But he is nearly twenty. He may wish to take a wife in a year or two.'

'You may well be married yourself by then.'

'I hardly think so. No one is likely to ask me—no one I would wish to marry.'

'Perhaps you may meet someone—at Massingham. One of Lord Massingham's friends…'

'There is always that possibility, I suppose.' Jane was thoughtful. 'I think I should prefer marriage—but only to the right man. I do not believe I could make a marriage of convenience.'

'Why should you?' Maggie smiled at her. 'You are still young and attractive, Jane. Why should you not—'

What she had been about to say was interrupted by the arrival of John and Amanda. They burst into the room together, laughing and clearly excited.

'Oh, Jane!' Amanda cried. 'You will never guess what we've been doing. It was so thrilling.'

'It was Massingham's idea,' John said. 'I would never have dared alone—but he supplied lamps and ropes. It was the greatest good fun. We explored together while Amanda kept watch.'

'They wouldn't let me go with them.' Amanda pouted,

then dimpled with pleasure. 'At least, not until Lord Massingham had made sure it was safe.'

'Are you talking about the secret passage?' Jane asked. 'You haven't actually found it?'

'By Jove, that's just what we have done,' John said, eyes bright with mischief. 'It leads from the ruins to a cellar under the house. But Lady Farringdon has no need to worry—it has been bricked up from the inside.'

'So no one can get into the house that way?'

'Only the cellar,' said Amanda. 'Lord Massingham took me there once he knew it was perfectly safe.'

'Well, that is a relief.' Jane laughed as she saw the excitement in their faces. 'Do you suppose the cellar was once used to hide contraband? Ormond is at least ten miles inland, you know.'

'That's exactly why it was used,' John said. 'The goods—mostly brandy, I expect—were brought on pack horses and hidden until they could be sold safely. It goes on everywhere. You know it does, Jane. Especially during those times we have been at war with France.'

'Even in peacetime,' she agreed. 'Many people, even the most respectable, will avoid paying excise duty if they can.'

'Farringdon's father must have had the cellar bricked up,' John said. 'He probably wanted to break with the smugglers after he inherited the place. Thought it too dangerous to carry on.'

'And now it has been found again.'

'It would have been great sport if the smugglers had still been using it,' John said. 'Who knows what we might have found?'

'I am glad it was empty,' Jane said, giving a little shiver. 'The kind of men who use a place like that would not take kindly to having their secret discovered. You might have been in some danger. You could not wish for that?'

'No, I suppose not.' John looked disappointed, as

though he might have relished an encounter with a smuggler, then brightened as he thought of something. 'Massingham is a complete sport. When we were introduced at Newmarket I suspected him of being a little high in the instep—but no such thing. He's the best of companions in an adventure—and he has promised to put me up for his club next year.'

'That is rather splendid of him,' Jane said, awed. 'But you mustn't take it for granted, John. You could be blackballed.'

'With Massingham as my sponsor?' John grinned. 'I agree it won't do to say so or appear to be too certain—but it's practically in the bag. I know you don't go about much, Janey, but Massingham is out of the top drawer. All the fashionable hostesses in London fall over themselves to secure him for their parties. If he puts in an appearance for the briefest time the evening is counted a success.'

'Oh, dear!' Jane looked startled. 'I hadn't realized he had quite that power and consequence.'

'No, I rather thought you hadn't. He has been amazingly cosy with us all—perhaps because you are Lady Farringdon's friend and he is known to think the world of her. He isn't always as approachable. Believe me. I've seen him give a tremendous set-down to persons he dislikes.'

'You might have told me this before!'

Jane was quite upset. She wasn't sure why it mattered, but it did.

'Since he so obviously approves of you it hardly seemed to matter. Don't look so shocked, Jane. It makes no difference.'

'No—no, of course not.'

'Well, I must go home,' Maggie said. 'I shall see you when you return from Massingham, Jane.'

'I think I'll walk home with you. It's such a pleasant day.'

'Just as you please.'

They walked in silence for a few minutes, then Maggie stopped and laid a gentle hand on Jane's arm.

'Is something troubling you?'

'No…at least…' Jane sighed. 'It is nothing—just something John said just now.'

'About Lord Massingham?'

'Yes.'

'You like him quite a lot, don't you?'

'He has been very pleasant to all of us—and I find him an amusing companion. Yes, I do like him, Maggie.'

'And you suddenly feel he is rather too far above you in rank and consequence?'

'Not exactly. Yes, perhaps…' Jane hesitated. 'I knew he had a large estate, but I thought it comparable to Ormond.'

'I have heard it is one of the finest in England. My aunt visited once when the present Lord Massingham's mother was mistress there. Aunt Fanny said she was a cold, proud woman.'

'Perhaps she had reason to be.'

'As to that…' Maggie shrugged. 'She died only two years ago, just after Lady Farringdon came here as a bride. They say she did not approve of the match, thought her daughter could have married a duke or an earl at least. It was his lordship who supported his sister and insisted that she should marry the man she loved.'

'I wonder if…?' Jane faltered. 'Do you think his mother's attitude might have been the reason why…?'

'Why Lord Massingham has never married?'

'Yes. I had thought it a little odd but now…'

Maggie nodded. 'He does seem very taken with Amanda. She may be the very bride for him—beautiful, innocent and amenable. His mother may well have turned him against clever, strong-minded women. Yes, I should not be surprised if you are right, Jane.'

'I think he is looking for a wife now.'

A wife to provide him with the sons he needed. A bevy of children in his nursery was just what was required, to keep him safe from cousins who would stop at nothing to inherit his estate.

'You believe that is the reason he has been so amazingly friendly towards you—because he wants your approval of his marriage to Amanda?' asked Maggie, looking at her thoughtfully.

'I can think of no other reason, can you? I mean, we are a respectable family, but our estate is small—insignificant compared with Ormond.'

'No...' Maggie frowned. 'No, I suppose there is no other reason. If John is right, you would not normally be noticed by a man of his consequence, except as a politeness, in passing. It is quite an honour to be asked to stay at his home.'

'I believe he intends to make an offer for Amanda during our stay at Massingham.'

'I should imagine that was in his mind when the invitation was given.' Maggie looked at her. 'But you can have no objection—that was what you hoped, wasn't it?'

'Yes. Yes...it was.'

Jane wondered why the match no longer seemed quite as ideal as she had first thought.

'You are not doubting him, are you?' Maggie asked. 'She may not be quite his equal either in birth or fortune, but she is an intelligent girl as well as being exceptionally pretty. Love can overcome far larger barriers, Jane.'

'Yes, of course. I'm not sure how Amanda would cope with being the mistress of a large estate...but she can learn. As you say, she is intelligent and no doubt her husband will help her to accustom herself to her new consequence.'

Amanda had plenty of spirit, and if she chose to accept Lord Massingham—which she was bound to do once the offer was made, for who could decline such a very flattering connection?—she would take it all in her stride. Jane was being foolish.

She determinedly thrust her doubts to the back of her mind as she said goodbye to her friend and started back up the lane towards her own home. John's revelations had given her cause for consideration, but on the whole she still believed that Lord Massingham would make her ward a very suitable husband. Besides, she was almost certain the girl's affections were engaged and if it was a love match between them it hardly behoved her to put obstacles in their way.

She would not do so. They were leaving for Massingham the next morning and, after further acquaintance with its owner, she would be in a better position to judge what manner of man he really was.

Chapter Four

Massingham surpassed Jane's expectation even after all she had been told about it. The grounds covered many acres and were diverse, having, besides a fine park, several more exotic areas. There was a large lake, woods, streams, a wilderness which was artfully contrived to appear the work of nature, and the walled gardens where a lady could walk in comfort and admire an amazing variety of flowers.

The house itself was splendid, both in its classical proportions and its interior. The main entrance hall had white marble floors, ionic columns supporting the domed roof, which was painted in the Italian style and caused Amanda to gasp when she first saw it.

'I fear my grandfather had rather grand tastes,' Lord Massingham seemed to apologize. His eyes rested on Jane, as if seeking her approval. 'He built the house so one has to forgive him, but I'm glad to say my mother had the west wing redecorated in a somewhat more refined taste. It is there I have requested your rooms, Miss Osbourne. I hope you will be comfortable.'

'It is a beautiful house, sir. You must be very proud to own it.'

'I admire beauty in all things—that is why I am happy to welcome both you and Miss Roberts to my home.'

Jane thanked him for the exquisite compliment, then smiled as he handed her over to the care of his house-keeper—a tall, stately lady who, had she been less strictly dressed in severe black, could have been taken for the mistress of the house. Although polite and attentive to their needs, she spoke very little as she conducted them to their apartments, and said nothing at all of a personal nature.

'Well,' Amanda remarked after she had left them alone in the suite of rooms they were to share. 'She frightened the life out of me.'

'Mrs Hurley is a little stiff in her manner,' Jane agreed, 'but you must not let her make you nervous. She is here to look after Lord Massingham's guests and therefore feels the full weight of this establishment on her shoulders, particularly as he is not yet married. It is always best to take things slowly with someone like that. Eventually she will thaw towards you.'

'It does not matter.' Amanda's eyes glowed. She glanced around the room at the soft, muted shades of green and cream mixed with a deeper gold. 'This sitting room is pretty, isn't it? More comfortable than the main rooms downstairs.'

'I believe Lord Massingham's mother influenced the decoration here. She had excellent taste—there is everything anyone could possibly want for one's comfort.' She ran her fingers over the keys of a pretty spinet. 'I feel these rooms have been used and loved, don't you?'

Amanda agreed. 'Do you suppose they belonged to Lord Massingham's mother?'

'Perhaps...' Jane's eye had been caught by the portrait of a woman. She went to look at it, studying the lovely face and proud eyes. A beauty indeed, but there was no warmth in her eyes. Amanda came to stand beside Jane. 'I think this must be her. She looks a little like her daughter...'

'She looks cold and proud,' Amanda said, and shivered. 'Lady Farringdon is much kinder.'

'Yes, she is,' Jane agreed, and turned away. It seemed Maggie had been right about the late Lady Massingham. 'I'm going to change my gown and tidy myself before I go down. Perhaps you would like to do the same?'

They parted company, each going to their own bed-chamber. Jane discovered that her trunks were being unpacked by a rather pretty young girl.

'I'm Ivy, miss,' she said, bobbing a curtsey. 'Mrs Hurley sent me to help you—being as you'd brought only the one maid.'

'Thank you, that was thoughtful of her. I see you have unpacked the dress I need.' Jane picked up a pale green muslin afternoon dress and went behind the dressing screen, slipping out of her travelling gown. 'Pray continue with your work, Ivy. I can manage very well.' She emerged a few moments later. 'If you could just fasten the hook at the neck?'

'Yes, miss.' Ivy did as she was asked. 'I'll press your gowns when I've finished unpacking. Mrs Hurley said as I was to serve you and leave the young lady to...' She faltered uncertainly.

'Bessie.' Jane supplied the name of her own maid. 'I am accustomed to dressing myself at home—but it was very kind of Mrs Hurley to send you to me.'

'I'm good at doing ladies' hair,' Ivy said. 'Yours is very pretty, miss—but if you wanted a different style I could do it for you. I used to do Lady Massingham's hair.'

'Then you must have known her well?'

'Oh, no, miss. Not what you call know...' Ivy blushed and looked at her oddly. 'I should like to do your hair, miss. If you would permit me?'

Jane looked at herself consideringly. She found it easy to put up her hair in a simple coronet of braids, but perhaps it would be interesting to try something different for once.

'Perhaps this evening, then.'

'Yes, miss.' Ivy looked pleased. 'May I say how nice it is to have you here—you and the young lady? It's what we've all been hoping would happen since…' She blushed and looked horrified. 'My tongue ran away with me, miss. You're so approachable, not like some others. I hope you won't take offence?'

Jane laughed. 'How could I? You have been very helpful, Ivy. I think I shall go and see if Amanda is ready.' She glanced a little doubtfully in the dressing mirror. Her dress was charmingly simple but made by a country seamstress and perhaps not smart enough for her present surroundings. 'What do you think—shall I do?'

'You look lovely, miss.'

'Respectable, anyway.' Jane smiled and turned as someone knocked at her door. 'Come in.'

Amanda entered, looking enchanting in a white sprigged muslin gown with tiny puffed sleeves and a red sash.

'So you are ready,' Jane said. 'Shall we go and find the others?'

'Oh, yes,' Amanda agreed. 'Lord Massingham promised we could walk in the gardens after tea. I can't wait to explore.'

'Nor I,' Jane said, smiling at her enthusiasm. 'It is all rather wonderful.'

They went along the passage together. It was softly carpeted with rich Persian runners over wood parquetry flooring. The walls were covered in a damask pink silk paper and there were matching pier tables with gilt-framed mirrors set at intervals the whole length of the hallway. The stairs were wide and impressive, leading down to the magnificent central hall.

'His lordship is expecting you in the green salon, miss.' A footman addressed Jane as they hesitated. 'Perhaps you would allow me to show you the way?'

'Thank you,' Jane said, 'that would be kind.'

She bestowed such a sweet smile on him that he was happy to agree with Ivy in the downstairs hall that evening when she said Miss Osbourne was a perfect lady, with better manners than many she could name of a higher rank.

As Jane entered the salon, she saw there were some people present she did not know. A tall, dark-haired man of perhaps thirty was standing before the fireplace with Massingham; another, younger, fair-skinned gentleman was seated on an elegant gilt and brocade sofa talking to a woman. Jane thought her extremely fashionable, beautiful, assured, but rather cold-looking, with dark gold hair and very green eyes. She smiled inwardly as she wondered if Ivy would find this lady approachable.

'Ah, there you are,' Max said, leaving his companion to come forward and greet them. 'Miss Osbourne, I want you to meet my friends—Amanda, you look beautiful as usual.'

Amanda dimpled and thanked him shyly.

'This lady is Helena, Countess Langdon.' Max turned towards the sofa, drawing Jane with him. 'Helena—may I present Miss Jane Osbourne and her ward, Miss Amanda Roberts?'

Was there something odd in his manner? Jane could not be certain.

'Max has spoken of you.' The countess inclined her head regally. 'I understand you are a friend of Catherine's.'

'Yes, we are neighbours.'

Jane looked into the narrowed, cat-like eyes of the older woman and felt her hostility. It was obvious the countess did not welcome their arrival. Why? She was wearing a wedding ring so she could not see Amanda as a rival—could she?

'This gentleman is my cousin—Richard Harte.'

Jane's attention was instantly diverted. So this was Lord Massingham's cousin! She was surprised. He was quite attractive though a little sullen-looking. Not at all what she had expected—and not in the least like a murderer. Except that she had no idea of what a murderer ought to look like, of course.

'Sir—I am pleased to make your acquaintance.' She bobbed a little curtsey.

'Miss Osbourne. Miss Roberts.' He had risen as the introductions were made and bowed over their hands. 'Any friend of my cousin's…always welcome…pleased, I'm sure…' His words came out indistinctly, almost mumbled.

He struck Jane as being awkward, a little ill-mannered but not by any means a scoundrel, which he must be if he had made three attempts on his cousin's life. He put her in mind of a sulky schoolboy, and she thought he needed a little more discipline in his dress, which was careless, his cravat badly tied—but was he really capable of murder? It was impossible to think so. Yet one could never be sure of these things.

'And this is Sir Andrew Forbes,' Max said, turning to the man standing by the fireplace. 'Andrew is the closest thing to a brother I've known. He spends more time in my house than at home. I sometimes wonder that he doesn't take up root.' His smile showed that there was perfect understanding between them. 'May I introduce Miss Osbourne to you, Andrew—and Miss Roberts?' He gave Amanda a quizzing look. 'I warn you, Miss Roberts—this man is a shocking flirt. You would be well advised to be on your guard with him.'

'No, damn it!' Andrew cried. 'That's shabby, Max. I won't have it. Do not believe him, Miss Roberts.'

'I know Lord Massingham likes to tease,' she replied. 'It was very bad of him. I am sure you are no such thing, sir.'

'Thank you.' His gaze veered towards Jane. Something about his eyes struck her as being unusual; they were very direct, even piercing. 'And you, Miss Osbourne—I hope this rogue has not destroyed your good opinion of me?'

'No, sir,' Jane replied. 'I take people as I find them. Until you give me cause to think differently I shall believe you blameless.'

'Be warned, Andrew.' Max threw a laughing challenge at her. 'Miss Osbourne is a deep thinker. She will find you out.'

What his friend might have replied was lost as the door opened to admit John and Lady Farringdon. The countess immediately called out to Catherine to join her and more introductions were made, by which time the butler and two maids had carried in the tea trays.

Jane found herself sitting near to Lord Massingham's cousin during tea. He regarded her for some moments in silence. His eyes were a pale blue, his mouth rather weak. Not a particularly charming young man, she thought as the silence dragged on.

'Have you known my cousin long?' He seemed to come to life all of a sudden, as if remembering it was considered polite to make conversation with one's guests.

'I first met Lady Farringdon when she came to Ormond after her marriage.'

'I meant Max, of course.' He glared at her as if he suspected her of deliberately misunderstanding him. 'He doesn't often invite strangers to visit Massingham, especially ladies.'

'Then perhaps he felt in need of a change of company,' Jane said, ignoring his rudeness. 'For we met only two weeks ago. He had been walking on the moors, looking for wild flowers, I believe. There was an accident and...'

'What's this?' Sir Andrew had been listening intently to their conversation. 'Not another accident, Max? That's damned odd.' His eyes seemed to fix accusingly on Richard's face. 'One too many, I'd say. What happened?'

Max looked annoyed. Jane bit her lip, realizing her mistake. She ought not to have said anything but had been driven to it by an unaccountable irritation of the nerves. To think that she was forced to be polite to a man who had tried to kill Lord Massingham! It was beyond endurance—but of course it must be endured.

'A stupid fall from my horse,' Massingham lied. 'All my own fault. A piece of carelessness. Nothing more. I bumped my head but Miss Osbourne came galloping up. An avenging fury to the rescue. I dare say she saved my life.'

'I did no such thing.' Jane reproved him with a look. It was all very well to make light of things but it made her blood run cold to think of him in danger. 'I merely bathed your…head.'

'You were an angel of mercy,' Max replied in a bantering tone. For a moment his gaze flicked towards his cousin. 'I dare not think what might have happened had you not arrived so opportunely.'

'Nor dare I.' Sir Andrew's mouth set in a hard line as he shot a rather odd look at his friend. 'I never knew anyone so accident-prone as you've become of late, Max.' There was a wealth of meaning in his voice which Jane could not mistake. He did not believe that any of the attempts made to injure Massingham had been accidental. He too believed that someone was trying to kill his friend!

Jane saw a deep flush creep up Richard Harte's neck. He was uncomfortable and ill at ease—as well he might be if he was guilty of attempted murder! How could he sit here if it were true?

'I think I shall take a turn about the rose gardens,' Countess Langdon said, apparently bored with the conversation. 'Will you come with me, Max? It is an age since we had any time privately together.'

The arch look she gave him was not lost on Jane. She felt a little disappointed as she realized what their relationship might be, though of course she had no right to any opinion. It was not unusual for men to have mistresses, and women of the countess's rank and status were accepted everywhere despite their private arrangements. Discretion was everything—but it seemed a little indiscreet of Lord Massingham to have his mistress staying at the same time as the young lady he intended to make his bride.

'You must excuse me for the moment, Helena,' Max replied, frowning. 'I have promised to show Miss Osbourne something of the house. It is so large that guests frequently lose their way, unless they have been shown where the main rooms are situated. Perhaps Richard will walk with you?'

His cousin scowled, then turned to her. 'If you can put up with me I'll come.'

Anger flared in the countess's green eyes. She was certainly not pleased by Max's rejection of what had clearly been an attempt to be alone with him. 'How can I refuse such a delightful offer? Come along, Richard—and do try not to slouch so!'

Jane looked at Max as they left, unable to keep a hint of reproach from her tone. 'You need not have refused on our account, sir. I dare say your housekeeper would have been glad to show us round.'

'I prefer to keep that pleasure for myself, Miss Osbourne. If you would care to come with me? I'm sure Andrew will keep Catherine company.'

'I'm going to lie down for an hour before dinner,' Lady Farringdon said. 'The journey was exhausting. You should let Jane rest, too, Max.'

'I am not in the least tired,' Jane assured her. 'Nor, I think, is Amanda. We should love to be shown some of the principal rooms before we go up to change.'

'I think I shall go for a walk,' Sir Andrew announced. He looked at Jane, his grey eyes seeming to dwell on her face for slightly longer than necessary. 'I shall see you this evening, Miss Osbourne.'

Jane experienced an odd flutter in her stomach, but did not quite understand its cause. Sir Andrew was a distinguished man—not as handsome as Lord Massingham, to be sure, but there was something about him, and his smile was attractive. And it was obvious that he liked her. She gave him an approving look as he turned to leave.

'Do you have a music room?' Amanda was asking her host. 'Or a ballroom?'

'We have both.' Max frowned slightly as he offered her his arm. 'Shall we start with the rogues' gallery?'

'What is that?' She gazed up at him, head to one side, eyes wide. 'I know you are teasing me, sir.'

'I meant the portrait gallery—all my wicked ancestors. Shall I tell you their secrets, Miss Roberts?'

'Oh, please do,' she cried, her face lighting up. 'Especially if they were really wicked. You tell such wonderful stories, sir—though I do not believe the half of them.'

Jane followed them, John walking beside her. He had been oddly quiet during tea, and she noticed that his eyes scarcely left Amanda. She felt a flicker of alarm. He must not fall in love with her! Not in a serious way. Jane tucked her arm through his.

'I believe you are in the east wing? We have our own sitting room. It is very comfortable.'

'It's a wonderful house, isn't it?' John looked gloomy. 'I should imagine anyone would be comfortable here.'

'Oh, yes.' She laid her hand on his arm. 'I think Amanda could be happy almost anywhere. She is so easy to please.'

'Yes, she is.' John smiled, his eyes flicking to the girl and back again. 'You do like her, don't you, Janey? I mean, really like her.'

'Yes, I do. I intend to do everything in my power to see her happy. She is very young yet…and she must have at least one season in town before she settles down.'

'Yes.' His expression lightened. 'By Jove, yes. She certainly deserves that—dances and all the rest of it. She must certainly have that before she settles down.'

Amanda glanced back at them mischievously. 'Lord Massingham is telling me his great-great-great-grandfather was a pirate. Should I believe him or is he telling tall stor
ies?'

'It is perfectly true,' Max declared, his eyes instinctively seeking Jane's to discover her reaction. 'The Massingham fortunes were founded on silver stolen from the New World—or rather Spanish ships on their way home from the Americas.'

'Oh, that's not piracy,' Amanda said, pouting. 'England was at war with Spain and the Queen encouraged her sea captains to attack the Spanish treasure ships.'

Max gave her a grave look which only made her giggle. 'I see you are unimpressed with Sir Rupert—perhaps a highwayman would please you more? He was an out-and-out scoundrel and narrowly escaped being hung.'

'Oh, I don't believe you!' Amanda went into a peal of delighted laughter. 'Now I know you are making it up. You are a wicked tease, sir.'

'Miss Osbourne.' Max threw a look of appeal at her. 'Your ward is casting aspersions on the veracity of my words—which must lead inevitably to doubts about my character. Pray reprimand her if you please.'

'When you have tried so hard to provoke her?' Jane arched her brows. 'Shame on you, sir! Pray be serious for a few moments. Amanda, my dear, walk with John, please. I should like a few words with Lord Massingham.'

'Yes, pray do take charge of this ungrateful child,' Max said, giving her a little push towards John. 'Continue down this gallery and you will come to the music room. We shall join you shortly.'

Jane had stopped to stare up at the portrait of a handsome man in Elizabethan costume. Max stood beside her in silence for a few moments, but his eyes were on her, not the painting, and there was an eager expectancy about him.

'Was he really a privateer?'

'Yes. He sailed under Elizabeth's orders and was given his title as a reward for services rendered.' Lord Massingham gave her a questioning look. 'You wanted to say something to me?'

'Your cousin—did you expect him to be here when you returned?'

'Richard has always come and gone as he pleases.' His forehead creased in a frown of displeasure. 'Are you afraid I have endangered your life and Amanda's? I assure you—you will be constantly watched over. You could not be safer in your own home.'

Seeing the pride in his face, Jane was reminded of what her brother had told her about his giving persons he did not like a severe set-down. She could see that he was quite capable of doing so, and that the charming manner he had shown to them was only a part of the man.

'I was not thinking of myself—or Amanda.' A little shiver ran down her spine. 'I cannot bear to think of you—' She broke off in embarrassment. 'If another attempt should be made on your life...' His look stopped her. She must not continue.

'Thank you for your concern,' he said, and she saw the steel in his eyes, giving her a further glimpse of the man she had until now only guessed was there beneath the surface. He would make a bad enemy once his anger was aroused. She was aware of strength and power, and something else she could not quite place, but decided must be pride. Not pride of person, but of his position, his heritage. 'It is, however, misplaced. I was caught off guard on the moors. Until then I had refused to take the idea seriously. Andrew warned me. It was he who pushed me to safety when the urn fell...he who suggested that my gamekeeper should check all my guns before I took them out.'

'He is a good friend to you, I think?'

'The best. I would trust Andrew above any other man—or woman—other than those I love, of course.' Jane nodded. Did he sound as convinced as his words implied?

'We have been friends for as long as I can remember.
Yes, I trust him completely.'

'I am glad you have a friend like that.'

She understood his feelings. He must be suspicious of
all those close to him, and that would hurt both his pride
and his inner self—that self she suspected had not often
been seen or touched by others. And with the suspicion
would come guilt for having suspected those he loved.

'At Massingham I am surrounded by faithful friends—
almost all my people have been with me for years and
would protect me with their lives. That is why I left them
behind when I visited Catherine. I knew that only "accidents" could happen here. If there was to be a deliberate
attempt on my life it would be when I was alone and
therefore more vulnerable.' He frowned. 'The devil of it
is that I still cannot be certain that shot was meant to kill
me.'

'Surely you cannot doubt it? A fraction of an inch and
it would have blown a hole in your brains.'

He clearly did not wish to accept the truth, and that
could be dangerous for him.

'Whoever made the attempt must have been a damned
poor shot—and my cousin is a better marksman than any
of us.'

'When hunting game—but if he were nervous? Might
his hand not have trembled at the last moment? Murder
is a desperate affair. And to carry it out in cold blood
calls for a determined nature.'

'You see Richard as a weak, spoiled boy perhaps?'

'Is that not what he is? I imagine you have encouraged
him to rely on you—and he has abused your kindness. I
believe it is often the way in such cases.'

'So I am at fault?' His eyes narrowed and she sensed
that he was annoyed with her. 'I have ruined him and now
I must pay the price for my foolishness?'

'No—yes, I think you may be partly to blame.'

He gave her a rueful, half-angry look. 'I wish I could

deny it, but I feel you are right. Richard's father was a wastrel, his mother a feather-brained woman who went into a decline when her husband died after blowing his brains out, leaving her virtually penniless. I had just inherited my estate and I brought Richard here out of pity. My mother warned me not to let him grow accustomed to the idea of being my heir, but I ignored her... On this occasion it seems she was right.'

There was a hardness in his voice she had not heard before, and his mouth was white-edged. It was obvious that he was very angry, though whether with himself or Richard she could not tell.

'And so, after years of indulging him, you decided to take a firmer stand against his gambling?' She dared to pry a little further. 'But you have something more in mind, do you not?'

Massingham nodded. 'I had begun to think it was time I married and got myself an heir. Richard will not be left high and dry. I intend to set him up with a small estate of his own once he has sown his wild oats and shown some signs of wanting to settle...'

'Does he know that?'

'He has not heard it from my lips.' His eyes burned with a cold blue flame. 'Besides, the estate does not compare with Massingham. If he hopes to inherit the title...'

'Which he could not expect if you were to marry...'

'Exactly.' Max smiled. 'The thing is, Miss Osbourne, I have impossibly high standards where your sex is concerned—or so I have been told. When I first came into my inheritance I was relentlessly pursued by matchmaking mamas and their daughters, but I refused to be caught. I have always preferred to be the hunter.'

Something in his eyes at that moment made her wonder if he was warning her against setting her hopes for Amanda impossibly high. She blushed and looked away, then brought her eyes back to his face, defying him.

'I should imagine that anyone who hoped to trap or

push you into anything would soon discover it to be impossible, sir. I believe you to be a man who knows his own mind.'

'Oh, indeed I am,' he said, and the anger died from his eyes. He was smiling again, at ease. 'And now I think it is time we joined Miss Roberts and your brother—don't you?'

Jane was not certain whether or not she had been given a gentle put-down. No one could have been more charming than his lordship as he continued his tour of the house for their benefit, but once or twice she caught him looking at her in an amused, slightly mocking way and she wondered if he had been warning her not to interfere in his pursuit of Amanda.

He was certainly a little out of temper with her. Perhaps she had let her discomfort at having found his mistress already installed at Massingham show too plainly? She was ashamed to admit it, but she had taken the countess in dislike almost at once.

Perhaps he had not quite made up his mind to marry Amanda after all? Jane decided that she had been too confident of his intentions towards her ward. Indeed, it was not surprising that he should want to get to know Amanda better before making her an offer—but she was still convinced that his reason for asking them to stay was to put doubt into the mind of whoever had made those cowardly attacks on him.

Chapter Five

'Isn't it a lovely day?' Lady Farringdon said, tipping her head to one side. 'Listen to those birds singing… I'm sure that was a nightingale. I remember we often had them in the park when I was a girl.'

It was the morning following their arrival. Amanda had gone riding with John and their host, Jane having declined in favour of a leisurely walk about the walled gardens with Catherine. They were very beautiful gardens, filled with masses of sweet-scented flowers, and both ladies carried a shallow basket on their arms, to which they added a bloom they particularly admired from time to time.

'Yes, it is a beautiful day,' Jane agreed, and breathed deeply of the perfumed air. It was a perfect day and a perfect place to be. 'Oh, look at that rose, Catherine. Such a deep crimson. It is almost too lovely to be picked. Indeed, I think I shall leave it there.'

'The gardeners will be pleased with you.' Catherine smiled. 'Poor old Jethro used to get quite cross with me for picking his best roses.'

'I have the same trouble at home,' Jane replied, and the two ladies smiled at each other in complete harmony. 'Shall we sit for a while under that tree?'

They rested for a few minutes, sitting on the wooden bench to watch and listen, enjoying the peace of the tran-

quil gardens. One of Max's dogs came ambling towards
them, lying at their feet, its tongue lolling out as it panted
from the heat. Jane reached down to scratch behind its
ears, and it rolled over in ecstasy.

'Jasper will be your slave for life,' Catherine observed,
but Jane merely shook her head and smiled. She had not
felt as happy as this for a long, long time.

'So—what do you think of my brother's home?'
Catherine asked as they returned to the house just before
nuncheon. 'I believe Max thinks the decoration a little too
elaborate, too majestic. He talks of having it changed.'

'It would be a pity to alter that magnificent hall,' Jane
replied. She thought privately that she had never seen a
more charming house, a house that wanted only a few
small changes to make it perfect. 'But private apartments
are a matter of personal taste, of course.'

'Max has excellent taste. You should see his house in
London—'

Jane was about to enquire further when she saw Sir
Andrew coming towards them with a purposeful stride.

'Lady Farringdon, Miss Osbourne.' His brilliant eyes
seemed to dwell on Jane with warm approval. 'It is an
excellent morning for a walk, is it not? May I join you?'

'Of course,' they agreed in unison, Lady Farringdon
adding, 'I must have a word with Mrs Hurley. If you will
excuse me, Jane, I shall leave you for a while. I'm sure
Sir Andrew will take good care of you.'

'Yes, of course. Delighted.' He looked and sounded
pleased as he asked, 'Would you care for another turn
about the rose gardens, Miss Osbourne?'

Jane considered. What she really wanted was to explore
the 'Wilderness' but had not liked to suggest it to Lady
Farringdon, who she suspected was still feeling a little
tired from the long journey.

'Yes,' she agreed after a moment's thought. Somehow
she was not sure she wished to be alone with this particular gentleman, not because she feared him in any way—

indeed, his manners could hardly have been bettered—but because of some foolish notion she had taken into her head. 'Perhaps we should not stray too far since the others will be returning soon?'

'Ah, yes…Miss Roberts.' Sir Andrew's expression was a little odd. 'I believe Max told me she is your ward?' His brows rose as she nodded. 'You will forgive me if I say that you seem rather too young to have the charge of a high-spirited girl?'

'Not so very young, sir,' Jane replied. 'Besides, I am accustomed to responsibility. I have had the care of my father's estate for the past few years—and Amanda is a sweet, obliging girl. She is no trouble to me. None at all, I do assure you.'

'Yes, of course,' he said hastily. 'I meant no criticism of her—or you. I just wondered at such a task having been laid on your shoulders.'

'Amanda's great-aunt was ill for some time before she died. I dare say she might not have been thinking too clearly when she made her will—and there really was no one else. Amanda has no other relatives. Her solicitors have written to me several times on the subject. Mr Bartlet is very good and takes care of all her business affairs. I have only to house and chaperon Amanda and that is no trouble to me. Indeed, it is a pleasure.'

He nodded, looking thoughtful. 'You must hope for a good match for her—since she is the heiress to a considerable fortune? A title perhaps? I should imagine you would not settle for less.'

Jane disliked the turn their conversation had taken. He seemed to be implying that she was parading her ward, as if Amanda were some kind of merchandise to be auctioned on the marriage market. The very idea was abhorrent to her, and made her frown.

'All I really care for is that she should be happy. Her husband must certainly be a gentleman—and both kind and considerate.'

'Ah…' Sir Andrew nodded. 'You are a woman of good sense, Miss Osbourne. I suspected as much from the first. I am certain Miss Roberts will have many suitors when she is properly out…her choice of the cream of society in fact. She is a fortunate young lady to have you as her guardian…very fortunate indeed. But you should think very carefully before setting your sights on a particular match. Much better to wait and give her the benefit of a season before reaching any decision, don't you think?'

Jane realized that she was being warned of something in a subtle way but could not imagine what. Sir Andrew could not possibly have taken Amanda in dislike, for there was nothing to dislike in the girl. She supposed that some might say that she was not quite Massingham's equal in birth or fortune, but she was intelligent and lovely—no one could deny that. Surely Sir Andrew was not that protective of his friend? He would not presume to direct or interfere in his lordship's choice of a bride without good reason? That would be impertinent indeed, even for such a close friend.

Jane did not know why but she felt a prickle of unease at the back of her neck. Something was a little odd here; she was tempted to probe further, but she was prohibited by the arrival of Richard Harte and Countess Langdon.

The countess was wearing a pale green muslin gown, which had been dampened slightly to make it cling to her curvaceous figure, and a large-brimmed straw hat adorned with a mass of yellow silk roses.

'So there you are, Miss Osbourne,' she said archly. 'We wondered if we might find you both here, didn't we, Richard?' Her tone suggested a clandestine meeting and made Jane grit her teeth.

She saw the glitter of hostility in the older woman's eyes. It seemed that they had taken each other in equal dislike, which was unfortunate since they were both guests under Massingham's roof and must make a show of civility if not warmth.

'Miss Roberts has returned from her ride and is asking for you,' Richard said, managing to look both sulky and uncomfortable. What an ungracious young man he was! 'I thought you were walking with Catherine and said I would find you. Miss Roberts and your brother were on their way to the gallery…'

'And now we have found you—*with* Sir Andrew.' The countess smiled falsely. 'You looked so serious too, the pair of you. What can you have been talking about? What secret plots were you hatching, I wonder?'

'For goodness' sake!' Andrew glared at her, a red flush creeping up his neck. He was clearly annoyed by her insinuations. 'We have merely been taking a turn about the garden. There was nothing secret about it. And I wish you will not make such ridiculous comments.'

Jane wondered at his show of temper. Why had he allowed the countess's taunts to irritate him to such a degree?

'Excuse me,' she said, not bothering to reply to the countess's insinuations, which were so ridiculous they deserved nothing but contempt. Unlike Sir Andrew she would not give the countess the satisfaction of seeing her barbs had struck home. 'I must find Amanda.'

She was thoughtful as she walked on, across the smooth lawns and into the house. Countess Langdon was obviously angry about something. Jane had learned that morning from Catherine that she was now a widow of some six months' standing. Was it possible that she had been hoping for an offer from Lord Massingham now that she was free to remarry? If so, the arrival of a beautiful young heiress must have been a considerable shock to her.

Jane suspected that none of Lord Massingham's closest friends were exactly delighted at the prospect of his marriage. Why? Richard's objections were the easiest to understand since it would blight his hopes of inheriting— but why should Sir Andrew dislike the idea?

She had at their first meeting thought him a very well

mannered gentleman, but some of his remarks that morning had not been quite to her liking—and she wondered at his sudden flare-up of temper. She was not completely sure she liked him, and that distressed her since Max had claimed him as his best friend.

It was very wrong of her to doubt him! She hardly knew him. No doubt he had meant well with his warnings. He obviously cared a great deal for Max's welfare, and that must redeem him in her eyes.

Jane entered the gallery to find Amanda and John seated together on a window seat. The sunshine poured in through the glass, turning Amanda's hair to spun gold as she and John put their heads together, studying something they clearly found of great interest. They were laughing, their eyes bright, both excited and enjoying themselves.

It was a pretty picture and Jane paused to watch for a moment, before moving towards them.

Amanda became aware of Jane's approach and immediately hid something in the pocket of her riding gown, a flush of guilt mingled with mischief in her face.

'Secrets?' Jane asked teasingly. 'I heard you were looking for me but perhaps I should go away again?'

'We have been discussing our costumes for the masquerade ball,' Amanda said. 'John has decided to go up to town himself and purchase what we want—and we wondered if you needed anything yourself?'

'If you are going, John, you may take a letter to my seamstress,' Jane said. 'I shall advise her that we shall be in town for a few days next month. I've given her your measurements, Amanda, and some idea of your requirements. She may make a start on some new gowns and fit them while we are there—though we shall not let it be generally known we are in London.' Seeing Amanda's face fall, she smiled in mild reproof. 'Remember John's main purpose in making the journey, my dear. Next spring you shall have your proper come-out, but for now you must content yourself with a few private parties.'

'Oh, I know I am fortunate to be allowed this visit and Lady Farringdon's dance,' Amanda replied. 'It's just that I lived so quietly with my great-aunt…'

'Well, you must make the most of this visit,' Jane said, frowning as she saw a flicker of something akin to rebellion in the girl's eyes. 'You are not bored here, are you?'

'No, no, of course not,' Amanda denied hastily. 'I have never been so happy as I am with you and John.' She glanced over her shoulder. 'It is just that I am a little nervous of…'

'Of being here in this house?' supplied Jane as the girl's words died on a sigh. 'Is that it? Do you find it a little too grand?'

'Not exactly.' Amanda blushed. 'Lord Massingham is so kind. I never dreamed he lived in a huge house like this…with so many servants and…and…' Her eyes were wide and frightened like a child's as she looked at Jane. 'I do not believe Countess Langdon likes me. Nor Mr Harte either.'

Jane nodded thoughtfully. Amanda *was* very young. It was no wonder if she felt a little overawed by her surroundings. And she could hardly remain insensible of the countess's hostility when Jane had felt it so very strongly herself.

'You will grow accustomed to your surroundings in time,' she assured her. 'As for Countess Langdon…' She was about to explain that the countess was not the only woman Amanda would meet who would be jealous of her youth and beauty, but was prevented from saying more by the arrival of Lord Massingham.

Max looked serious as he entered the gallery, but his expression softened as he saw them, his mouth quirking at the corners.

'So this is where you have been hiding yourself, Miss Osbourne. Tell me, what would you say to the investigation of several trunks from the store rooms, Miss Roberts? You will find much that may be of use to you in your search for a period costume. I believe nothing has been thrown away for a couple of hundred years or more.'

'John and I have decided on our costumes,' Amanda said, the lilt of enthusiasm in her voice. Her eyes glowed like jewels as she gazed up at him. 'He is going to London tomorrow to purchase what we need—but I should like to look through the trunks all the same.' She jumped up in eager anticipation as if she would have liked to begin that very moment.

'And I,' agreed Jane, realizing that Massingham had already gone to some trouble to have his servants bring down the trunks. The least they could do was show some interest. 'Shall we all go together after we have eaten?'

'As always you remind us of our duty,' Max said, a glimmer of amusement in his eyes. 'Catherine and the others will be waiting for us. We should join them at once.'

He arched his brows at her, offering his arm. She laid her hand on it, feeling very much the sensible chaperon. Surely she was not yet that old or that staid?

'I trust you and Catherine have had a pleasant morning?'

'Yes, indeed. Your grounds are very beautiful, Lord Massingham. I have not yet been further than the walled gardens, but I am looking forward to exploring further another day.'

'You were kind to keep Catherine company,' he said, a slight crease between his brows. 'Does it seem to you that she is not quite herself?'

Jane hesitated. She had noticed a certain tiredness in Lady Farringdon's manner and suspected there might be a good reason for it. Maggie Graham had experienced something very similar during the first month or two after discovering she was with child. However, Lady Farringdon had said nothing of her hopes in this direction and it was not for Jane to anticipate her by mentioning

her own suspicions. Catherine would tell her brother in
her own time.

'I expect it was the journey,' she said. 'I'm sure Lady
Farringdon will feel more herself tomorrow.'

'Yes…perhaps.'

His concern for his sister could only do him credit and
Jane found herself once again in harmony with him.

Her goodwill was, however, severely tested when they
all sat down to the excellent cold collation provided in
the small dining parlour, which was used for informal
meals. Everyone sat where they chose, which meant that
Countess Langdon took the seat at Massingham's right
hand. As he had already requested his sister to sit beside
him, Jane found herself being ushered into the chair at
the opposite end of the table—the position more properly
belonging to Lady Farringdon or Maximilian's wife, had
he been married.

Sir Andrew had drawn the chair for her and seated himself on her right. Richard Harte took the space to her left,
leaving Amanda and John to fill the empty places opposite
one another.

As the two men closest to Jane were obviously hostile
to one another, and continued to glare at each other
throughout the meal, she began to feel very much like a
bone between two snarling dogs. Her attempts to make
polite conversation met with scowling monosyllables from
Mr Harte and terse comments from Sir Andrew, who
played continuously with the stem of his wineglass and
seemed slightly on edge. She was relieved when the meal
ended and Catherine rose, inviting Jane and Amanda to
follow her upstairs.

'Max tells me he has had the trunks brought down,' she
said, a sparkle in her eyes. 'I remember Mama giving a
costume ball once. She permitted me to help her choose
something from the trunks.' She glanced at her brother. 'I
was only fourteen—do you remember, Max?'

'Yes, I remember very well.'

There was a harsh note in his voice. Jane wondered at
it. She noticed that his sister also seemed puzzled by his
manner, which was introspective and unlike him.

'Max—is something wrong?'

He made a visible effort to dismiss whatever had
brought that bleak look to his eyes and smiled at her.

'Nothing at all, Catherine. Please take Miss Roberts and
Miss Osbourne on your treasure hunt. I will engage to
entertain our other guests.' He looked directly at John.
'Would you care to take a gun out this afternoon? I know
Andrew has no love of the sport and I am hoping he will
oblige me by amusing you, Helena—while I accompany
John and perhaps...' His thoughtful gaze came to rest on
his cousin. 'Richard? Would you care to shoot with us?'

As she left the room in Lady Farringdon's wake, Jane
noticed two things—a deep flush was creeping up Richard
Harte's neck and the Countess Langdon was quite clearly
furious. Sir Andrew seemed lost in his own thoughts,
which, from the rather brooding expression in his eyes,
were obviously not particularly pleasant ones.

Beneath the surface deep emotions were simmering.
Jane could sense something...old secrets, anger, even hatred. She frowned as she trailed behind the others. What
had brought that look to Lord Massingham's eyes earlier?
His mood had changed abruptly at the mention of the
costume ball given by his mother. What was it about that
particular memory that caused him so much pain?

The next hour or so passed pleasantly. Amanda was
excited by the variety of garments stored in cedarwood
trunks, all of which had been carefully packed with layers
of lavender and herbs to keep away the moths. Efforts
made long ago to deflect the passage of time had not
always succeeded and some of the material crumbled beneath their touch, but other gowns came out whole and
looked much as they must have done before being packed
away.

'Oh, look,' Amanda cried, holding up a beautiful silk gown that might well have been worn during the reign of Queen Anne. 'Isn't this gorgeous? Look at the elaborate stomacher—and the headdress! I think it would suit you, Jane.'

'It is lovely,' Jane agreed, 'but I think it would be heavy to wear. I was thinking of something simpler.'

'If neither you nor Amanda wants it...' Lady Farringdon took the gown and held it against herself. 'I think it is the very thing for me.' She gave Jane a shy smile. 'I fancy you may have guessed my secret?'

Jane nodded but said nothing, waiting for her to continue if she so wished.

'I have not yet told my brother—though Farringdon knows I had my suspicions before I came away. He was half inclined to forbid me to travel, but I told him I would not be fussed over. My mother had no trouble in...well, you know...' She glanced at Amanda, who was at the other end of the room delving into yet more trunks. 'I shall not ride, of course, and I promised to rest if I felt tired...which I confess I do.'

'I think it is quite normal,' Jane said, a faint blush in her cheeks. 'Maggie Graham says...for the first few weeks.'

Lady Farringdon nodded. It was not thought quite proper to discuss such things with an unmarried lady, but Jane was so sensible and not a green girl. Had she not devoted herself to her ailing father she might have been married with a nursery of her own long before this. Besides, Catherine felt drawn to her in a way she seldom had towards other ladies of her acquaintance.

'Have you found nothing you like?' she asked as Amanda returned to them empty-handed.

'Oh, I might have seen something,' the girl replied airily. 'But John and I are to go as a pair, you know. We have drawn sketches of our costumes and shall have them made up in town—so that no one has the least idea of what we plan.'

'Nothing too outrageous, I hope?' Jane picked out a circlet of gold mesh. 'I shall borrow this, I think. My seamstress will supply the rest—but this cap has given me an idea.' She looked thoughtfully at Lady Farringdon. 'Shall you invite Countess Langdon to your dance?'

'Not unless I am forced to it,' Catherine said. 'She is not my favourite of Max's friends. I had thought...' She coloured slightly. 'I believed their friendship to be not as close as it once was. I was surprised to find her staying at Massingham, though I know Max feels...a certain sympathy towards her.'

'Sympathy?' Jane arched her brows.

'She was trapped in a most unfortunate marriage. Her husband...' Catherine screwed up her mouth in distaste. 'It is best not to speak of such things. Nor have I been told very much. I know only that both Farringdon and my brother have spoken of Langdon with dislike. Max gave Helena a standing invitation to join him here whenever he had guests staying—though I understood that it was some months since she was last here...'

Jane wondered if she had mistaken the relationship between the countess and Lord Massingham. She had jumped to the conclusion that there must be an intimate connection—but perhaps she was wrong? It was unusual for a lady to presume on a gentleman's hospitality and, finding her installed in Massingham's home, Jane had assumed she must be his mistress.

Such arrangements were not unknown in polite society. The Prince Regent and other gentlemen of high rank had discreet arrangements, often with married ladies of their acquaintance. The unfortunate husbands turned a blind eye or had arrangements of their own. Only those who sported ladies of dubious reputation on their arms raised a censorious eyebrow.

Maria Fitzherbert had, of course, been received everywhere. Her reputation was unsullied, many people believing her to be the prince's true wife—though, of course, it could not be openly admitted, because the King had forbidden such marriages by an act of parliament. Even after the prince's official marriage to Princess Caroline many had continued to support Mrs Fitzherbert and think her hardly used, though the relationship had been at an end for some years now.

If the countess was not Max's mistress but had hopes of becoming his wife… Jane caught herself up on the thought. It was presumptuous of her to have decided Amanda was a suitable match for a man she herself hardly knew. And she ought to have no opinions about the woman to whom he had given an open invitation to his house…and yet she did! She disliked the countess, was ashamed of her uncharitable emotions, but unable to rid herself of them.

'And Sir Andrew?' Jane asked, giving herself a mental shake. 'Shall you invite him to your dance?'

'Why, yes,' Lady Farringdon said. 'If he cares to come.' Noticing Jane's faint flush, she arched her brows in a teasing way. 'I believe you have taken a liking to him, Jane?'

'I like him well enough,' Jane said, shaking her head and laughing at her friend's quizzing look. 'No, no, Catherine. There are no such thoughts in my head, I do assure you.'

'Well, I shall not tease you for you have only just met,' Lady Farringdon said. 'But I know that he was very taken with you from the first.'

Jane shook her head again and the subject was dropped. She too had noticed a certain warmth in Sir Andrew's manner—except for the few minutes in the rose garden when he had seemed to warn her of something—but she did not flatter herself that it meant he had a particular liking for her. It was merely his pleasant manners which made him smile that way.

However, later that afternoon, when Sir Andrew again sought her out as she took a turn in the rose garden, she had cause to wonder if Lady Farringdon might not have been right. He went out of his way to be courteous to her, his slight moodiness at nuncheon apparently forgotten, and at dinner that evening proved an entertaining companion, making her laugh several times. After dinner, Jane was invited to make a four at whist with Sir Andrew partnering her against the countess and Lord Massingham.

Jane and her partner won easily, but she felt that Lord Massingham's heart was not in the game, his gaze straying again and again to where Amanda, John and his cousin were playing a noisy game of Fox and Geese watched over by an indulgent Lady Farringdon.

'You are careless this evening, Max,' the countess cried, throwing down her cards in disgust when Sir Andrew trumped her hand because of a mistake her partner had made earlier. 'I shall see if Catherine can be persuaded to play something for us on the pianoforte.'

She left the table, obviously in a temper. Max gave Jane and Andrew a smile of apology.

'I fear Helena is right. I am poor company this evening. Forgive me. My mind was elsewhere.'

Jane watched as he rose and went over to join the noisy game of counters.

'You must forgive Massingham if he sometimes seems careless of your feelings,' Sir Andrew said, making her look at him. 'If he seems cold at times…harsh…he has his reasons.'

Jane was astonished at his saying such a thing. 'I do not understand you, sir.'

'Does it not appear to you that he appears moody on occasion?'

'What are you suggesting?'

Jane had not suspected Massingham of any such thing—at least, not until a few hours previously, when she had caught that brief look of brooding grief in his eyes.

'Both he and Catherine had an unhappy childhood, you know,' Sir Andrew said. 'Their parents were not particularly fond—perhaps that's why they cling to each other. I believe it to be the reason Max has never married—may never marry.'

'Because his parents…?' Jane glanced at Massingham. He was smiling and relaxed as he leant over Amanda's shoulder to move her counter. The girl glanced up at him, eyes bright with laughter. 'But surely that cannot be reason enough for him to…'

'If he marries it will be to get himself an heir. He told me once that he believed himself incapable of love. Such men can only cause grief to the women who love them, don't you think?'

Jane frowned as she turned back to meet Sir Andrew's intense gaze. Something about him then sent a tiny shiver down her spine. Why had he thought it necessary to tell her this? It was most improper on such short acquaintance. 'I think you should not be saying these things to me, sir.'

'I do so only to save you hurt, Miss Osbourne.'

'To save me…' Her cheeks burned. He was making her very uncomfortable. 'I think you forget yourself, sir.' She got up and walked over to stand beside her brother.

John glanced up at her, his smile warm and loving. 'I'm glad you've come to lend me your support, Janey. Massingham is helping Amanda and between them they've stolen half my geese.'

'Shame on you,' she teased. 'If you do not pay more attention you will lose another…' She laughed as Amanda pounced on the counter. 'There, it is already too late!'

Amanda's triumphant squeal of joy made Lord Massingham turn his head to look Jane's way. As their eyes met in shared amusement she suddenly felt much better, her spirits lifting. What a very comfortable man he was, which made his friend's hints all the more unpleas-

ant—as if Sir Andrew had gone out of his way to turn
her against him. Surely he could not have meant to do
that? No, no, he would not do such a thing. What was
she thinking of? It was far more likely that he was trying
to warn Jane not to hope for a match between her ward
and Massingham—because he knew something she did
not.

Jane wondered what that might be. It was obvious that
there was an understanding of some sort between
Massingham and Countess Langdon. Was that perhaps the
reason for Sir Andrew's hints?

Another half an hour passed swiftly, then Lady
Farringdon announced her intention of seeking her bed
and the party broke up.

Amanda walked beside Catherine up the magnificent,
wide staircase. Jane paused a moment to speak to John,
then bid him goodnight and started after the other ladies.
Sir Andrew caught her at the foot of the stairs, detaining
her with his hand on her arm.

'A moment if you please, Miss Osbourne.' She turned,
a slight crease in her brow. She looked regal, slightly dis-
approving but never more lovely. 'Forgive me,' he said,
a note of humility in his voice. 'I fear I have displeased
you. I should not have spoken so openly but…'

'You need not apologize, sir.'

'Then you are not angry with me?'

He looked so contrite that she smiled and touched his
hand, feeling guilty over her own less than charitable
thoughts. 'I assure you I am not angry with you, sir.'

'Then you will walk with me tomorrow? I believe you
have expressed a wish to explore the Wilderness?'

Jane hesitated but felt a refusal would seem rude.
'Thank you,' she said. 'Yes, I should like that. I'm sure
Amanda would also like to explore more of the grounds.
Perhaps we could make up a party?'

'Andrew, would you…?' Max had come into the hall
in search of his friend. He hesitated, eyes narrowing as he

saw what appeared to be an intimate moment. 'Forgive me. I was not aware… I intended to suggest a nightcap, Andrew.'

'I shall be delighted to join you,' Sir Andrew said. 'Goodnight, Miss Osbourne. I look forward to our walk tomorrow.'

Jane hesitated. Why was Lord Massingham giving her that hard, almost accusing stare? Or was that merely her fancy?

She smiled, bid them both goodnight and walked up the stairs.

Jane had changed into a nightgown and was brushing her hair when someone knocked at her door. She reached for a deep blue satin dressing robe and slipped it on then gave permission for the visitor to enter. She was expecting Amanda and felt a start of surprise as Countess Langdon walked in.

'You were not expecting me, of course.' The countess smiled, her eyes hard and cold with dislike. 'Forgive me if I impose, Miss Osbourne. We have had little opportunity to make each other's acquaintance. It was a shock to me when you arrived with Max. He had not told me he would be bringing two young and rather beautiful guests. Of course, now that he has explained…'

'Explained?' Jane's head went up as she tensed. 'I do not understand you, ma'am.'

'That you helped him after he was attacked by that rogue of a highwayman…' The countess inclined her head graciously. 'Naturally I understood at once. Max wished to extend the hospitality of Massingham as a way of repaying your kindness. There is clearly no need for me to feel jealousy.' She gave Jane another of her cool smiles. 'We have an understanding of several years' duration. It was naturally impossible for me to leave my husband, but now that I am a widow…'

In an effort to retain her composure, Jane turned away

to fiddle with a fine blue glass scent bottle on the dressing chest. 'Am I to offer you my congratulations, ma'am?'

The countess laughed. It was a harsh, brittle sound. 'Nothing has been settled. There is no hurry after all. I must wear my blacks for a while longer for the sake of propriety. We have always been very discreet. You were a little shocked to find me here when you arrived, I think? Max had written to me to tell me his sister was coming to stay, so I knew he wanted to see me—and Catherine and I are old friends, of course.'

Jane declined to answer. She waited patiently for the countess to take her leave, but she gave no sign of doing so, seemed in fact to want to linger.

'Miss Roberts is a pretty child,' Helena Langdon went on. 'And a considerable heiress, I hear. Your brother will be well advised to fix his interest with her before she becomes the latest rage—which she will undoubtedly be once you introduce her into London society.'

Was she to be warned yet again that Massingham was out of bounds for her ward? It took every ounce of Jane's self-control but she held her temper.

'Amanda will be given every opportunity to make a good match,' she said with quiet dignity. 'She is too young to think of marriage just yet. When she does her happiness will be my main concern.'

'You will be wise not to set your sights too high,' the countess said. 'Beauty is well enough, and her fortune may secure her a title—but even so there are some families to which she may not aspire…'

Jane had listened to her spite long enough.

'Amanda is fit to be the wife of any gentleman,' she said. 'Yes—even Lord Massingham if he should ask her. I know that you claim to have a prior understanding but you do not yet wear his ring. And I think if you were certain of his affections you would not be here.'

'You are impertinent, Miss Osbourne.'

'And you are unwelcome in my rooms, madam.'

Countess Langdon turned red and then white. She raised her head, eyes flashing with temper. 'How dare you? I shall speak to Max about this in the morning.'

'You must do as you think fit, madam. Now—if you please?' Jane stood by the door and held it open, her face pale but remarkably calm. 'I should like to retire.'

Green eyes narrowed to dangerous slits. For a moment Jane thought the countess would strike her, but she merely walked past her, head high, face like thunder.

Closing and locking the door behind her, Jane leaned against it, breathing deeply. She was trembling and indignant. How dared that woman come here? How dared she make such insinuations about John's intentions towards Amanda?

Jane was so angry that she paced about the room, unable to settle. Helena Langdon was insufferably rude! To imply that Amanda was not good enough to marry into the best families!

Several minutes had passed before Jane began to feel calmer and think clearly, but then she began to see what lay behind the countess's behaviour. If she had felt it necessary to pay Jane a visit at this hour she must be seriously concerned. She had obviously noticed Max's manner towards Amanda that evening. He had seemed to cast off his cares all at once, joining in the childish game with every sign of pleasure…which could only mean that he enjoyed the girl's company. And that Helena Langdon was not as secure in his affections as she claimed.

Sir Andrew had suggested that Lord Massingham intended to marry simply for the sake of an heir…that he was incapable of feeling love for any woman. If that were true it would give Jane cause for concern. She would not care to see Amanda trapped in a loveless marriage.

She had been so certain that Lord Massingham had felt some deep emotion when he had first seen Amanda. He had been so very considerate towards her…his manner

always attentive and charming, exactly like a man court-
ing the woman he intended to ask to marry him.

It was no use, Jane thought as she retired to bed at last,
determined to put it all from her mind. She would get
nowhere by worrying.

Her first impressions of Lord Massingham had been
favourable—indeed, she had liked him excessively! She
still liked him, she decided as she tried in vain to sleep.
It was just that she was no longer certain he was the right
husband for Amanda.

It was no use—she was never going to sleep! Jane left
her bed, pulling on a silk wrapping gown and tying the
sash about her waist. If only she had a book to read,
something that would take her mind off the unpleasant
interview with Countess Langdon.

She was foolish to let that awful woman upset her. Jane
sighed. If she were at home she could have taken much
comfort from one of her favourite books. There was a
wonderful library at Massingham; she had noticed it particularly, but had not yet had the opportunity to explore
its shelves.

When the idea first came to her, she dismissed it.
Whatever was she thinking of? Her wits must have gone
begging. She could not simply wander about Massingham's house in the middle of the night—or could she?

Surely there could be no real harm? Both guests and
servants must long ago have retired to their beds; the only
person likely to be still up was the hall porter, but since
she need not venture as far as the front hall there could
be no impropriety there.

She would go down to the library. It need only take a
few minutes and she would be back in her own rooms
with no one the wiser.

The passageways were still lit by flickering candles.
Jane took a branch from a pier table outside her room,

just in case she come to a part of the house that had fallen into darkness where the candles had flickered their last.

She knew her way to the library and it took her a very few minutes to reach it. Pushing open the door, she went in, set down her heavy candelabra on the large circular table in the middle of the room, and lit one of the smaller ones from it, carrying that carefully as she began to search the shelves for a book she might enjoy.

'What is this, Miss Osbourne?' The familiar voice speaking from behind her made her jump, almost causing her to drop her candlestick. She turned, her cheeks flushing with embarrassment as she looked into the questing eyes of Lord Massingham, who must have been sitting quietly in one of the deep armchairs. 'Could you not sleep?'

'I was a little restless,' Jane confessed. 'It is my habit to read if I am wrestling with a problem that will not let me sleep. Forgive me, sir. I should not have intruded on you had I known you were here.'

'So you too have troublesome thoughts?' His eyes moved searchingly over her face. 'Is there any way in which I may be of service to you? A problem shared is often halved—or so they say, though I confess I have not found it so.'

'Nor I,' Jane said. She wondered why she was finding it unaccountably difficult to breathe. 'It is nothing, sir. Nothing at all.'

'Perhaps I may at least help you choose a book?' He smiled at her. 'Is your preference for the poets this evening, or perhaps a work of great literature—or even a novel?' His eyes teased and challenged her.

'You have a vast selection,' Jane said. 'I think perhaps something light, to amuse…'

'I have it on Catherine's authority that Fanny Burney is guaranteed to relax one's nerves,' he said. 'Or perhaps your namesake—Miss Jane Austen. I believe the Regent thinks highly of *Emma*, though Miss Austen's novels are not as popular as they might be, being a little too subtle for the majority of readers.'

'That is perhaps why I like her,' Jane replied with a smile. '*Emma* will suit me very well, sir.'

He reached up to a high shelf and took it down for her. As their hands touched, Jane felt a very odd tingling sensation and it was all she could do not to gasp. She gazed up into his face, eyes wide with surprise as he reached out, trailing the tips of his fingers down her cheek.

'You are a very beautiful and desirable woman,' he said in a husky voice. 'Perhaps you should go now, Miss Osbourne. I might otherwise say or do something we might both regret.'

'Yes, of course. Forgive me…'

Jane took a step back, her eyes seeming unable to let go of his. He was drawing her to him, making her aware of feelings she had not until this moment dreamed existed.

She should not be here!

'Excuse me.'

She dragged her gaze from his, turned and left the room as quickly as she could. Once outside, she breathed deeply to recover her composure. As she ran upstairs, she knew that sleep was impossible. Even Miss Austen's excellent novel would not help her now!

Chapter Six

John left for London early the next morning, promising to return very soon. Amanda, Jane, Richard and Sir Andrew spent the morning exploring the Wilderness, at first on horseback and then, having left the horses with a groom, on foot.

'How beautiful this is,' Jane said as she stood watching a small waterfall tumble over dark, gleaming rocks. 'I think I could happily stay here for ever.'

'But the countryside around your own home is beautiful, too,' Amanda remarked thoughtfully. 'You love to ride on the moors, don't you?'

'Yes, indeed I do. You are very right to remind me.' Jane smiled at her. 'It was but a passing thought. I am content to live at the Lodge…though I shall have to find a new home when John marries.'

'Why?' Amanda stared at her, clearly dismayed. 'Surely you will stay?' A faint blush stained her cheeks. 'John wouldn't want you to leave your home.'

'But his wife might feel differently. She will naturally wish to be mistress in her own home.'

'Yes, but…' Amanda's cheeks were bright pink. 'I think—I am sure—you would always be welcome in John's house…even if he were married.'

'Well, we need not concern ourselves just yet,' Jane

said. 'I do not believe my brother intends to marry for a while.'

'Oh, no,' Amanda replied airily. 'Not for a while.'

'Shall we catch up with the others?' Jane asked. Richard Harte and Sir Andrew had wandered further down the mossy path that wound past the stream. They seemed to be having an argument, though they were too far ahead for Jane to be certain. 'Lady Farringdon preferred to stay at home and write her letters, but it was a shame Lord Massingham could not join us.'

'He had some urgent business,' Amanda said. 'We spoke earlier this morning…a few moments before you joined me in the breakfast room.' She smiled happily at Jane. 'He said he was disappointed but promised to spend time with us this afternoon.'

'That was kind of him,' said Jane, careful to keep her voice light. She must not put any pressure on Amanda, nor give her any reason to think she was expected to accept an offer if it was made. 'He has been most attentive…don't you think so, my dear?'

'Oh, yes, so kind,' Amanda agreed instantly. 'He makes me laugh.'

'You like him, don't you?'

'No one could dislike Lord Massingham,' Amanda declared. 'He is such a wicked tease—besides, he says nice things about you, and that naturally makes him a favourite with me.' She pressed Jane's arm. 'You must know that all this seems like a fairy tale—and none of it would have happened but for you, dearest Jane. I am so lucky that Great-Aunt Mary sent me to you and not one of her other friends. Some of them were so old. I should have died of boredom—and you are so kind to me.'

Jane was touched by her show of affection. What a sweet, considerate girl she was! It made Jane all the more determined to make sure she was given every advantage.

'This is only the beginning, my love. Next spring we shall go to London. I have many friends…people who will invite you to their parties. You will have lots of pretty clothes…and a wonderful time.'

'And John?' Amanda asked, frowning just a little. 'Will John come to town with us?'

'I expect so…at least for a part of the time.'

The men had disappeared from view. Jane looked around her, experiencing an odd sensation, as though they were being watched.

'Come along, Amanda,' she urged. 'We must catch up with the gentlemen. I do not care to be here alone.'

'You have your instructions, sir. I shall wait to receive your report.'

'Your lordship may rely on me.' The man glanced round as they heard impatient footsteps. 'Excuse me, sir. I shall make myself scarce.' Lord Massingham's visitor made a hurried exit through the French windows.

'Max!' Countess Langdon burst into the room angrily. 'Why have you been avoiding me?'

'Helena…' Max frowned. 'Forgive me if I have neglected you. I have had many things on my mind. You wished to see me?'

'I demand to know if you intend to marry that chit of a girl!' she cried, eyes flashing with temper.

'I believe that is my business, Helena.'

'How can you treat me so shabbily?' she asked. 'After all we have been to each other?'

'*Have been*,' he said mildly. 'I thought you understood that our relationship was at an end.'

'I refuse to accept dismissal,' she said. 'Your attitude is unreasonable, Max.'

'Indeed?' His brows arched. 'I believe not, ma'am.'

She moved towards him, clearly intending to throw herself into his arms, but he turned away, walking to the window to gaze out at the smooth lawns, which stretched away to a pretty summerhouse.

'I need an heir, Helena,' he said, his back to her. 'Even

if I still wished to continue our relationship, I could not make you my wife.'

'Why not?'

He turned to face her, his eyes as cold as deep-water ice. 'I think you know the answer to that, Helena. A man in my position needs to be sure that the children his wife bears him are indeed his own. If you were my wife I could never be certain—could I?'

Her face paled and she flinched as if he had struck her.

'Max...' she whispered. 'Please...'

'There is no reason why we should not be friends,' Max said. 'But I think I must ask you to leave my house today.'

'I suppose Miss Osbourne told you what I said to her last night?' Countess Langdon flashed angrily. 'She has pride above her station. I merely intended to warn her against expecting too much for her ward.'

'You said something to Miss Osbourne—last evening?' Max's mouth thinned. 'I suppose I can imagine what you told her...' The countess stepped back as she saw the menace in his face. 'Please oblige me by leaving at once, madam. My godmother is arriving this afternoon and she will not wish to find you here.'

'Very well, if that is your wish.' Her green eyes narrowed. 'I see how it is. I was mistaken.' She laughed harshly. 'In that case, I wish you joy of her, sir. I dare say you are well suited...'

With that, she turned on her heel and stalked from the room.

Max frowned. The little mystery of Miss Osbourne's midnight excursion to his library was now solved—and in a manner that did not displease him.

Jane was relieved to see Sir Andrew patiently waiting for them at the end of the narrow path. Richard Harte could be seen disappearing into the woods ahead.

'Has Mr Harte decided to leave us?' Jane asked, surprised at his abrupt departure.

'That young cub needs a lesson in manners,' Sir Andrew said, clearly angry. 'As you must have realized we do not get on. I'm afraid he knows I dislike the way he takes advantage of Max's good nature.'

'He is a little sulky at times,' admitted Jane thoughtfully. She found Richard rather immature but was unable to see why Sir Andrew should dislike him so much— unless he suspected him of being behind the attempts on Max's life! If that were so, she could not but think that the sooner he was banished from Massingham the better.

'You do not know the half…' Sir Andrew hesitated, seeming to think better of what he had been about to say. 'But it is not for me to interfere. If Max sees fit to keep his cousin here it is his own fault if…' He shrugged and glared at nothing in particular, seeming absorbed in his own thoughts, then, as he turned, he smiled at Jane, his mood slipping away as if it had never been. 'Well, Miss Osbourne—what do you think of this wild place now you have seen it?'

'One would think it had always been this way,' she replied, a slight frown on her brow. Once again she was aware of something…of hidden tensions simmering beneath the surface. 'I can hardly believe it was not the work of nature—it must have taken so much labour to build the streams and that waterfall.'

Sir Andrew shrugged. 'As to that…there is nothing money cannot buy. If one has enough of it one may do anything, I suppose.'

'Yes, perhaps.' Jane looked at him, feeling puzzled. Was that a note of resentment in his voice? 'Do you believe that money can buy happiness, sir?'

'No, that was not my meaning. I spoke of material things. For myself I would prefer a more simple life. You must not imagine I envy Max his wealth, Miss Osbourne. Far from it. I am not poor—though my fortune cannot equal Massingham's—but I believe there are more important things.'

'And what would they be?' Jane walked by his side, Amanda a little behind them. 'You intrigue me, Sir Andrew.'

'What do I consider important?' He smiled slightly. 'Loyalty…truth…decency. Love. Yes, above all else love. For without that what is all the rest?'

'You are a romantic, sir.' Jane laughed, a little surprised at this new insight into his character. She would not have thought it. 'But I am prepared to agree—though I believe life in a hovel would be a severe test for any romance.'

'You disappoint me,' he said, lifting his brows. 'I am sure Miss Roberts would agree with me that love is all…' He turned to enquire for her opinion but Amanda had stopped to gather some wild flowers, her skirt spread out around her on the woodland path so that she looked almost an exotic flower herself. 'What an enchanting picture. I am inclined to think Max could not do better than to make that child an offer.'

'You did not think that yesterday,' Jane said, slightly accusing.

'You saw that? Forgive me.' He was immediately apologetic. 'So many matchmaking mamas have tried to catch Max…but I know he must marry and Miss Roberts has such a sweet nature. I believe she may be the very wife for him. And I am sure he is very fond of her. Most men would find her a delightful companion.'

'Yes, she is a lovely girl.' Jane turned her face aside. Why could she not be happy that someone else agreed with her own opinions?

'And we should be almost related—for Max is like a brother to me.' An odd, wistful, half-angry expression entered his eyes. 'Once I believed we should be truly brothers…brothers-in-law. My sister was also a sweet girl…but she died of an infection of the lungs last year. She was just eighteen.' A deep sigh escaped him and his eyes darkened with remembered grief.

'That is terrible!' Jane stopped walking to stare up at

him in shock. 'I am so very sorry. You must have been devastated.'

'It was a severe blow to me—and to my mother. She took to her bed at once, and has scarcely left it since Marion's death.'

She saw his hands clench at his sides and knew he was struggling against very deep emotions. 'Forgive me, I cannot speak of it without…' He choked and turned his face from her, unable to continue.

'I am so sorry,' Jane said again.

She looked at his averted face. His expression was unreadable, controlled, but then when he turned to her once more he was suddenly calm, as if he had cast off his feelings…the way a snake might shed its skin.

'It was unfortunate—but we shall not dwell on an unhappy past. Lady Farringdon tells me she is to give a costume ball. Have you decided on your disguise, Miss Osbourne?'

'It is to be a secret,' Jane replied, readily accepting the change of subject. She felt a rush of sympathy for him. It must be so painful for him to speak of his sister. 'Shall you be there, sir?'

'Most certainly. I am already looking forward to the occasion.'

Jane smiled. The atmosphere had lightened and they continued to talk of this and that until they reached the groom and their horses. Richard Harte had taken his own horse and ridden off alone, which was rather ill-mannered of him.

Jane was sure he and Sir Andrew must have quarrelled earlier, something it seemed they often did. It was clear to her that neither man liked the other and that there was resentment on both sides. Both Sir Andrew and Massingham's cousin seemed to be rather temperamental—though in Sir Andrew's case with good reason. His sister's death was certainly a tragedy: the kind of thing that might play on a man's mind, causing him to be sometimes rather introspective.

She was thoughtful as she changed out of her riding clothes some half an hour or so later. Despite Sir Andrew's obliging manner towards her personally, Jane suspected he disliked the idea of Massingham marrying a young and beautiful girl. Or he had at first. Why? Was it because he had once hoped for a marriage to unite his own family to the Massingham's...? Yes, it was understandable that he might feel a pang of distress just at first, might feel resentful towards the girl his friend was thinking of marrying. But he had gone out of his way to praise Amanda to Jane that morning, which was probably his way of apologizing for any offence he might have caused previously.

Jane could sympathise with his natural grief over his sister's untimely death, and the continuing ill health of his mother must be a source of worry to him. When you thought about what must be going through his mind it was not surprising that he should sometimes seem to be brooding. And one must always make allowances for grief, for the ill-judged thought or careless word. His revelations had made her see him in quite a different light, and so when they met again in the dining parlour she greeted him warmly and smiled in a way that brought a frown to one other's brow.

'Did you enjoy your morning, Miss Osbourne?'

Jane turned to her host. 'Yes, very much,' she said. 'Your wilderness is a delightful place, sir. Sir Andrew tells me we have seen but a small part of the whole. Perhaps I shall ride that way again another day.'

'Perhaps I may have the pleasure of accompanying you,' Max said. 'I must tell you I expect friends this evening. Sir Thomas Howard and his wife Lady Elizabeth, Viscount Roxborough—and Lady Fairley. She is my godmother and a formidable woman. She visits me once a year and has decided now is the time.' A gleam of humour entered his eyes. 'I must warn you, Miss Osbourne, my godmother disapproves of what she terms my ramshackle ways. She delights in giving me—and anyone else who arouses her wrath—a severe set-down. However, I believe you have nothing to fear. She will undoubtedly approve of your good sense.'

'We must hope so,' Jane answered, well aware that she was being mocked. As he offered her his arm to escort her into nuncheon, she glanced over her shoulder. 'Countess Langdon does not sit down with us?'

'She was forced to return to town,' he said, such an odd note in his voice that Jane glanced up in surprise. His expression was grim, his eyes hard and cold. 'Her decision may have been hastened by the news of Lady Fairley's imminent arrival. My godmother and Countess Langdon do not agree.'

'Oh…' Jane wondered at his expression. Had the countess complained of her rudeness the previous evening? If so it seemed he was not going to mention it. 'I see…'

'Do you?' He glanced down at her, his frown easing. 'I take leave to doubt that—but perhaps all will be made plain in time.'

'You intrigue me, sir.'

'Indeed?' The harshness had left his face. 'I should be pleased to think so, Miss Osbourne.' He was smiling again, smiling in a way that made her heart quicken. 'But these things must not be rushed—though I confess I am not always so patient. Be warned, I am not a man to be led by the nose.'

Now what was he hinting at? She arched her brows at him but he shook his head, leading her to the seat Countess Langdon had thought hers by right.

'Will you please me by sitting here?' he asked, pulling out a chair for her before his footman could forestall him. 'You must know, I have a favour to beg of you. I want you to give me your true opinion of my home, Miss Osbourne. I value your thoughts on this matter. Will you tell me, if you please—should I embark on a complete refurbishment of the house?'

'I have not yet seen all of it,' she reminded him. 'But it would be a pity to change that magnificent hall, do you not think? Perhaps your own apartments are not to your particular taste? I should be happy to give you my personal opinion.'

'It is your own feelings I require.'

'Then, by all means, let me see them.'

'Until recently I have not spent a great deal of time here,' he replied. 'I have a house in town and a small shooting lodge in Scotland. Also my maternal grandfather's estate in Hampshire, which has a smaller, more comfortable house. However, when I marry I shall bring my wife to Massingham and the apartments we shall occupy must be refurbished to accommodate my wife's tastes and needs.'

So he did intend to marry! Jane fixed her gaze on the exquisite glass into which the butler was about to pour a rich deep ruby wine. She felt as if pins and needles had been stuck all over her body. What could be the matter with her? The pain was so intense that for a moment she was unable to speak.

'It is your intention to marry quite soon?' she asked, keeping her voice carefully light.

'Oh, yes,' he said. 'I believe so. When I am certain of the lady's mind—but in the meantime I should be grateful for your opinion, Miss Osbourne. I have come to respect you as a lady of both taste and sense. Tell me, please, is my house too formal to be a comfortable home? What must I do to make it acceptable to a young and very beautiful lady?'

He was surely not speaking of Countess Langdon! The countess was indeed beautiful, but sophisticated and well past the first flush of youth. Besides, she would insist on any refurbishment being to her own taste. This was the clearest indication yet that Lord Massingham was thinking of making Amanda an offer. He was asking for Jane's opinion because he thought Amanda's taste as yet unformed—or perhaps because he wished to surprise her.

'Perhaps if you were to show me the apartments?'

'Certainly. I should be delighted to hear your thoughts. You must be quite frank with me—perhaps later this afternoon?'

He was eager to begin making plans. It seemed that his mind was made up. He had been struck immediately by Amanda's beauty, of course. And her nature was so sweet and amenable that he had decided she was the wife for him—but was he in love with her?

He had certainly enjoyed her company the previous evening. Was that sufficient? Had he considered the difference in their ages? Jane had thought the match ideal at first but now she had begun to wonder. It would be a splendid match for Amanda, of course—but would either of them be happy?

Her thoughts were confused and uneasy. So when Sir Andrew asked her if it was her intention to go up to town when she left Massingham she turned to him with a feeling of relief.

'Yes, just for a few days,' she agreed. 'Amanda is to have some fittings for the new gowns she needs—and I have some errands of my own.'

When she felt able to glance at Lord Massingham again, he was in conversation with his sister. Jane kept her silence for some time, and when her host spoke to her again it was on quite a different matter.

Richard suddenly announced his intention of riding out to dine with friends of his own that evening, surprising them all. Obviously he was still in a black mood.

'You know our godmother always puts me in a blue quake,' he said, looking straight at Max. 'If she is to stay, I may visit Mama's cousins for a while.'

'As you wish,' Max said. 'But remember what we discussed yesterday, Richard.'

'I haven't forgotten.' Richard scowled. 'You need not go on about it, Massingham.'

'It was not my intention to nag you, Richard.'

'Oh, damn!' The younger man had turned bright red. He scraped back his chair and stood up. 'I can't stand this...' He rushed from the room, almost knocking a tray from the butler's hands in his desire to escape.

'Richard!' Max called, but was ignored. 'The young fool...'

'Let him go,' Sir Andrew advised. 'It would do him the world of good if you left him to fend for himself for a while.'

'Oh, Max!' Catherine looked at her brother anxiously. 'I do not like you to quarrel with Richard.'

'We have not quarrelled,' he replied. 'Please do not worry, Catherine. Everything is under control. I promise you.'

She said no more but was obviously concerned, picking at her food without the least interest. After a few minutes she pushed her plate away, still visibly distressed.

Richard's departure had hastened the end of the meal. Lady Farringdon asked Amanda if she would care to walk with her in the rose gardens, then invited Sir Andrew to accompany them.

She turned to Jane with a smile. 'I know Max wants to show you some of the private rooms so I shall not tease you to come with us—but later I should like to talk to you, Jane.'

'Of course.'

Jane found herself alone with her host as the others left the room. He seemed distant, lost in thought...anxious? She wondered if he had regretted giving her an invitation to voice her opinions on the refurbishment of his house, but when she took a tentative step to follow the others he laid a restraining hand on her arm.

'You must think me an odd fellow, Miss Osbourne.'

The wistful note in his voice caught her attention, but

she could see nothing in his expression to help her discover its source.

'Why so, sir?'

His eyes were serious as they met hers. 'I have a dilemma—of which we have spoken previously. It causes me some unease. There are things I wish to say—important things—which might be better left unsaid for the moment...'

'I understand perfectly.'

'Do you? I wish I thought you did.' His mouth quirked at the corners and he seemed to shake off his mood. 'No more of this. We shall not be diverted from our work, Miss Osbourne. Your opinion must be sought and the refurbishment shall be commenced. Richard's sulks shall not be allowed to spoil our pleasure.' A mocking smile lurked in his eyes, his good humour quite clearly restored. 'I do trust it will be a pleasure for you, Miss Osbourne?'

'I have been wanting to see more of the rooms,' she admitted. 'And it is always a pleasure to plan the refurbishment of a house—especially one such as this. I fear my own home has been sadly neglected for some years. My father was too ill to consider changes—and now it will be for John's wife to refurbish the house when he marries.'

'Ah, yes...' His gazed fixed on her face. 'And have you thought of your own plans, Miss Osbourne? What will you do when John decides to marry?'

'I am not sure. I must make a new home for myself—perhaps in Bath.'

'You have not thought of marriage?'

Jane kept her gaze fixed straight ahead. They were in a part of the house she had not seen before. She thought the colours a little sombre—dark purples, dusky gold, crimson and brown.

'I have not yet been asked to marry anyone I could consider as a husband,' she replied after a lapse of several seconds.

'But you have been asked, surely?'

'Oh, yes!' She gave him a laughing glance. 'Several times. I do not boast when I say I could marry almost at once if I chose, but...' Mischief lurked in her clear eyes. She had no idea of how enchanting she looked at that moment. 'You once told me your own standards were impossibly high in the matter of a wife, Lord Massingham. I believe mine to be impossible. I fear I have grown too accustomed to being my own mistress. I should not find it easy to obey...'

Max gave a shout of laughter. 'You delight me, Miss Osbourne! I must cast about in my mind for a suitable husband for you—a man who would not demand obedience but merely...love?'

The warm, intimate look he gave her made her blush. How wicked he was to tease her so! And how foolish her heart was to beat so very fast just because of a charming smile. She pulled her gaze away, looking about her once more, trying in vain to control the wild tumult of her racing pulses.

'I think whoever decorated these apartments must have been in a sombre mood,' she said to steady herself. 'All these autumn tones. If I were you I would strip all these heavy colours away and replace them...with shades of green and pale lemons...or perhaps a pretty rose and cream in here.'

She glanced around the room, which was clearly intended to be a lady's boudoir. It led through to a bedchamber connecting through a small dressing room to yet another bedchamber. As she glanced briefly inside this furthest room she realized it was in present use—was in fact Lord Massingham's own. Seeing a gold and black brocade dressing robe lying on a chair where he must have discarded it earlier, she felt a very odd sensation, which made her slightly breathless. She moved away, her cheeks warm, back to the boudoir.

'Yes, this would look charming in shades of pink and

cream—and yellows for the bedroom, I think. Something bright and sunny. And for the small salon...perhaps shades of green or turquoise.'

She had wandered back to the salons, which were part of the suite of private rooms, and, glancing round, said, 'Some of this furniture is rather gloomy—could it not be replaced with some pretty pieces? A writing desk and a display cabinet here...and a pianoforte?'

'These were my grandfather's rooms,' Max admitted. 'I believe he had them changed after his wife died and he was in mourning. Indeed, he never ceased to mourn her. Theirs was a happy marriage, you see.' Something in his tone made Jane look at him, but his expression gave nothing away. 'Grandfather liked majestic colours...the purples and gold you see here. I chose these rooms when I came into the estate, for a particular reason of my own, but have always meant to change them...' He smiled at her. 'I knew you would see immediately what was needed and I shall set the work in hand at once.'

'Do you not think...?'

Jane had been about to ask whether he ought to seek his prospective bride's opinion first but before she could do so they were interrupted by the arrival of a somewhat flustered Mrs Hurley.

'Forgive me, sir,' she said as he gave her a very direct stare, clearly not pleased at the intrusion. 'Lady Fairley has arrived and demands to see your lordship at once.'

'Ah...' His expression changed to one of understanding coupled with a rueful amusement. 'Cutting up rough, is she? Very well, I shall go to her now. Pray conduct Miss Osbourne to...wherever she wishes to go.' He looked at Jane thoughtfully, lingering, as if reluctant to leave. 'If you need a little more time to think about what needs to be done here Mrs Hurley can come back for you. Feel free to stay as long as you wish. I am grateful for your assistance—and now I must go. My godmother is inclined to become a little fractious if kept waiting.'

Jane hesitated as he strode away. She felt awkward and wondered what the housekeeper must be thinking at finding her alone with Lord Massingham in his private rooms. It might seem rather odd to someone who did not understand the reason for her visit.

'Lord Massingham was asking my opinion,' she said as carelessly as she could. 'He intends to have these apartments completely refurbished.'

'And not before time,' Mrs Hurley replied in a manner that conveyed approval without a hint of the expected censure. 'If I may be so bold, Miss Osbourne…we are all of us below stairs anticipating the future with pleasure. We shall be happy to see the master settled at last.'

Jane nodded, unsurprised by her little speech. It was never possible to keep a secret from one's servants. They seemed to be aware of one's intentions even before the decision was made. Naturally Max's people would have guessed his intentions towards Amanda.

'Thank you,' she said. 'If you could furnish me with some sketching materials I might make a few notes—and there is no need for you to wait on me, Mrs Hurley. I am sure I can find my own way back to the main rooms.'

'You will find all you need in here.' The housekeeper pulled open the top drawer of a heavy mahogany desk. 'If you have no need of me, Miss Osbourne, I have much to do…'

'Of course. Please do not concern yourself for my sake.'

Jane wandered back through the rooms after the housekeeper had departed. She was not sure why—she could have sketched the rooms from memory—but she had a foolish fancy to spend a few moments alone in Max's rooms. It was, after all, the only time she would see them. The next time she visited this house it would undoubtedly be as a wedding guest.

Somehow she found herself drawn to Max's bedchamber. Nowhere else in the house could possibly tell her so much about him. And there was so much she wished—needed—to know.

She moved about the room slowly, touching the silver-backed combs and brushes on his dressing chest, and picking up the heavy silk robe, holding it to her face, inhaling the scent of him which still clung to the material. Her heart twisted with sudden pain. She had become so fond of him!

But she must not allow herself these feelings. Max had made his intentions perfectly plain. He was going to ask Amanda to marry him. It was the reason they had come here, of course, just as she had thought at the beginning.

Jane blinked hard to halt her foolish tears. What was she thinking of? She stroked the soft material of Max's dressing robe before laying it carefully back in its former place, then, hearing a slight noise behind her, she turned to see a man watching her. He was tall, thin and quite elderly, but his eyes were bright and curious.

'Oh…' She was flustered. 'I did not hear you come in.'

'Excuse me, Miss Osbourne.' He inclined his head. 'I'm Thorne—his lordship's valet. I came to tidy the room. You must excuse the state of it, miss. I was busy this morning and neglected to put this away.' He picked up the dressing robe and carried it to a large walnut armoire. 'I am ashamed that you should have found this lying around.'

'Oh, please do not distress yourself,' Jane said hastily. 'I'm afraid I was…' Her cheeks felt warm. 'Lord Massingham was called away and I…am helping him to…'

'Exactly so, miss,' Thorne said, and smiled at her. 'His lordship has told me of his intentions, Miss Osbourne. I've taken care of him man and boy for the whole of his life and he has formed the habit of confiding in me.'

'Yes, of course. You must be…very close to him?'

Thorne cleared his throat, obviously emotional. 'I believe his lordship thinks well of me. And I know my duty.'

'And you are fond of him? You would be pleased to see him happy?'

'It is the wish of all his people, Miss Osbourne. We had begun to think it might never happen. We were all very gratified when you arrived—you and the young lady.'

'Thank you.' She nodded and smiled. 'Well, I must not keep you from your work. I think I have seen enough now. I shall make some notes and a few sketches.'

'May I offer my best wishes, Miss Osbourne—if I am not presuming?'

'I—nothing is settled yet.'

'Forgive me…' He looked awkward. 'I have said too much.'

'Not at all. I believe you may see things as you would wish here at Massingham in the near future—but that is between us, Mr Thorne. Not to be communicated to anyone else.'

He looked pleased. As Lord Massingham's most trusted servant, he clearly understood the way things were going. Max had undoubtedly told him of his decision to marry— and, as such a very flattering offer was not likely to be refused, Thorne had presumed the offer had been made and accepted.

'I am gratified with your confidence, Miss Osbourne. Nothing could be better for his lordship.'

Jane felt the warmth of his approval. She nodded and turned away. Max's servants had clearly taken to Amanda, which was a good thing. The girl would need all their goodwill if she was to be mistress here. Massingham was an important house and certain standards would be expected of its mistress. Amanda would have a great deal to learn, of course, but no doubt Max would help her.

If Jane had been able to hear a particularly interesting conversation that took place in Mrs Hurley's parlour later that afternoon she might have been surprised, but perhaps it was best for her peace of mind that she would never know exactly what Thorne had said about a very intimate moment he had witnessed in his lordship's bedchamber. Or that Mrs Hurley had entirely agreed with him, she having formed a very similar opinion about the feelings of a certain person.

Making her way back to the main part of the house, Jane struggled to bring her own emotions under control. It had been very unwise of her to give way to her feelings in Max's room. She only hoped Thorne had not seen her holding the dressing robe to her face in that foolish way! What would he have thought of her?

What a very silly thing to have done! She must not allow herself to think of Lord Massingham as anything more than a friend. She liked him very much, but that was all it was. To imagine anything else was quite ridiculous.

She wasn't falling in love with him. Of course she wasn't! That would be a mistake…something she might have done if she had been a young girl, but not something Miss Jane Osbourne would consider.

'I thought I should find you here,' Sir Andrew said, entering the library to see Max standing before the fire-place. It was a large room with lofty ceilings, usually a little cool, and, since it was the room most often favoured by the master of the house, there was usually a small fire kept burning there. 'I wanted to speak to you—if it is convenient?'

'Of course, Andrew. You know I always have time for you.'

'It is a delicate matter,' Sir Andrew said cautiously. 'I have no wish to tread on your toes, Max. I believe it is your intention to ask Miss Roberts to be your wife?'

'And if it is?'

'Then I should be relieved,' Sir Andrew confessed. 'As

I said, I have no wish to tread on your toes—but I have developed a very great liking for Miss Osbourne.'

'Indeed?' Max's brows arched. 'I have not yet made up my mind that I wish to marry at all—but if I do I shall not fear your competition, Andrew. If the lady concerned prefers your suit, you need not fear that I should blame you.'

'I felt it only fair to warn you,' Sir Andrew said, an odd smile on his lips. 'But, as you say, if the lady should prefer my company to yours, it would not be the fault of either of us. Do they not say everything is fair in love and war?'

'I have never been a man to resent healthy competition.'

'I was sure you would say that,' Sir Andrew said, and smiled at him. 'You have relieved my mind, Max. For you know that what I value above all else is your friendship?'

'Yes,' Max replied, and turned away to glance along the shelves. 'Yes, I know that, Andrew.'

Jane heard the rather querulous tones coming from the drawing room when she and Amanda went down to dinner that evening. Lady Fairley was clearly displeased about something. She turned as they entered, a tall, thin, slightly forbidding lady, very elegantly dressed, her gold-handled quizzing glass directed at Amanda.

'So you're the chit I've heard so much about,' she said in a sharp tone. 'Humph! Pretty enough, I suppose.' Her penetrating gaze fell on Jane. 'Much too young to be a chaperon. What's this I hear about Mary Roberts making you Amanda's guardian, Miss Osbourne? She had much better have sent the gel to me.' Her eyes moved back to Amanda and she pursed her mouth in disapproval. 'What's this—wearing colours so soon?'

It was clear Lady Fairley had known Amanda's great-aunt. Jane's heart sank as she saw disapproval in the el-

derly lady's face. In her position as Massingham's godmother, her opinions of the girl he intended to make his
bride must carry some considerable weight. If she were
to disapprove, it might even make the difference between
his making the girl an offer or not. Especially if he was
not perfectly certain in his own mind.

'Godmama.' Max came to their rescue. 'You are terrifying Miss Roberts. Pray do not frown so; it will make
your head ache. You are well aware that it was Amanda's
great-aunt's express wish that she should not wear black.'

'That's as it may be; doesn't mean it's proper or that I
approve,' Lady Fairley said. 'But I suppose if it was
Mary's wish…' She glared at Amanda. 'Well, child—
have you nothing to say to me?'

Jane realized they must have met previously at Mary
Roberts's house. From the reluctance in Amanda's face
she guessed that Lady Fairley was not a favourite with
her and gave her an encouraging nudge forward.

'Good evening, Lady Fairley,' Amanda said, remembering her manners, though a trifle belatedly. 'Forgive me
if I did not greet you at once. I did not like to—to presume. In case you had forgotten me.'

'Forgot?' Lady Fairley wielded her quizzing glass with
a vengeance. 'My memory is as good as it ever was. I am
hardly likely to forget the ward of one of my greatest
friends.'

Amanda was silent, her usual confident manner crushed
beneath the weight of Lady Fairley's displeasure. Even
when Max introduced her to his friends Sir Thomas and
Lady Howard and Viscount Roxborough a few minutes
later, she was unable to raise more than a faint smile.

Unfortunately, Amanda had been placed next to Lady
Fairley at dinner and was forced to endure several lectures
during the course of the meal. Looking at her wan face,
Jane longed to rescue her, but when the ladies retired,
leaving the gentlemen to their port, she herself was accosted by the dowager and spent the next half an hour

listening to her ladyship's opinions of the ramshackle ways of modern society.

'When I was younger we called a spade a spade, but we knew how to be discreet,' she said in a loud voice. 'I don't say our morals were superior, for they weren't—but washing one's dirty linen in public is something I won't put up with. And so I've told that godson of mine.'

'I'm not sure I understand you, ma'am.'

'Humph!' The bright, bird-like eyes were intent on Jane's face. 'At least you know how to be discreet, Miss Osbourne. I'm relieved that Massingham had the good sense to get rid of *that* woman at last. If I'd had my way he would have sent her packing long ago. She should never have come here in the first place. Max assures me he did not invite her and I believe him.'

Jane could not pretend ignorance in the face of Lady Fairley's frank words: there was only one person to whom she could be referring. 'I believe Countess Langdon had urgent business in town.'

'Business that will prevent her return. I have it on good authority that she will not be a guest at Massingham again—unless the future Lady Massingham cares to invite her, which if she has half an ounce of brains in her head she won't. A more spiteful piece of goods I've yet to meet. Max is well rid of her.'

Had Massingham asked the countess to leave? Why? Was it because he realized the impropriety of her being here—or because she had complained of Jane's rudeness?

'I believe I agree with you, ma'am.'

Lady Fairley gave her an odd stare. 'I should hope so, miss. Massingham needs a wife who cares for him, not a cold fish in his bed. It would be a pretty thing if Lady Massingham condoned the presence of that woman here!'

Jane's cheeks took fire. 'Lord Massingham has spoken of his intentions, ma'am?'

'He wrote informing me of his desire to marry. Why

else do you suppose I'm here? I wanted to see the chit he—'

She was interrupted by the arrival of the gentlemen. Two card tables were set up almost at once and Jane was asked to join Amanda, Richard and Sir Andrew in a four at whist, while Max chose the privilege of partnering his godmother. In doing so he showed himself both considerate of his guests and possessed of endless patience.

Jane could not help but admire the way he behaved towards Lady Fairley. As the evening wore on she gradually mellowed under his attentions and went off to bed an hour before anyone else was ready to retire, leaning heavily on Lady Farringdon's arm and quizzing her about the state of her health.

'You must forgive me for subjecting you to this,' Max apologized to Jane after Lady Fairley had left them. 'I know she is a little trying…but she cares for me and I am fond of her in my way. She would have been hurt had I not invited her to join us here.'

'You need not apologize to me,' Jane said, and glanced across the room. 'But I believe Amanda is feeling crushed. Perhaps you should do what you can to raise her spirits. I am well able to cope with Lady Fairley's lectures, but I fear Amanda finds them oppressive.'

He gave her a slightly puzzled look. 'Yes, of course— but perhaps there may be another reason for Miss Roberts's subdued manner this evening.'

'I'm not sure I understand your meaning, sir.'

'Do you not?' He smiled, an odd, mocking expression in his eyes. 'But I must not tease you. I shall do as you bid me, Miss Osbourne. We cannot have Miss Roberts falling into a fit of the sullens, can we?'

Jane watched as he crossed the room to Amanda's side. Within minutes she was all smiles, her pretty laugh ringing out as he began to tease her.

'So serious?' Sir Andrew was at Jane's side. 'You must not let Lady Fairley upset you. Max will do as he pleases no matter what she says—though I dare say he would be happy to have her approval.'

'Why should she disapprove?' Jane asked. 'Lord Massingham assures me his godmother cares for him. Surely she must want only his happiness?'

Jane's gaze went back to Amanda. Lord Massingham had persuaded her to play a piece for him and was standing by her side at the pianoforte, turning her music, smiling down at her.

'They make a pretty picture, do they not?'

'Yes…they do…'

No one could doubt that they looked well together. Jane wondered why her own heart felt so very heavy. Max glanced at her, a slight frown creasing his forehead. She smiled, then turned to Sir Andrew as he suggested a turn on the terrace.

'It is such a warm night, Miss Osbourne. We need not go far…but would you not care for a little air?'

'Yes…' Jane was cross with herself. She had asked Lord Massingham to bring a smile back to Amanda's face—so why did she find it so painful to watch them together? 'Yes, Sir Andrew. I think I would like a breath of fresh air…'

Chapter Seven

It was cooler on the terraces. A soft, sweet perfume floated on the air and the moon was full, touching everything with its silvery light and giving the night a mystery all its own. Jane breathed deeply, letting her breath go on a sigh as she fought against the ache inside her.

'That was a deep sigh,' Sir Andrew said, giving her a searching look. 'Is something troubling you?'

'No...nothing at all.'

'If I can be of help?' He hesitated, then reached out to take her hand, covering it with his own, holding it briefly before touching it to his lips. His eyes were intense, glowing oddly as he looked at her in the moonlight. 'You must be aware that I have a high regard for you, Miss Osbourne? That I would count it a privilege to be your friend and confidant...much more if you would grant me the right.'

His voice throbbed with passion. Jane felt a thrill of sudden fear as she gazed up at him. That look in his eyes...passionate...almost wild...unnerving! He was not himself, but a stranger...someone she did not recognize.

He was making her very uncomfortable. She knew a moment of panic. What on earth had made her come out here with him?

'Please...' She pulled her hand from his, pulses racing.

What could he mean? What was he saying to her? They hardly knew one another. Even if she had wanted an offer from him this was much too soon. And she did not. No, she certainly did not! 'You must not say such things to me, sir. Please do not…'

'You think it is too soon to speak of such feelings?' he asked, his voice hoarse with the force of his emotion. 'Because we have known each other only a few days?' He seized both her hands this time, holding them so fast she could not escape, his face tight with a queer blind look that once again frightened her. What could be wrong with him? 'I am not a man to hide my feelings, Miss Osbourne…Jane. Do not fear that I mean any disrespect. I speak of love. The love of a man for the woman he would honour above all others…would cherish, protect and worship for the rest of his life.'

'No, no!' she cried, her embarrassment growing by the second. Had he lost all sense of propriety? This was not the behaviour of a gentleman. 'Please, I beg you. Do not say any more.'

'Forgive me if I embarrass you—but I had to speak. I could not bear to lose you to another because you were not aware of my very deep feelings.'

'Please do not!' She wrenched her hands from his at last, heart hammering in her breast. 'You are too impulsive, sir. I will not listen to this. It is not proper.'

'Forgive me…dearest Miss Osbourne. I would not willingly have offended you.' He dropped to one knee before her, face turned up, eyes very bright—too bright. 'I beg you not to turn from me…not to refuse me without consideration. If you granted me the honour I seek, I would do everything in my power to make you happy.'

'I…we do not know each other, sir.'

'I knew you from the moment I set eyes on you. I knew instantly that you were the woman I wished to make my wife.'

'Oh, no!' she cried. 'I beg you, Sir Andrew. Get up,

please. Do not speak so to me. It causes me much distress.'

'I would not hurt you for the world.' He rose, looking a little uncertain, pleading, the heat fading from his eyes. 'Is there no hope for me—none at all?'

She turned away, her breast heaving. This was so unexpected, so sudden—and she had encouraged it by coming out here alone with him! His rash, almost wild behaviour had shocked her, but now she saw that she was at least in part to blame.

'You—you should not have spoken,' she said. 'It is much too soon. Even if… Excuse me. I must go.'

She walked away from him, entering the house by a side door that led to the large dome-shaped conservatory in which orange trees and vines were growing. Alone, she pressed her hands to her hot cheeks, shame and embarrassment flooding over her. Sir Andrew's passionate declaration had startled her. He had seemed so…so strange. Too intense, almost desperate.

She had been afraid of him and it had made her react badly. At first she had thought he was offering to protect her, to make her his mistress. She ought to have been a little kinder in her refusal—as she had always been with the Trio, turning their clumsy attempts off with a smile and a gentle apology—but she had been overcome with a sense of panic, a feeling of such revulsion that she had followed her instincts without thought or consideration.

Oh, how awful it all was! She could not face Sir Andrew again this evening. She would go immediately to her own room and ask one of the maids to convey her apologies to Lady Farringdon and her host.

She walked quickly through the house but was stopped at the foot of the main staircase when Lord Massingham came out into the hall.

'You are not deserting us, Miss Osbourne?'

Jane could hardly bear to look at him. She felt shamed, sullied by what had just happened. What would

Massingham think if he knew? He would blame her for encouraging the advances of his friend only to cruelly reject them. She could not bear him to think so ill of her. She longed to escape to the quiet of her own room, and though she sensed his eyes upon her would not meet them.

'You must forgive me,' she said, her voice muffled as she fought against the raging emotions inside her. 'I have a headache. I wish to lie down.'

'Is that why you went outside with Andrew? To take the air—because you felt unwell?' His eyes searched her face, seeing more than she cared to reveal.

'Yes…' She refused to meet his accusing gaze as she lied. 'But it has not helped. Indeed, I feel quite wretched. Please excuse me, sir. I really must lie down.'

'Are you truly ill, Jane?' There was concern in his voice now, a caressing warmth that almost brought her to tears. 'Shall I send for my physician?'

His concern was almost her downfall. She felt the tears well up inside her, but held on desperately. He must not guess what was going through her mind. She was so ashamed of her own behaviour. She must have done something to bring on such a passionate avowal from Sir Andrew, though she could not imagine what.

'There is no need,' she said. 'It is just a foolish headache. Please let me go.'

'Of course,' he replied. 'I shall make sure you are not disturbed—but promise me you will ring for Mrs Hurley if you feel worse in the night. Please, Jane?'

'Thank you…'

Jane fled before the tears she was trying so hard to suppress could fall and shame her. What a show she was making of herself, behaving so stupidly, and so unlike her usual self. She did not know what had come over her.

When she reached her own room she could no longer contain her overwrought emotions. It was all too much! For the first time since the death of her beloved father, Jane wept. She lay on the bed sobbing for a long time, feeling so wretched that she wished she might die that very night. It was some minutes before she was able to recover her composure enough to sit up and wipe her face.

What a foolish wretch she was! Behaving like a schoolroom miss! Just because the wrong man had declared his love for her. Oh, why couldn't it have been Max out there on the terrace? How differently she would have reacted then!

A hot wave of shame washed over her. Shocked at her own thoughts, she looked at her face in the dressing mirror. She could no longer hide the truth from herself. She had fallen in love with Max! Oh, this was terrible! How could she have so far forgotten her duty? They had come here to allow Amanda and Lord Massingham to get to know one another better. He had already made up his mind to ask Amanda to be his wife.

If only she could leave this house tonight! If she could go home…away from all that caused her such pain. Jane felt the tearing ache begin again inside her, striking deep into her heart. Hers was the most unenviable of positions. She was compelled by both duty and affection to do all she could to promote a match between her ward and the man she herself loved.

And that would break her heart!

Jane sat in the window embrasure, looking out at the gardens. How foolish she had been earlier! Yet she could not deny the force of her own feelings. She had given her heart unwisely, and that would cost her a great deal of pain throughout the coming weeks and months, but it was done and she could not undo it.

What was that out there in the garden? Surely she could see a shadow in the shrubbery? Was it a man? Someone hiding, keeping a watch on the house?

A chill went down her spine. She was not mistaken. There was someone out there.

What ought she to do? Wild thoughts of a murderer

breaking into the house to kill its master filled her mind.
She should warn Massingham. And yet she dared not go
down to the library at this hour again. Knowing how she
felt about him...knowing that if he looked at her again in
that intimate way...she might fall willingly into his arms.

She had sensed he was tempted the previous evening.
She was not particularly shocked, even though he was
intending to make her ward an offer. It was not surprising
that a man might feel drawn to a woman who came to
him as he sat alone, brooding in his library.

Had Max been brooding? He had certainly been unable
to sleep, but so had she.

She saw the man move, step into a patch of moonlight.
It was Max himself! What on earth was he doing out there
alone? And why had he stood in the shrubbery, almost as
though he wished to keep watch on the house without
being seen?

Just what was the master of this great house up to—
and why did she feel he had been staring up at her room?

She longed to go down to him, but was afraid of giving
herself away. She must never, ever let either him or
Amanda guess what was in her heart.

Max saw her sitting by the window. He drew back into
the shadows, not wanting her to glimpse him. She had
been very distressed by whatever Andrew had said to her
on the terraces—but why?

Miss Osbourne was usually very adept at concealing
her feelings. He sensed that she enjoyed his company, but
could not be sure it was more than that—at least, he had
nothing substantial to confirm his own belief that she felt
more than mere liking.

If it were not for this damned threat hanging over his
head he could have found a way of breaking through the
barrier she seemed to keep so firmly in place. He had been
sorely tempted in the library the previous evening—

tempted to sweep her into his arms and give way to the fierce longing seeing her like that had aroused in him.

His mind pictured her, hair loose on her shoulders, her soft body draped only in the flimsiest of coverings. Coverings that he had longed to tear aside so that his eyes could feast on her sweet flesh. He imagined the smell and taste of it and groaned with desire.

'Damn! Damn! Damn!'

It had taken all his strength to control himself when Andrew had announced his own feelings for her in the library that afternoon. He had wanted to strike his friend, to forbid him to think of her! Somehow he had remained outwardly calm.

He had no right to influence Jane's feelings either way. If her heart was still her own—but it was not. It belonged to him. He was almost certain it was his, had been his from their first meeting.

He must speak to her. How could he continue to hold back when every nerve in his body was on fire with this longing for her?

And yet to speak might be dangerous, both for himself and for her. Perhaps he ought to wait for just a little longer.

In the morning Jane was much calmer. She had slept very little, but, having wrestled with her conscience, and come to terms with the hopelessness of her situation, knew that she could not abandon her ward. It would be very painful for her, but she must not ruin Amanda's chances by being selfish. She had agreed to this visit and must see it through to the bitter end. So when Amanda knocked at her door a little later to ask if she was better she was able to greet her with a smile.

'Yes, much better, thank you, Amanda.' She held out her hand in greeting. 'You look very pretty, dearest.'

'Thank you.' Amanda dimpled, taking her hand for a

moment. 'Do you think John will be back today? He promised he would not be gone long.'

'I doubt he will return before tomorrow at the soonest,' Jane replied. She wondered a little at the girl's impatience. 'Has he said he will bring you something special?'

'Oh, no,' Amanda said. 'I just wondered. Are you well enough to come riding with us this morning? Lord Massingham said he thought you would prefer to stay here and rest.'

'Yes, I think perhaps I would—but you must go, my love.'

'Are you sure you don't mind?' Amanda looked at her doubtfully. 'Is there nothing I can do for you?'

'No, nothing. Of course I don't mind. That is why we came here—so that you could enjoy yourself. And get to know…people.'

'You are so kind to me.' Amanda kissed her cheek. 'You're not really ill, are you?'

She looked so anxious that Jane took her hand and squeezed it reassuringly. 'No, of course not. It was just a silly little headache, that's all. I am feeling much better. You go along now and have a lovely time. There is no need for you to worry about me.'

Amanda hesitated for a moment. She seemed as if she wanted to say something, then turned away without speaking, the opportunity for confidences lost.

Jane sighed when she was alone. Of all things she would have loved a good gallop—but it was better to avoid Lord Massingham's company as much as possible. She was afraid that she might give herself away, and that would make her situation impossible.

She stood up, touching her hair as she studied her reflection in the mirror. She was a little pale but no one would know she had lain awake half the night with an aching heart. There was no point in sitting here alone. She would have to face the others some time—so it might as well be now.

* * *

Catherine was in the small sunny parlour that looked out towards the rose gardens. She had an embroidery frame in her hand, but she laid it down and got up to greet Jane as she entered the room, her expression one of concerned affection. They kissed each other on the cheek.

'Jane, dearest! How are you? I wanted to visit you earlier but Max strictly forbade it. He said Lady Fairley had worn you out and given you a headache, and that you must be allowed to rest.'

'That was kind but also a little unfair of him,' Jane said, responding with a faint smile. 'I do not blame Lady Fairley for my headache. Actually, I rather liked her.'

'She has often been the cause of mine,' Catherine said, and laughed. 'How wicked I am! She is really very good-hearted. Both Max and I went to her with our troubles when we were young.' Her lovely face clouded. 'I don't know if Max has told you—but our mother was not at all affectionate towards us. Papa was kinder when he thought about it, but he was seldom at home—and then, you know, he died when Max was eighteen. It was a hunting accident. He fell from his horse and broke his neck.' She frowned. 'It happened a few days after the costume ball…'

Jane felt a prickling sensation at the nape of her neck. That look in Lord Massingham's eyes when his sister had mentioned their mother's costume ball…was it possible it had reminded him of his father's tragic accident?

'Max grew up very quickly after that,' Catherine said, her expression thoughtful, as though she too wondered at something. 'He was never quite the same again. I suppose it was the responsibility of the estate.'

'Yes, I expect so.'

'Oh!' Catherine looked at her oddly. 'I almost forgot, Jane. Sir Andrew asked me to give this to you.' She took a sealed letter from the pocket of her gown. 'He was most insistent that I give it to you privately.'

Jane hesitated, then took it reluctantly.

'Do you wish to be alone while you read it?'

'No, I most certainly do not!' A flush stained Jane's cheeks as she slipped the note into a pocket. 'I must read it later, I suppose, but I am in no hurry.'

'Is something wrong?'

'I…' Jane was uncertain. She felt it wrong to betray Sir Andrew by discussing what had happened, but was uneasy in herself. It could do no harm to confide in her friend. 'It is a little awkward. Did—did you ever receive an unwanted declaration of love?'

'Oh, Jane!' Catherine stared at her in astonishment. 'You mean Sir Andrew proposed to you—so soon? I thought he would, but I confess I did not expect him to speak so quickly. Whatever did you do?'

'He asked me last night—when I was foolish enough to take the air with him. I was so embarrassed, Catherine. He was so very intense. He frightened me. I mean, I like him but…'

'He should have waited until you knew him better,' Catherine said, a little frown wrinkling her smooth brow. 'I do know how you feel, dearest. Some men do frighten one with their passion. I received at least ten proposals before dear Farringdon saved me from further embarrassment. One young man—my goodness!—he swore to end his life if I would not have him, and I had met him only twice before. It upset me terribly. I was afraid that he would really kill himself, but Max told me it was all nonsense, so then I felt better.'

'I'm so glad to have spoken to you,' Jane said, feeling relieved. She had been inclined to think Sir Andrew a little unbalanced the previous evening, but since Catherine had also experienced something similar thought now she must have made too much of the whole affair. 'I'm afraid I was not very gracious. I—I was feeling low and he took me by surprise.'

'Poor Jane!' Lady Farringdon sympathised. 'Lady Fairley had been lecturing you half the night and then—

But at least you will not have the awkwardness of having
to meet Sir Andrew immediately. He left for London an
hour since. I suppose he could not bear to meet you
this—' She broke off as Amanda came running into the
room. Her hair had fallen down her back and she was
clearly in a state of acute distress. 'Why—what is it,
child? What has happened?'

'Someone fired a shot at us as we were out riding near
the woods,' Amanda cried, her eyes wide with fright. 'At
least, Lord Massingham said it was probably a poacher
who had misfired, but it caused Max's horse to bolt and
he was almost thrown.'

'Is he hurt?' Jane and Catherine cried together.

'No. He held on despite his horse's wild flight. He was
wonderful—so brave and calm, more worried about any
distress I might be feeling than himself.'

'Were you thrown?' Jane asked, looking at her in sudden anxiety. 'You are sure you are not hurt, Amanda?'

'Oh, no. I was some distance ahead of him. We had
been racing, you see, and he gave me a start, because I
could never keep up with him otherwise, of course. Please
do not look so worried, Jane. I am quite unhurt.' She
turned as they heard a man's step and her face lit up as
John came into the room. 'Oh, John! Thank goodness you
are here.'

John back already? He must have travelled all night and
day to return so quickly, thought Jane, and wondered at
it. Why had he not spent a little time in town with his
friends?

Amanda ran to him at once. He caught her hands, looking down at her with such undisguised longing that Jane
felt a pang of distress. That explained his desperate hurry
to return to Massingham. Oh, no, not that—not poor John
too! It was surely enough that she should be suffering an
aching heart. She would not have had her brother fall in
love unwisely for all the world. What a pair they were!

'I came as soon as I could,' he said. 'I told you I would,

didn't I?' He glanced over Amanda's head at his sister. 'I've just seen Massingham. He looked dashed queer. Something wrong?'

'He was almost thrown from his horse,' Amanda said. 'A poacher in the woods shot at him and his horse bolted. I was terrified. I thought for sure he would be hurt—or killed.'

'Papa was killed by falling from his horse,' Catherine said with a little moan. 'His horse was spooked by something, but they called it an accident. So many accidents keep happening to Max. I am afraid for him—afraid that he will be killed. I could not bear it, really I could not.'

'That's damned odd,' John said, meeting Jane's worried look. 'If I'm not mistaken that's the sec—'

'John!' his sister warned swiftly. 'Please don't make things worse. Lady Farringdon must not be upset.'

'Why should it happen now?' Catherine asked, seeming on the verge of hysterics. 'It must be because Sir Andrew is no longer here to keep an eye on—' She broke off, biting her bottom lip. 'No, no, I cannot think that. It is too awful.' She stood up. 'Excuse me, I must speak to my brother.'

She almost ran from the room, clearly in deep distress. After she had gone, John gave his sister a knowing look. 'There's something dashed queer going on if you ask me. A man don't get shot at by accident twice running.'

'Is someone trying to kill Lord Massingham?' Amanda cried. 'Who would do such a wicked thing?' Tears started to fill her beautiful eyes. 'Oh, Jane! I cannot believe it. To think that his life may be in danger…it is too terrible to be borne!'

'We don't know for sure,' Jane said. She too felt like giving way to the violence of her feelings, but knew that she must not. 'It may be just a coincidence.'

'You don't really believe that?' John raised his eyebrows at her. 'Come off it, Janey, that's doing it too smoky. I dare say you know more about this business than either of us, but I shan't ask you to betray a confidence. It ain't my business—nor yours either.' He gave Amanda a straight look. 'Don't breathe a word of this—to Massingham or anyone. Do you hear me, Amanda?'

'No, of course I shan't say anything—not if you say I mustn't, John.'

'It is best that we say nothing,' Jane said, a little surprised at her ward's obedient answer. Amanda's face was very pale. She was clearly very shocked and concerned for Lord Massingham—further proof if it was needed that she felt a deep affection for him. 'Shall we go upstairs, dearest? You need to tidy yourself—and perhaps a sip of brandy for the shock? And I dare say John would like to wash and change after his journey?'

'Indeed, I must,' John agreed. 'Take Amanda and make her drink that brandy for the shock.'

'I hate the taste of it,' Amanda said, pulling a wry face. 'I would prefer a cup of hot chocolate—if that would not be too much trouble for Mrs Hurley?'

'I will ring for her,' Jane promised. She smiled at her brother. 'I'm glad to see you back so soon, John.'

She was thoughtful as she accompanied Amanda upstairs to their apartments. Was Catherine right? Was it because Sir Andrew had left for London that the would-be assassin had struck again? Had Richard seen his chance and seized it? Because Andrew was not there to watch over Max?

The thought made her feel guilty. Max's friend had undoubtedly left to avoid causing her more embarrassment. She had been very foolish to take fright like that. It was not as if it was the first time anyone had proposed to her...but it was his odd manner...

She put the memory resolutely from her mind. She was wrong; his manner had not been unnatural—just the intense passion of a man deeply in love.

'Where is Jane?' John Osbourne asked, looking eagerly into the face of the girl he adored as they met in the garden later that afternoon. 'Is she all right? I think she was more upset about the shooting than she let on.'

'She said she wanted to be alone for a while,' Amanda said, reaching for his hand. 'Oh, John, I was so frightened. I could not bear it if anything happened to dear Max. I am so very fond of him.'

'Yes, yes, I know you are... It's no wonder that you should be. He's a damned fine chap. I like him a lot myself.'

John sounded so gloomy that Amanda stared at him in surprise, then, as she realized what he was thinking, she laughed.

'Oh, John, you silly thing,' she cried, looking at him in such a way that his heart quickened and he began to hope. 'I don't mean that I like him more than you. Of course I don't. I cannot imagine ever caring for anyone more than you...' Her cheeks blushed fiery red. 'Oh, dear! Is that terribly forward of me? I shouldn't have said it—should I? But I did miss you so very much...'

John was so overwhelmed by the lovely, innocent way she had declared her feelings that for a moment he could not speak. When she lowered her lashes, looking distressed, he seized her hands, holding them so tightly that she had difficulty in suppressing a cry of pain.

'Did you really miss me that much, Amanda?' he asked in a voice laden with humility. 'Could you possibly have missed me as much as I missed you? Is it possible that you...?'

She raised her wonderful sparkling eyes to his, mischief lurking in their depths. 'Of course I love you, silly! There—now I've said it. I'm a shameless hussy. You will be disgusted with me, I expect?'

'How could I ever do anything but adore you?' he asked, looking at her with such hunger and slavish adoration that she gave a little cry and flung herself into his arms. 'Oh, my dearest, dearest girl. I have been so wretched thinking that you must naturally prefer Massingham. He *is* far superior to me, you know.'

'Oh, I love him as a friend,' Amanda cried, lifting her face for John's kiss. 'But I could never love anyone else in the way I love you, my dearest, kindest John.'

'Amanda…' he breathed, kissing her gently on the lips, then more deeply as she pressed herself against him, yielding the softness of her body to him with all the confidence and eagerness of an innocent girl newly awakened to passion. 'I love you, my darling. I want you to be my wife.' He touched her face as she gazed up at him. 'But you must be sure. It is only fair that you should have a season in town, dearest. I do not want to rob you of that, though I long to make you my own.'

'I should enjoy all the parties and balls,' Amanda agreed. 'Besides, I don't think they would let us marry for a while. But I don't mind…this will be our secret.'

'Our secret,' he agreed, stroking her cheek again. 'You have made me the happiest of men, my beloved.'

'When shall we tell Jane?' Amanda asked with a slight frown. 'Only…only I hope she won't be cross with me.'

'Why should she be?' John asked, puzzled.

'I think she is expecting me to marry Lord Massingham.'

'Yes…perhaps she is,' John agreed, looking at her anxiously. 'You see, she thinks she ought to give you the very best chance of making a good match. I'm not a wonderful catch, Amanda. I can't offer you a half of Massingham's wealth.'

'But I don't want it,' Amanda cried, a hint of mutiny in her face. 'I have enough money, John. All I want is to be with you—and to go to dances and balls, of course.'

John smiled at her indulgently. She was very young and it was natural she should crave excitement. He would not begrudge it to her for the world. Especially now he knew her heart was his.

'We shall go to as many balls as you like when we're

married,' he promised her. 'We'll visit London and Bath often—France and Italy too if you wish it.'

'Oh, John, dearest,' she said, smiling happily at him. 'I wish we could marry at once—but I know it wouldn't be proper just yet.' She sighed deeply. 'I suppose we shall just have to wait for a few months.'

He took her hand, carrying it to his lips, kissing the palm with tender reverence. 'I can wait for a while,' he said. 'Much as I love and want you, my darling, I would do nothing to upset Janey. She has been so very good to me.'

'Yes, I know—and to me,' Amanda said, looking worried. 'I love her too. You know I do, John. I don't want her to be cross with me. Let's not tell her just yet.'

'Perhaps that would be best…'

'Need we go back to the house for a while?' Amanda asked. 'Could we not walk for half an hour or so? I want to be alone with you.'

'And I with you,' he agreed. 'We shall slip away to the rose arbour so that I can kiss you as much as I like…'

Chapter Eight

Jane really had a headache now. It had started when she'd come up to help Amanda settle her nerves. The girl had looked so pale and frightened. And no wonder! Jane was feeling sick with nerves herself. She had no doubt that someone had deliberately fired at Max—that his life was in terrible danger. This was the second time someone had fired at him; they might be luckier the next.

'Oh, Max…' she whispered, the emotion making her throat tight and painful. She felt like weeping. 'If you were to die I should not know how to bear it.'

She must stop this at once! She had no right to feel this way. It was very wrong of her. Amanda was going to marry Lord Massingham. He was in love with her.

Jane bathed her forehead in lavender water, then picked up a light shawl and, wrapping it around her shoulders, left her bedchamber. She knew from past experience that her headache would not go if she stayed indoors. What she really needed was a good gallop. If she were at home she would order her mare from the stables and ride out on the moors, but she did not like to ask Massingham's grooms without permission from her host—though she knew it would be instantly granted.

She did not want to speak to anyone for the moment. She was so upset that she might burst into tears again.

How very missish of her! Jane smiled at her own foolishness as she walked down the stairs and escaped into the
rose gardens without seeing anyone. Only a few weeks
ago she would have taken a hundred-guinea wager against
her behaving like this. She had always prided herself on
her strength of mind. But falling in love was a new experience—and she was in such a difficult position.
Besides being half out of her mind with worry over this
latest attack on Max.

She had been strolling for some minutes in the sunshine
before she heard the laughter coming from a secluded
arbour. That was surely Amanda's laugh? Jane hesitated,
about to turn away, when she heard a man say something
and then Amanda started giggling. She sounded very
happy.

Even as Jane paused the two of them came into view,
their arms about each other's waists. As she watched in
surprise and growing horror, Amanda lifted her face for
the man's kiss.

She was kissing John! And in a way that showed she
had done it before. Jane was shocked beyond anything.
How could Amanda behave so wantonly? She was on the
verge of becoming engaged to Lord Massingham...how
hurt he would be if he ever learned of her betrayal. It was
very wrong of Amanda, and selfish.

'What are you doing?' Jane demanded angrily. Her tone
was so sharp that it startled even her. But all she could
think about was Max's pain when he discovered the girl
he loved had been playing fast and loose with him. 'How
dare you sneak away like this? I have never been so
shocked in my life.'

'Jane...' Her brother stared at her in dismay. 'I...
we...it isn't what you think...'

'I can see what it is,' Jane said. 'Amanda, you look like
a hoyden. Go to your room and tidy yourself at once. I
am ashamed of you. I thought you had more sense than
this.'

Amanda hesitated, looking to John for help, but he was too stunned by his sister's unexpected arrival—and her unusual anger—to say anything of substance.

'Janey…you don't understand.'

'This is not one of your larks,' Jane said in a voice colder than any she had ever used towards him. 'Amanda is my ward. You should know better than to bring her here alone. What do you think people will say of her? Her reputation would have been ruined if anyone else had seen what I saw. No one would receive her!'

Amanda gave a little moan of distress and broke away from him. Picking up her skirt with one hand, she rushed past Jane and disappeared in the direction of the house. John made to go after her, but Jane stopped him.

'Let her go,' she commanded. 'I am disappointed in you, John. What were you thinking of? Don't you know that people will say you have taken advantage of her innocence? That you are more interested in her fortune than…'

'That's a damned lie!' John said, recovering somewhat. 'You know it is, Jane. I love Amanda. I would never do anything to harm her. You know I wouldn't!'

'You have already harmed her,' Jane said, some of the harshness leaving her face as she acknowledged the truth of his words. He did love her. 'Yes, I dare say you had not thought—but she has been robbed of the chance to grow up. To enjoy a little flirting…'

'Damn it, no!' John said. 'We know we can't marry at once. We are prepared to wait…to let Amanda have her fling in town.'

'Oh, John,' Jane said sadly. 'You are not listening to me. If you are secretly engaged it will not be the same. And supposing…just supposing she did meet someone else?'

'Then I should let her go,' John said stiffly. 'No matter what it cost me—but it won't happen. We have talked of this, Jane. I am not a fool though you clearly think me one.'

He looked so put out that Jane might have laughed under other circumstances, but this was not the time for laughter.

'No, dearest, I do not. I want only what's best for you—and Amanda.'

'You want her to marry Massingham,' John flared. 'She told me so. Just because it's a good match, you think…'

'Yes, I do think it a good match for her,' Jane said, stung by his manner. Why had he gone behind her back like this? It was very hurtful. 'She would be very lucky to secure him for a husband.'

'She doesn't love him. You can't make her marry him. She loves me.' John glared at her. He was too angry now to think sensibly. 'We won't let you ruin her life and mine.'

'I am not trying to ruin your lives,' replied Jane, irritated beyond bearing. 'You are both of you so selfish. Have you no thought for others? For what Lord Massingham might be feeling? Or are you so selfish you cannot think of anyone but yourselves?'

'To hell with Massingham and with you!' John cried, pushed beyond the limit. 'I love Amanda and I mean to marry her. You cannot stop us.'

He walked away, his back stiff, his walk quick and angry.

Jane stared after him. She was shocked by the bitter quarrel. It was the first time she and John had ever had angry words, except those of childhood, which were soon forgotten. She could have bitten off her tongue for what she had said to him and Amanda. The shock of seeing them like that had made her say such terrible things. She had no idea why she had lashed out like that, except perhaps that her nerves were in such a state.

'Oh, John…' she whispered to the air. 'I'm so sorry…so very sorry…'

* * *

Jane returned to the house feeling very chastened. John and Amanda *had* behaved thoughtlessly, but perhaps they had not meant it to happen...had not meant to hurt anyone. It had been such a shock to her seeing them together...and it *would* cause people to talk if they married too soon. People would say that John had taken advantage of the girl because of her fortune... But that could not matter if they were truly in love. She ought not to have flown into a temper like that. Jane felt the sting of remorse. She had not meant to hurt either of them.

'Miss Osbourne.' The housekeeper's voice broke into Jane's thoughts. 'Lady Fairley has been asking for you. She is in the small parlour next to the library, miss. She requested that you come to her as soon as you returned.'

'Oh...' Jane hesitated. She was not in the mood for one of Lady Fairley's lectures at the moment. She wanted to talk to Amanda, to apologize and make up their quarrel, but it would be rude if she refused a request from Max's godmother. Amanda must wait for a few minutes, and perhaps that would not do any harm. It might give her a moment for quiet reflection. 'Yes, thank you, Mrs Hurley. I shall go to her now.'

When Jane entered the room, Lady Fairley was sitting by the window with a book in her hand. She glanced up, then nodded, indicating that she wanted Jane to sit with her.

'You have pink cheeks,' she announced. 'You have been walking in the garden, I dare say? The air has done you good. That scamp of a godson of mine says I gave you a headache last night. I had not thought you such a poor dab of a thing?'

'Nor am I,' Jane said with a smile. 'It was most unfair of Massingham to blame you. I certainly did not, ma'am.'

'And so I should think.' The elderly lady nodded approvingly. 'If we are to be connected I should like to think you could stand up to me—that we might become friends in time?'

'Of course…' Jane felt her cheeks getting warm. How dreadful this was! Max had asked his godmother here believing Amanda was about to accept his offer. He would be deeply offended when he discovered that she had no intention of becoming his wife. 'That is, I see no reason why we should not be friends, ma'am…whether there is a connection between us or not.'

'You mean that ramshackle godson of mine hasn't come up to scratch yet? What is he waiting for?'

'Perhaps he is not yet certain of…'

'Stuff and nonsense!' Lady Fairley grunted. 'Any fool can see he's head over heels in love. I know him too well to be mistaken. He hasn't led the life of a saint, nor should you expect it. But all that nonsense will finish once he has the right wife—and I think he has chosen well for once in his life. I couldn't have picked a better gel for him if I'd had the choosing myself.' She raised her quizzing glass and studied Jane. 'Well, well, you have my approval—though it makes not a jot of difference to the outcome, as I well know. Max is his own man. Run along now, Miss Osbourne. I am going up to my bed for a little nap. At my age an hour in the afternoon makes all the difference. Don't stare like that, chit. Go on with you!'

Jane knew herself dismissed. She felt deeply distressed as she left the room. All Max's friends and relatives expected an imminent announcement of his engagement. He would feel such a fool when he discovered the truth. Jane's heart took a flying leap as she saw him coming down the hall towards her. How tall he was…and so handsome! How could any woman prefer another man?

She waited for him to come up to her, gazing up at him with concern. He was such a proud man. He would not enjoy being made a fool of by a young girl.

'Mrs Hurley told me where you were,' he said, his eyes going over her with concern. 'I trust you are feeling better today? I was coming to rescue you. You must not let my godmother bully you, Jane.'

'She doesn't,' Jane replied. She was finding it very difficult to breathe when he was standing so close to her. How could she tell him? How could she prepare him for the hurt he was bound to suffer? 'I am not such poor stuff. I like her. I dare say she can be difficult at times—but all she needs is a little consideration and understanding. But I do not need to tell you. I saw last night that you can manage her very well.'

'I am very fond of her,' Max said, his eyes warm with approval. 'So—if it was not my godmother, what did upset you last night?' He frowned. 'It wasn't Andrew—was it?'

'No, of course not.' Her cheeks were pink and she could not look at him as she lied.

'You are not telling me the truth, Jane.' His tone was so commanding that she found herself compelled to look at him. 'Did he make advances to you? Did he try to touch you...to make love to you? Did he do something to make you afraid of him?' His voice rose on a note of anxiety. 'You must tell me, Jane. It is important. Perhaps more so than you might imagine.'

'No! No, of course not,' Jane said in a muffled tone. 'Excuse me—I must go!'

'Jane…' Max caught her arm as she would have turned away. 'I know Andrew likes you. Do you like him? Is that why you cannot look at me?'

'Naturally I like your friends,' Jane said. 'Now, I must go to Amanda. Please let go of me.'

He was so close to her. She was breathing in the scent of him, the faint perfume of cedarwood, a heady masculine mixture of leather, horses and his own personal musk that she found so intoxicating. She gazed up into his eyes, feeling herself drawn towards him, longing to be held in his arms, to be kissed and loved. Oh, how she wanted him to make love to her! What a wanton she was. Surely he must read it in her eyes?

'I'm sorry, I must go,' she cried, and broke away from

him, running up the stairs before her overwrought emotions caused her to betray herself.

'Jane,' he cried, a note of exasperation in his voice. 'Damn it! Don't go. I want to talk to you. It's time we got this sorted out... I have to talk to you, to explain...'

She could not stay and hear him now. She needed time to calm herself, to decide how to tell him that Amanda did not wish to be his wife. It was bound to cause him pain, to hurt him—and she could not bear the thought of giving him such pain. Jane's heart twisted at the thought of what she must do. It could not be long delayed—but first she must make her peace with Amanda.

She knocked at her door, then tried the handle. It was locked against her. Her ward must be in a terrible state and Jane was overcome with remorse for upsetting her.

'Amanda, dearest,' she said. 'Please let me in. I have come to apologize to you. It was very wrong of me to say those things to you. What you did was foolish—but not as wicked as the things I said to you. Please, my dear. Let me in. I am not angry. Please don't be angry with me.'

There was no reply. Jane tried the door again, rattling the handle.

'Please, Amanda...we must talk about this.'

'It's no use, Miss Osbourne—she isn't there.'

Jane turned as she heard the voice of her maid. 'What do you mean, Bessie? The door is locked; she must be there.'

'No, she isn't, miss.' Bessie frowned, then glanced over her shoulder to make sure they were alone. 'She locked it from inside then went through the little parlour door.' Bessie took a deep breath. 'Like a scolded cat, she was...in such a state as I don't know what. I asked her what was wrong but she just stared at me—tears in her eyes—then ran off down the hall to Mr John.'

'She is with my brother?'

'Yes, Miss Osbourne.'

'Thank goodness. No doubt she will return soon. I can speak to her then.'

'No, I don't think so, miss.' Bessie screwed up her mouth in an expression of distaste. 'Not by what I heard them saying...'

'What are you talking about?'

'As I understood it, they was planning to run off together, Miss Osbourne—to Scotland, I think. I dare say you're shocked, but as true as I stand here I heard them speak of it.'

Jane went white. She took hold of the maid's arm, her heart beginning to beat wildly. 'Tell me what you heard, Bessie,' she said, struggling for control. 'Exactly what was said and by whom.'

'Miss Amanda was in a terrible state,' Bessie said, 'crying and carrying on, near hysterical. She kept saying they must run away, that you would force her to...marry against her will and she would rather die.' Bessie hesitated, looking uncomfortable. 'Mr John put his arm round her to comfort her—and then he said something about no one forcing her to do anything...and that they would be married straight away and he had come to take her to Scotland.'

'Gretna Green,' Jane gasped, feeling slightly dizzy with the shock. 'They are going to be married over the anvil.'

'Surely not, miss?' Bessie looked at her in concern. 'It was just nonsense, wasn't it? They wouldn't do that— not after you've been so kind to Miss Roberts.'

'It is my fault,' Jane said, her heart filled with dread. 'I have driven them to it. You don't know, Bessie. I was so angry! I said terrible things to her—to both of them. If they have run off to Gretna Green it is my wicked temper that has driven them to it.'

'Now, that I can't and won't believe,' Bessie said. 'You're the kindest, most generous lady and if you were cross with Miss Amanda she probably deserved it. Such wickedness as this is none of your making, and that I dare swear.'

'Oh, no, Bessie.' Jane was lashed by remorse for what she had done. 'No, no, it was quite my fault—but what must I do?'

Her maid had no solution to offer—or none that she dared voice. In Bessie's opinion her mistress had indulged both her brother and the young miss beyond what was sensible. If it was up to her she would give them both a good smacking and send them back to the schoolroom until they learned to behave themselves.

Jane walked away to her own room, still reeling under the shock of what had happened. She went into the small parlour that connected Amanda's room to hers, and from it to Amanda's. There was no one there but the dressing table was in disorder, as if the girl had snatched up some of her personal possessions in a hurry.

Bessie was right—she had run away! It was all so awful that Jane did not quite know how it had come about. Oh, why had she flown at them in a temper? It was so unlike her. Why hadn't she dealt with the situation calmly, talked to them sensibly? If she had asked them to wait for a few months...but it was too late now.

She returned to her own room and sat down at her dressing table, staring at herself in the mirror. What on earth was she going to do? It was quite shocking that her brother should elope with her ward to Gretna Green: it would cause a terrible scandal that might ruin both their lives. It had to be stopped! And yet what could she do?

A loud knock at her door caused her to spring up, her heart leaping in fright. Perhaps it was John, come to have it out with her? Surely *he* would see the impropriety of a flight to Scotland!

She ran to open the door, but halted as it was abruptly thrown wide and Lord Massingham walked in without ceremony. He looked so angry! She took a step back, her heart quailing. Had he heard? How could he? Unless

Bessie was not the only servant to have overheard Amanda's rash words.

'I'm so sorry,' Jane cried, her words coming out in a jumbled torrent. 'I know you must be offended and angry but…I fear it is all my fault. She thought I meant to force her into marrying you, which of course you must know I would never have done—and you could not have wanted if I had been foolish or unkind enough to try. But when I saw them—embracing!—I flew into a temper, because she…they have behaved badly, but Amanda is more to blame because she must have known of your feelings. And now to run off like this, and the scandal…' Jane was forced to draw breath and in that moment he caught her in his arms, kissing her with such force that she was silenced and gazed up at him in dismay, her breath quite gone.

'That's better,' Max said, frowning down at her as he released her. 'Calm down if you please, Jane, and tell me what that wretched girl has done to upset you now.'

'She isn't a wretched girl.' Jane defended her ward instinctively. Her eyes were on his face. Why had he kissed her like that? 'I know she has not behaved well—and I could never condone what she and John have done. But they are in love and it is my fault they have run off.'

'Run off?' Max stared at her in disbelief. 'What on earth made them do such a stupid thing? She is too young to be married yet, but in a few months it might easily have been arranged. I know Amanda is a madcap but I should have thought your brother had more sense. What drove them to such a desperate act?'

'It was my fault,' Jane said. 'I was upset because of the way she had treated you, letting you think— And I told her her reputation would be ruined if people saw them kissing in your gardens—that no one would receive her.'

'Good Lord!' Max was astonished. 'No wonder she flew into his arms. What were you thinking of, Jane? That is not like you. I know it is rather soon…that she ought properly to have a season before they marry…but there is nothing so very bad about the match, is there? John is obviously in love with her and if she loves him…'

'But what of your feelings?' Jane asked, bewildered. 'You were intending to make her an offer. Everyone is expecting it.'

'Are they indeed?' His eyes glittered like sapphire beads. 'Then everyone is making a foolish mistake. Believe me, I have never once thought of making Miss Roberts an offer.'

'But I thought…' Jane could not breathe. 'You said you were thinking of marrying. Lady Fairley said…'

Her voice trailed away as she saw his mouth go hard with anger. He glared down at her, his hands clenching at his sides, obviously fighting against an urge to do some violence to her.

'And you?' he asked grimly. 'Is that what you have been thinking all this time—that I intended to make an offer for that girl? Good grief, Jane! What sort of a man do you think I am? She is almost young enough to be my own daughter. Please credit me with enough sense to want someone a little more sophisticated—a woman able to share my interests, and hold an intelligent conversation now and then.'

'But you seemed to enjoy playing silly games with her?' Jane was bewildered by his outburst.

'Because you asked me to look after her.' He made a sound of exasperation in his throat, turned away and paced about the room for several seconds. When he looked at her again his expression was hard, distant, quite unlike anything she had ever experienced from him before. 'I suppose you want me to go after them?'

Jane curled her nails into the palms of her hands. 'Would you?' she asked. 'They haven't thought…they don't realize what it will mean…that many of the people they call their friends will refuse to receive them.' She smothered a sob, wondering why she felt so very miserable. 'I know I have no right to ask it of you, but...'

'Stop looking at me like that,' Max said harshly. 'And don't talk such fustian! We shall discuss at another time what right you may or may not have to command me—for now there are plans to be made.'

'Yes, Max.' Jane could hardly bear to look at him. 'I should be so grateful if—'

'Damn your gratitude!' he flared. 'I shall do what I can to save them from the consequences of their own folly, but I must know your wishes in this. Do you want them to marry or would you rather I brought Amanda back—and gave the charge of her to Lady Fairley? At least she would know how to control the girl. Which is plainly more than you can.' His eyes narrowed in frustration. 'It was foolish of Mary Roberts to thrust such a task on your shoulders. You are hardly out of the schoolroom yourself.'

'Indeed I am,' Jane said, stung to anger by his high-handed manner. 'I am six and twenty. Amanda has been no trouble to me.'

'Because you have indulged her every whim,' Max growled. 'When you very rightly reprimanded her for behaviour that can only be called foolhardy at best—and something far worse if we are being straight about this!—she runs off with your brother and lands you in a scandal. If you do not call that trouble, I most certainly do.'

'You must not blame her,' Jane cried. 'I know you are angry with her but...please do not fly into a temper.'

'We are wasting time,' Max said grimly. 'While we stand here arguing about something that matters not one jot they are well on their way. I shall have Thorne pack my bag and set out after them at once. You do not know whether they took your brother's carriage, I suppose?'

'I think they must have done,' Jane replied. 'I cannot suppose John to have been so lost to decency as to borrow your horses when he was making off with the woman he believed you wanted to marry.'

'And that is your fault,' Massingham said, glaring at
her. 'If you had not got such a ridiculous notion into your
head none of this need have happened.'

Jane felt as if he had slapped her. The colour drained
from her cheeks and she was only just able to stop herself
giving a cry of distress. She caught at his arm as he would
have walked from the room.

'Where shall I meet you?'

'Meet me?' An expression of disgust came into his
eyes. 'You do not imagine I shall let you come with me?
You cannot keep up with me, Jane. You will slow me
down, hamper my chances of reaching them before they
get past London.'

'I am coming with you,' she said, giving him a haughty
look. 'I want to be there when you catch up with them—
and as for not keeping up with you I can ride as well as
any man.'

'Indeed?' He was very angry, but as she met his fierce
stare she saw a flicker of respect. 'Have you no thought
for your own reputation, Miss Osbourne?' he asked, a hint
of the old mockery in his voice. 'What will people think
if you ride off with me? They may say that we are elop-
ing.'

'My friends will know differently and as for the rest…'
Jane shrugged carelessly. 'I do not mind what people
think of me. I have no plans to go into society. It is my
brother and Amanda who matter—and we are wasting
more time, sir!'

'Very well, bring no more than a change of clothes,'
Max commanded. 'And be waiting in the hall in fifteen
minutes or I shall not stay for you.' With that stern warning he turned and strode from the room.

Jane called loudly for Bessie, who came so quickly she
must have been in the next room with her ear to the door.

'I have only a few minutes,' Jane said, tearing at her
gown. 'I must change into my riding things and pack
some undergarments.'

'Yes, miss,' Bessie replied, and ran to the closet. 'You get out of them things and leave the rest to me...'

They had been riding hard for several hours now and it was beginning to grow darker. Jane kept her eyes on the man's back as he rode just ahead of her. She was tired and she knew her mare must also be weary but she dared not ask him to slow down or call a halt, because he would very likely send her home and carry on alone.

They had had news of an open carriage driven by a young man with a very pretty girl as his passenger at one of the toll stations a few miles back, and Massingham thought that they might be lucky enough to catch up with the runaways before nightfall.

'There is a good coaching inn some ten miles ahead,' he had told her as they'd left the tollgate. 'John would know of it—and it is the only decent place for miles. If we can catch them before they spend the night together all may not be lost.'

'Spend the night together?' Jane was shocked at the very idea. 'Surely they would not do anything so foolish?'

Massingham's mocking look had silenced her. Would John anticipate his wedding night? He was very much in love with the girl, and might think it the best way of making sure they could not be parted. Oh, no, no, he would not! And yet she had seen another side of her brother that day, and could not now be certain of anything.

It must not happen. Jane urged her mare on, determined to keep up with Massingham: Amanda's innocence and reputation should not be lost for want of a lack in her!

It was raining now. A slight drizzle that dampened her hair and clothes and made her uncomfortable. She noticed that Massingham's pace had slowed slightly, allowing her to catch up with him.

'I have friends nearby,' he said, glancing at her. 'I could take you there and then go on alone.'

'I am coming with you.' Her face was pale but determined. 'I must be there when you find them.'

'You may regret your decision before long,' he said. 'I think this rain will get worse.'

'I have been soaked before when out riding. I shall not give up now. And we are wasting time, sir.'

A flicker of respect showed in his eyes. He nodded, gave his reins a little shake and started off again at his former pace, leaving Jane to keep up as best she could, but never going so far ahead that she could not follow his lead.

She knew that he might have been faster if she had not insisted on accompanying him, but it would not make that much difference—and if they were lucky they would reach the inn before dark.

The rain started to lash down within half an hour. It drove into Jane's face as she rode, stinging her eyes and soaking into her clothes. She ducked her head low over her horse's back, gritted her teeth and prayed that it would not be for very much longer. It had turned very cold all of a sudden and their quest had become a matter of endurance. She could not keep this up for very much longer, but she must. She must!

The inn came in sight after another twenty minutes or so, though to Jane it could have been eternity. She was chilled to the bone, weary and thoroughly miserable when at last they rode into the courtyard and two grooms came running to take their horses.

Max jumped down, questioning one of the grooms for some seconds before coming to Jane, who had remained in the saddle, afraid to get down lest he tell her they must set out once more. She knew she would be incapable of getting back into the saddle again that night.

'An open carriage with a young man and girl arrived just over half an hour ago,' he said. 'They are in the parlour having supper.'

'Oh, thank goodness,' she said, relief sweeping over her. 'We are in time.'

'Let me help you.' He held her as she slipped from the saddle. She was so exhausted that if he had not had his arm about her she might have fallen, though in a moment she had recovered. He gazed into her face for a second, his brow furrowing. 'You are weary. You should not have come. I warned you I would be riding hard.'

Jane's head went up. 'I am perfectly all right,' she said. 'Let us go and find them before they finish their meal and go upstairs. We must do all we can to reduce the harm that has already been done.'

The innkeeper came towards them as they entered his house. He bowed low when Max requested to be shown to the parlour.

'Yes, my lord,' he said. 'If your lordship won't mind sharing it with two others? I have a gentleman and his sister dining this evening.'

'Very well,' Massingham said. 'Give us a few moments to thaw ourselves by the fire, landlord, then you may serve us a meal—something warming. My cousin is chilled to the bone as you can see.'

'Yes, my lord. Of course, my lord.'

'You have stayed here before?' Jane asked as he strode ahead of her. 'Why did you tell him that I was your cousin?'

'For the sake of your reputation,' Max said, smiling oddly. 'And my own. I would not want to be the latest scandal in the drawing rooms of London—and depend upon it, someone who knows me will see us.'

Jane's cheeks were flushed as she followed him. She had been all on fire to come with him, because of her natural concern for Amanda—and her brother, who might be tempted to do something very foolish if accosted by Massingham—but she knew in her heart that her own behaviour would be censured if it became common knowledge. But if her being there averted the threat of a fight—

or perhaps a duel!—between the two men she loved she would count her disgrace as nothing.

Massingham walked into the dining parlour, Jane two steps behind him. There were only two persons seated at the tables—and neither of them was known to Jane.

'Oh…' she cried, feeling a rush of disappointment. 'It isn't them.'

'Good evening, Ravenscourt,' Max said with easy affability. 'I didn't know you were in the country. Miss Ravenscourt.' He turned to Jane with a lift of his eyebrows. 'May I introduce Miss Osbourne—a distant cousin.'

'Massingham.' The man stood up and bowed to them. 'Miss Osbourne. Pleased to meet you.' He sat down again and went on with his supper, making no attempt to introduce his sister. His behaviour was so particular that it was obvious what he thought of her.

Jane felt her cheeks flush bright red as the girl looked at her curiously. She was suddenly aware of what she must look like, splattered with mud, wet through and wind-blown—and what they must be thinking.

She looked at Max, lowering her voice to an urgent whisper. 'We must leave now—we must go on.'

He took her arm, directing her to a table at the far end of the room. 'Sit down,' he said quietly but with a firmness she was compelled to obey. 'You cannot go further tonight—and I am not going back out in this weather. We could ride for miles and never find them. John has clearly thought this out and will avoid all the well-known inns. We shall stay here this evening and tomorrow I shall make enquiries in the district. Until we know for certain which way they are headed we shall have no chance of finding them.'

'Stay here?' Jane met his stern gaze. 'Yes, I suppose you are right.'

'Ah, here comes our host,' Max said as the innkeeper

entered the room. 'I shall bespeak our supper and two rooms for the night...'

He would also have a quiet word with Viscount Ravenscroft before they left the next day. Jane's flush of embarrassment at not being introduced to Ravenscroft's sister had not gone unnoticed, and Max did not intend such a thing to happen again!

Chapter Nine

'We shall come to an inn soon, dearest,' John said, looking anxiously at Amanda's pale face. The storm had come upon them with such ferocity that he had had no chance to look for shelter for them. 'I know you are wet and cold but I dare not stop anywhere I might be known. We shall probably be followed.'

'Oh, do not say so,' Amanda begged, her eyes wide and frightened. She was shivering and felt close to tears, beginning to wonder why she had come on this mad adventure. She had thought it would be simple to run away, and she *was* terrified that Jane meant to force her to marry Lord Massingham, but being bounced about in an open carriage on a wet night was not very romantic. She thought longingly of her own warm bed. 'What shall we do if they catch us? Jane will be so very cross with me.'

'I shall protect you, dearest,' John said, smiling at her. he took her hand in his, holding it comfortingly. 'Besides, when she has had time to consider I am sure…'

Whatever he meant to say was lost as the carriage wheel suddenly hit a rut in the country road they were travelling, gave a sickening lurch sideways, which was followed by an ominous crack as the leading pole snapped. Amanda was thrown against John's shoulder as he struggled to keep his hold on the reins and quieten the nervous horses.

It was several minutes before he had them under control, and one glance at Amanda's white face told him that she was close to exhaustion. This was all too much for a girl as fragile and delicate as he believed her to be.

'Damn,' he muttered beneath his breath. 'Now what are we to do? I'll have to get down and unharness the horses, Amanda. We must abandon the carriage and...' He cursed and looked around him at the gathering gloom. The rain was starting to bucket down now and he knew they were miles from any decent inn. 'I think we shall have to let the horses go free and walk—unless I could put you up on one of them and lead it. Do you think you could manage that, dearest?'

'Yes, I think so.' Amanda's teeth were beginning to chatter. She was so cold and getting wetter by the minute. 'Do you think we shall find an inn soon?'

'Yes, of course we will,' John said, sounding far more confident than he felt. He was a stupid fool to have subjected Amanda to this! If he had stuck to the main roads someone would have been bound to come along but they were miles from anywhere...in fact he was lost and had no idea of where he was. 'Stay here while I see to the horses, dearest. Here, let me put my cloak around you; it will keep off some of the rain.' He placed the warm cloak tenderly around her shoulders and she managed to summon the ghost of a smile.

He freed the fretful horses from the wreck of his carriage, then went back to help Amanda down. For a moment his arms closed about her, holding her pressed to him. He felt her shiver and frowned in the gathering darkness. This was all wrong! He should never have brought her on such a wild flight.

Her hysterical tears had made him act impulsively, but now that he was calmer he knew it would have been far better to face up to things like a man. He should have stayed put and stood his ground. Jane could not—would not if he admitted the truth—have forced Amanda into anything she really did not wish to do. They might have had to wait for a few months but in the end Jane would have agreed to the match between them. Anything would have been better than his darling girl having to put up with such discomfort.

He was thoughtful as he put Amanda up on the back of the steadiest of the two carriage horses. His first priority must be to find somewhere they could safely stay for the night, and then, in the morning, he would talk to Amanda. Perhaps if he took her home they could brush through this, make it seem as though it had been their intention all the time.

'The landlord has supplied me with a rough guide to the lesser country roads in this area,' Max said the next morning as he and Jane left the inn after partaking of an early breakfast. 'There are two directions John might have taken if he was heading for London—which he would if he meant to take Amanda on to Scotland. They could lose themselves there for a few days, allow the trail to go cold and then continue without fear of detection.' He showed her a pen-and-ink sketch which had obviously been roughly done. 'This is the main road we took here...'

'Yes, I see,' Jane said, following his pointing finger. 'So they could have branched off here to avoid the high road—or here.'

'The first turn leads only to farms and small villages,' Max said. 'It is very rough according to the landlord and almost impossible for a carriage to pass after about this point. This road is better and joins up with the main highway again at a crossroads some miles further on. If John had any idea of his whereabouts he would choose that, thinking to avoid detection for the first stage of their journey in the hope of losing anyone who tried to follow them.'

'Yes,' agreed Jane. It did seem probable that her brother would have chosen the secondary road. 'Are there any inns this way? Would they have found shelter for the night or gone on travelling?'

'In that rain?' Max raised his brows. 'It was a wonder you did not catch your death of cold, and you have been used to hard riding on the moors. Amanda has not the half of your resilience. If John has any sense at all he will have sought shelter at the earliest opportunity. I happen to know that there is only one inn on that road. We shall no doubt discover that they stayed there—or are perhaps still there if we are fortunate.'

'Then we must go there at once.'

'Will you not let me take you to my friends?' Massingham asked. Jane was looking much better after a night's rest but despite his words of encouragement he knew that searching for the fugitives would be a thankless task and might well take days or even weeks. If he was wrong, they could miss them altogether. 'You could stay there—or go back to Massingham and wait for me.'

'Why will you not accept that I intend to see this through?' Jane asked, a sharp note in her voice because she was anxious. 'Amanda is my ward—and I am responsible for this. It is my fault. If I had not upset her they would never have run off.'

'That girl is a selfish minx,' Max said harshly. 'If you don't give her a good talking-to when we catch up with them I certainly shall.'

'Indeed you will not,' Jane said. 'She will very likely run off again if you scold her.'

'I suppose you will fall on her neck and beg her forgiveness?' he said in a tone of sarcasm. 'That will teach her not to behave so recklessly in future, won't it?'

'You are in a temper, sir,' Jane said, glaring at him. 'If you do not wish to waste more of your time give me the map and I shall go on alone. I dare say I can find this inn you spoke of quite easily.'

'I've a good mind to let you try,' Max growled, then, as she made to walk off towards where the groom stood waiting with their horses, he caught her arm, swinging her back to face him. 'Ridiculous child! You are scarcely more able to look after yourself than Amanda!'

'And you are a tyrant!' she countered, furious with him now. Surely he must know how very anxious she was? 'Whatever made me imagine you might be a suitable husband for Amanda I cannot think!'

'Nor I,' he said, and scowled at her. 'However, I must have done something to foster this ridiculous idea in your mind—therefore I am as much to blame as you in the matter. Besides, I happen to like the girl—as wilful and thoughtless as she is—and I have no intention of abandoning the search just yet. We shall go together since you will not be sensible.'

Jane had reached the groom. She allowed him to help her mount, keeping her face averted from Max as she gave her horse a little nudge with her heels and started off at a brisk trot. She knew he was following her and was secretly very relieved, for it would have been impossible for her to go careering all over the countryside without his assistance. Improper as it might be for her to be travelling with a man who was not a member of her family, it would be far worse for her to continue alone. She knew it in her heart, but was still angry with him.

'Jane…' Max steadied his horse to trot beside hers. 'Whatever you may think of me, let us not fall out over this. I know you are worried to death over Amanda, but she is with your brother, not some blackguard of a fortune hunter. He cares for her truly. I cannot think that he would harm her intentionally and I dare say we can hush all this up—come up with some feasible excuse for their sudden disappearance. Catherine is aware of the truth, of course, but she knows how to be discreet. Do not fear that she will be ruined, and stop blaming yourself.'

Jane gave him a grateful smile. She blinked hard, feeling a rush of foolish emotion. He was arrogant at times and had a temper—no one could deny that!—but he could also be very considerate. And just now she was very much in need of a strong shoulder to lean on. It would have been such a relief to lean her head against his chest and give way to her overwrought emotions.

'Thank you. I should not pull caps with you when this is all my fault. I just wish that we could find them—that I could tell them I am willing to forget this nonsense and allow them to marry. Perhaps next spring.'

'Stop worrying,' he said again. 'We shall find them. I promise you. Do not despair, Jane. We shall find them at the inn; you see if I am not right.'

They very soon discovered that the landlord's sketch was far from accurate. Several times during the long, wearisome day that followed, they missed their way, had to turn back and start again, finding themselves miles from anywhere, lost and seeming to go round and round in circles. Jane felt a mounting sense of frustration, and knew her companion must feel the same. She could see by his expression that his mood was worsening, but he said nothing, and it was not until it was growing dusk that evening that they eventually came to the inn Max had spoken of that morning.

And what a terrible place it was! Jane's heart was filled with dismay as she saw it. This was not the kind of hostelry used by persons of quality. Not at all like the comfortable inn they had stayed at the previous evening. Could John really have brought Amanda here? Surely not! The yard was a midden, with hens and pigs nosing about in the rubbish that had accumulated through years of neglect, and the house itself was little better than a pigsty.

It smelt unpleasantly of stale beer and cabbage water as they went in. Jane held a scented kerchief to her nose and tried to ignore the impertinent stares of a gathering of yokels drinking ale in the taproom. She had never been so uncomfortable in her life and wished herself a thousand miles away.

Max glanced in the direction of the inn's customers once, frowned and took hold of Jane's arm, moving closer as if to protect her with his powerful body.

'Yes, sir.' The landlord bowed low before Max, obviously overcome at having two persons of quality in his humble establishment. No doubt it was the first and, as far as she was concerned, most definitely the last time a lady had ever set foot over his threshold. 'What can I do fer yer Honour?'

'I am looking for some friends,' Massingham said. 'A young man of about twenty and a girl—a very pretty girl with blonde hair.'

'Runaways, are they?' The man's crafty eyes ogled Jane. 'You and your good lady come after them, have you?'

'Are they here?' Jane cried, her patience almost at an end. 'Have you seen them?'

'Can't say as I 'ave.' He scratched at his middle, a sour odour of stale sweat wafting out from his filthy clothes. 'Don't have many visitors round 'ere, miss—or is it madam?'

'You are addressing my wife,' Max said, at his haughtiest. 'We shall want food in your best parlour, man—and a room for the night. Quickly, man! Stir yourself if you please. We have come a long way.'

'Ain't nothing but some of me wife's stew,' the landlord said. 'And there's a room…used to be me son's afore the rascal run off to join the army. Left his poor ma and me, he did—ungrateful wretch. Ain't been used in a while, with us not having many visitors, like. Well, not them as I'd let 'ave me best room.'

'Well, tell your wife to run a warming pan over the linen,' Max said impatiently. 'And show us to your parlour. I cannot dine in this place. You do have a parlour, I suppose?'

'Yes, sir. Not much of a one but you can be alone with your good lady, sir. I'll see to that. You just trust me, sir. I'll see as you're comfortable.'

Jane followed silently in Max's wake. She was filled with horror at the idea of staying in this terrible place overnight but knew that they had little or no choice. It had taken them all day to find it, and if they left now they would inevitably become lost again. Besides, she was too weary to venture out again. Her body ached so much that she could have wept, except that she would not have dreamed of doing so in front of her escort.

Alone in the parlour, which was slightly better than the taproom but still disgusting, the floor in need of a good scrubbing, Jane sat down and stared at Massingham as he began to strip off his leather gloves.

'Why did you ask for only one room?' she asked. 'We cannot possibly share a room. You cannot think I would consent to share a room with you?'

'Do you imagine I shall leave you to sleep alone in a place like this, Jane?' He glared at her, on his mettle, angered by her seeming distrust. 'I doubt if the door will have a decent lock—and who knows what might happen in a house like this? Those fellows in the taproom were eyeing you in a way I did not like. This looks like the haunt of rogues—maybe even a highwayman or two. I intend to sit up all night and keep guard over you. Otherwise they might slit both our throats and take our purses.'

Not to mention what they might do first to a lady who was as beautiful and desirable as Jane! He kept this last thought to himself, naturally, cursing himself for being fool enough to have allowed her to accompany him on this mad escapade. If any harm were to come to her—it did not bear thinking about!

'Surely not?' Jane looked at him in alarm. Her very proper objections to his sharing her room were forgotten as her heart started to thump uncomfortably. Her throat was suddenly dry and she could only croak as she asked, 'Would we not be better to leave now if you think this house so dangerous?'

'And risk being followed and set upon in the dark?' Massingham frowned and glanced over his shoulder as if he feared they might be overheard. 'Those men downstairs—they were not merely country yokels. At least two of them had a desperate look about them. Especially the one with the scar on his cheek. If I am wrong I shall lose a night's sleep for nothing, but if I am right—' He broke off as a rather sluttish woman brought in a tureen of steaming hot stew and set it down on the table before them with some bread, dishes, pewter mugs and a jug of water.

'Would you be wanting some ale, sir?' she asked, glancing towards the door and lowering her voice. 'I shouldn't if I were you—need your wits about you in a place like this.'

'What do you mean?' Jane asked, her heart leaping with sudden fright. 'Are we in danger of being attacked here?'

The woman looked nervous, and was obviously afraid of being overheard by someone. 'We don't get many visitors here,' she said in a harsh whisper. 'You'll be all right if you bolt your door and your man keeps his pistol at the ready.' She jumped as someone called for Bella and put a finger to her lips. 'Don't say nothing. I didn't tell you nothing.'

'Oh, Max!' Jane looked at him in alarm as Bella went out. 'May we not go now, please? I don't like it here.'

'Nor I,' he agreed, 'but I think we shall be safer if we do as she says. I have a pair of pistols and every intention of using them if need be. Don't worry, Jane, you will be quite safe. I give you my word.'

He looked so grim that Jane shuddered. What a terrible place their mad adventure had brought them to, and it was all her fault.

'I am glad Amanda and John did not come here.'

'We may think ourselves lucky for that much,' agreed Max. He lifted the lid of the tureen and smelt the stew. 'I think this is edible. Try to eat a little if you can, Jane—then we'll go upstairs.'

Jane was silent as he ladled some of the meat and gravy into a bowl for her. She did not think she could eat a mouthful, but the stew was surprisingly good and she ate most of what he had given her, also swallowing a few sips of the cool water. Max did the same. When the land-lord came in with a jug of ale he accepted it, but tipped it out into a wooden spittoon after he had left them.

'It is probably spiked with a drug of some kind,' he observed grimly. 'If mine host or one of his friends comes to visit us during the night they will imagine me fast asleep and be in for a nasty surprise.'

'Oh, pray do not!' Jane stood up, her nerves jumping. 'Can we go up now?'

'Yes, I think we may as well,' Max said. He took hold of her arm. 'I don't think they will try anything until later, when they think the drug has taken effect. They will have supposed me to be armed and now hope to take me off guard.'

Jane nodded but said nothing. She was nervous but Massingham was in command; he was a man of experi-ence, and she could do nothing but accept his judgement. As they went out into the hall, Bella came to meet them, carrying a chamberstick and lighted candle. She led the way upstairs, opened a door, went inside and lit several candles, then turned to look at Jane.

'I'll wish you a pleasant night, ma'am...' As she turned she looked straight at Massingham, her eyes flashing a warning. 'Take good care, sir. I can do nothing to help you, except warn you to be alert.'

'Thank you. I understand, and would not have you en-danger yourself further for our sake.' He took half a guinea from his pocket and gave it to her. 'You'd best hide that—for your own safety.'

She smiled, bit the gold coin and tucked it into the dipping neck of her filthy gown before departing.

Max examined the door. There was a bolt, which he slid into place. It looked as if it might hold unless a great force was used against it—which meant that they would come in another way. Crossing to the window, he looked out and nodded. It was possible for a man to climb up using a ladder, and there was no catch on the window.

'That's the way they will come,' he said to Jane, and set the only chair in the room to face it. 'You might as well lie on the bed and get what rest you can. I'm afraid it may not be very clean, but you must make the best of it. We shall leave as soon as it is light in the morning.' He sat down, stretching out his long legs in front of him.

Jane pulled back the covers. The linen looked grey and worn but there were no stains and hopefully no lice. She took off her travelling cloak and her bonnet and piled up the pillows, lying against them to watch Max as he prepared for the attack he suspected would come during the night. He had two pistols, each of which he checked to make sure that they were primed and ready. Becoming aware of her watching him, he smiled, his expression somehow comforting her despite their perilous situation.

'Close your eyes and try to rest,' he advised. 'They will not come yet—and I shall warn you when they do.'

'I couldn't sleep a wink,' Jane said, but closed her eyes as he blew out all but one candle. 'I am sure I shan't sleep at all…'

When her shoulder was shaken quite roughly, Jane awoke to a room in pitch-blackness. Her cry of alarm was immediately stifled by Max's hand over her mouth.

'Quiet,' he whispered against her ear. 'They are coming. I think there are two of them…perhaps more. Stay calm and do not move unless I tell you. '

Jane tensed, her nerves jangling. This was the stuff of nightmares. She had never been this frightened in her life.

If she had been that kind of woman she might have given in to a fit of the vapours, but she was determined not to cause more trouble for Max. He had quite enough to cope with already.

As her eyes became more accustomed to the gloom she began to make out shapes, and then she heard the scuffling noises that had alerted Max. They were coming from somewhere outside and it sounded very much as if someone was climbing a ladder.

All at once, a head poked through the open window, followed seconds later by the bulk of a man's body. Jane felt the scream rise in her throat, but before she even realized what was happening Max sprang at the intruder and struck him a hard blow on the back of the neck with the butt of one of the pistols. The man gave a cry of pain and slumped to the floor, lying so still she was sure he must be dead.

'What's going on?' A harsh voice called from outside. 'Are you in, 'enery? 'Enery…?'

Massingham leant out of the window and fired two shots. There was a scream of pain, then several warning shouts and another loud scream from below as a second man fell from the ladder with a thump, taking it crashing down after him. Jane shrank up against the pillows, stifling her own desire to scream as Massingham turned to her with a look of grim satisfaction.

'I winged one in the arm and another hurt his leg as he fell,' he said. 'He has hobbled off, and I think that's the last we shall see of those fellows tonight. Now, I'd better take a look at this one.'

'Is he dead?' Jane asked a little fearfully as Max bent over the man he had felled. 'He hasn't moved once.'

'He will be unconscious for a while,' Max replied grimly, 'but he isn't dead. I had best bind and gag him, too, if we are to get any rest this night.'

'Rest! With a murderer in the room?' She was horrified. 'What can you be thinking?'

Jane had got out of bed and stood watching as Max held a candle he had lit near to the intruder's face. She noticed a livid scar on one cheek—a scar that once seen would not be easily forgotten.

'What is it?' she asked as she saw the expression on Max's face. 'You know him, don't you? That's why you were expecting this attack...you've seen him before somewhere.'

'I wasn't sure downstairs,' Massingham admitted, 'but I believe I have seen this rogue a couple of times recently...following me.'

'Oh, Max!' Jane gave a cry of alarm. 'You don't think this could be the man who has been trying to kill you? Did he follow us here? Do you suppose he enlisted the others to...kill you?'

If he had killed Max, he must have killed her, too, because a witness could not be left alive to testify.

She was pale and trembling. Max did not notice at first, because he was busy binding the man's wrists behind his back, but when he finally had his victim trussed like a boiling fowl, complete with gag and blindfold, he looked up at Jane and saw that she was crying, the tears running silently down her cheeks.

'What is it, my dearest?' he asked, such a tender note in his voice that she could not bear it. 'You've been such a good brave girl. There's no reason to cry now. You are quite safe.'

'I w-wasn't th-thinking of me,' she stammered, quite unable to control the shaming sob that escaped her lips. 'I c-can't bear the thought of someone wanting to kill you.'

'Oh, my poor darling,' Max said in a soft, caressing tone and reached out to draw her into his arms. He gazed down at her, wiping away her tears with his fingertips. Then he bent his head and kissed her very tenderly on the mouth. 'I should never have told you of my foolish suspicions. I dare say it is all imagination anyway.'

Jane was enjoying the sensation of being held in his arms, but at this she fired up and remembered that this was all quite improper. What was she doing? To let him hold her—when they were alone in a bedchamber! Afraid that he would guess her reason for withdrawing, she flew to the attack. She wrenched away from him.

'Are you saying I'm one of those missish women from whom everything of a worrying nature must be hidden to save their fragile nerves?'

Max smiled at her truculent look. 'No, my very dear Jane, you must know I am not. I have never met a woman I thought more sensible or felt more able to confide in.'

'Oh…' His words worked wonders on her, drying her tears instantly and restoring her equilibrium. She turned a jaundiced eye on the unconscious man on the floor. 'What are you going to do about him?' she asked. 'Shall you turn him over to the authorities?'

'They would undoubtedly hang him,' Massingham said, considering. 'And, while he probably deserves it, I have no real desire for his blood. If he is the rogue who has been trying to kill me he has made poor work of it—and must be in the pay of the real culprit. I think I shall have a few words with the wretch when he wakens…and then we shall see. I am more interested in discovering who is behind it all than exacting punishment.'

He had such nobility of character. It was hardly to be wondered at if she had lost her foolish heart to such a man; he was just the kind of man she had hoped to meet one day. While her father had been ill she had had little chance to meet anyone other than her close neighbours, and after his death she had felt so dispirited, but since knowing Max her heart had begun to sing again. Something inside her swelled and reached out to him, and she longed to touch his face, to tell him that she loved him, but knew she must not.

'Shall I watch him while you rest for a while?' Jane asked. 'If he makes a move I can shoot him.'

'My fierce warrior queen,' Max said, a teasing smile lurking in his eyes. 'The poor fellow is trussed up securely; what harm do you imagine he can do to either of us?'

'None, I suppose,' said Jane, and laughed at herself. 'But will you not rest a little now? I have slept and feel much better for it.'

He must be so tired, and it had all been done for her sake. How kind and generous he was. If only she dared to reach out to him, to show him how she was feeling.

'I suppose I could lie down beside him,' Max teased, a wicked gleam in his eyes. 'Or would you trust me to share your bed, Jane?'

She gasped as her heart took a dizzy leap. For one moment she thought he meant it and knew that she was so far lost as to what was proper that she was tempted to agree; then she saw the mocking smile and realized he was funning her.

'I am perfectly certain I can trust you to behave as a gentleman,' she said, very much Miss Osbourne on her dignity. 'You may lie beside me if you wish.'

'What would people say of you, Jane?' he chided, obviously delighted at her daring. 'You have already risked everything on this mad venture. If it were ever known we had shared a bed...'

'And who will tell them?' she asked, a note of asperity in her voice. Could he not see that she longed for him to sweep all her protests aside and make her his own? 'I certainly shall not—and I had not taken you for a rogue, sir, which you certainly would be if you breathed a word of this to anyone.'

She climbed back onto the bed and curled over on her side, her back to him, daring him to follow. If he touched her, if he whispered her name she would not resist him.

Several seconds passed before she felt the bed sag beneath his weight, and the closeness of his body, almost but not quite touching her, sent a thrill of something she

realized must be desire rushing through her. She was longing for him to reach out and take her in his arms, and
then—goodness me!—she would surely have been lost for
she could not have summoned the will to resist him.
Indeed, she would quite possibly have thrown herself willingly into his arms and counted all well lost for love!

What a terrible wanton she was! It was quite, quite
shocking.

Fortunately for Jane's virtue, Massingham was well
able to control any feelings of lust he might be harbouring, and after a while she relaxed sufficiently to drift into
a peaceful sleep. Had she but known the thoughts passing
through the mind of the man who lay so still and quiet
beside her, it is doubtful she would have slept a wink, but
Massingham had always been a man to keep his own
counsel and he had good reason for his silence…an unpleasant doubt that had been growing in his subconscious
for a while now. A suspicion so horrible to him that he
could not bear to admit it even to himself.

As Jane slept peacefully at his side, Max knew that he
must be very careful from now on. He was almost sure
who his enemy was, and he suspected that he was very
much more dangerous than he had previously thought. He
must do nothing that might endanger the woman he loved,
even if that meant keeping silent for a while longer.

Something he was finding increasingly difficult!

When Jane woke the next morning it was to discover
there was no sign of Massingham or the creature who had
disturbed them the previous night. For a moment she wondered if it had all been a wild dream, but one look at her
surroundings brought it all back only too vividly. She
yawned and stretched, getting up to discover that there
was warm water in a jug on a washing stand in the corner
of the room, and soap and towels that had seen better
days.

Max must have sent Bella up to bring her these com-

forts, she realized. No doubt he had woken early and gone
downstairs to speak to the landlord and discover if he had
been a part of the plot to rob and perhaps murder them.

She dreaded to think what might have happened to her
if Max had let her come alone, but of course he was far
too much of a gentleman to do that—no matter how tiresome all this was for him.

His behaviour the previous night had shown him to be
a real gentleman—unless he had felt nothing as he'd lain
beside her? She considered it for a while, then decided it
was unlikely after the way he had spoken to her in the
library at Massingham. He had as much red blood in his
veins as any man, and if he had not taken advantage of
her vulnerability it was out of a gentlemanly consideration
for her virtue.

She had just finished tidying herself, and was wondering whether she ought to go down or wait, when Max
knocked at the door and asked if he might come in.

'Yes, of course,' she said, and turned with a smile as
he entered. 'Thank you for the water. It was good of you
to think of it, when I know you've had so much on your
mind.'

'I knew you would feel better for the chance to wash,'
he said. 'If you would care to come down, Jane, there is
some fresh bread and butter waiting in the parlour for
you—and Bella has managed to make you a cup of tea.'

'That would be very welcome,' Jane admitted. She discovered that she was very hungry. 'Have you finished
your business with…whoever he was?'

'That rogue has been sent on his way a trifle sorry for
himself,' Max said, a grim set to his mouth. 'He knows
he will hang if he should ever cross my path again. And
the landlord swears he knew nothing of any of it, of
course—but it's my guess this place has been a meeting
place for gentlemen of the road for many a day. However,
I have accepted his apologies and he has promised to send

a lad with us to show us the quickest route back to the main highway.'

Jane nodded and looked thoughtful. 'I believe you were right, Max. I have been nothing but a hindrance to you. If I had let you go alone in the first place you might have caught up with John and Amanda, but I fear it is already too late.'

'I very much doubt it,' he replied. 'John has simply been too clever for us. I think we should go back to the main roads and make more enquiries. If we have no luck today I shall go on alone to Scotland and arrange for you to return to Massingham in a hired carriage.'

'I think I should prefer to go home,' Jane said decisively. 'It might be best if everyone thinks that is what I intended when I first left Massingham.'

Max studied her in silence. What had changed her mind? He did not believe that she had been frightened by that unpleasant episode the previous evening, so why was she looking so subdued?

'If it is your wish,' he said, and inclined his head. 'But we shall have one more stab at finding them—or at least someone who has seen them—before we part. I know you will worry until they are found, and if I can at least give you some hope...' He stopped speaking as he saw the tears building in her eyes. 'Jane—is something wrong? You are not angry with me for embroiling you in that unfortunate episode last night? I truly had no choice. Out there in the darkness they would have had the advantage.'

'Of course I do not blame you,' she denied, blinking hard to stop herself giving way to the foolish emotions that threatened to overset her. 'I simply wondered if we had been mistaken in John's intentions. Perhaps he has thought better of it and taken her home.'

'We can only hope for the best,' Max said. 'Go and have your breakfast, Jane. I have a few things to finish here and then we shall be on our way.'

She must have given him a poor opinion of her, Jane

thought as she went downstairs, so lacking in resolution that she had faltered at the first hurdle. It was no such thing, of course. She really did think that John might have come to his senses and taken Amanda home—and if she went on with this mad adventure she would end by betraying herself.

It made her hot with shame to remember the way she had longed for him to make love to her the previous evening. He had been very kind to her, even calling her his dearest Jane when she was weeping on his shoulder, but she was not going to jump to foolish conclusions this time. It would be terrible if she did anything that caused Lord Massingham to believe he had preyed on her affections or compromised her reputation so much that he was forced to make her an offer out of sheer decency. She really would not be able to bear that!

No, it would be much better if she went home and let him get on with the search for Amanda and John alone. Which was exactly what she ought to have done in the beginning.

Chapter Ten

John looked down at the flushed face of the woman he loved and cursed himself for the fool he undoubtedly was for endangering her health in that ferocious storm. If she died—a terrible pain gripped at his heart—if she died it would be his fault and he would never forgive himself. Indeed, he knew that his life would become intolerable, for she had come to mean so much to him.

'John…' Amanda tossed restlessly on the pillows, calling out in her fever. 'John…don't leave me…don't go…'

'I shall not leave you, my darling,' he promised, catching hold of her hand. She felt so hot, so terribly hot. 'I love you, Amanda. Rest. Please rest, my little love…'

He turned as the door opened behind him and a pleasantly plump woman came in; she was carrying a bowl of steaming liquid which smelled rather strong and made John want to gag.

'How is she now, sir?' the woman asked kindly. 'I've brought this to help her breathing, poor lass. It's a remedy my gran used to swear by and might ease your young lady. The soaking she had the night my husband found you both has gone to her chest. She ought by rights to have a doctor, but there's none nearer than ten miles that we know of—and I doubt he would come if we could find a way of fetching him.'

'She seems worse,' John said, watching anxiously as she bent over Amanda, bathing the girl's forehead with cool water. 'You were very good to take us in like that, Mrs Winters. I was quite lost and do not know what I should have done without your husband's help.'

'That reminds me,' the farmer's wife said. 'Bert has taken some men and gone to fetch your carriage back; they'll mend the leading pole and it will be right as rain again. Not that I want you to leave, sir. I wouldn't think of it while the young lady is so ill.'

'I only wish she could be mended as easily as the carriage!' John's eyes were on Amanda as she tossed and turned restlessly in her fever. He feared she was very ill indeed.

There was such anguish in his tone that the good-hearted woman was moved to pity. 'Now don't you take on so,' she said. 'I'm warming some good goose grease for the poor young lady's chest and that will help draw out the evils. I'm sure she will be better in a day or so.'

'I wish Jane was here,' John said fervently. He had never been really poorly himself, and did not know how to cope now that he was faced with what was clearly a serious illness. 'She nursed both my mother and my father. I'm sure she would know what to do.'

'Could you not send for her?'

Jane would come if he asked her. She might give him a good scolding, but she would not fail him. He looked eagerly at the farmer's wife.

'If I wrote a letter could Mr Winters send it for me by the post? I would pay the charge, naturally.'

'We've never had much to do with things like that,' she said doubtfully. 'But he could take it to the vicar and he might know what to do. I'll speak to him directly he gets back.'

'I should be grateful,' John said. Jane would be so angry with him for bringing Amanda to this sorry state, and he deserved everything she might say to him. He was torn by remorse as he heard his beloved's moan of distress. If Amanda recovered he would do anything his sister demanded of him. Anything! Even if it meant giving her up.

Oh, please God, let her not die! Take me instead.

John had never prayed so fervently for anything in his life.

'You go and write your letter,' the farmer's wife advised. 'I'll tend to her and perhaps she'll sleep for a while.'

'Now this is the only other turning they could have taken,' Max said, glancing at Jane as she reined in beside him an hour or so later that morning. A cool breeze had sprung up, whipping the colour into her face, heightening her beauty. It was not fit weather for her to be riding about the countryside and he knew a moment of anger with her wretched brother and Amanda. 'We'll ask at the villages for the next ten miles or so and if we hear no news of them I'll take you to a decent inn and arrange for you to go home...'

'Max...' Jane's gaze was fixed on a point just beyond him. 'Over there—those men by the carriage!'

'What?' He looked in the direction she had pointed out, wondering at the look on her face. He could see nothing out of the ordinary. 'They are mending the leading pole, that's all.'

'It's John's phaeton,' she said, a note of near hysteria in her voice. 'I'm sure it is... Look at the yellow rims to those wheels... It has to be his! I am sure it is. Oh, Max! Do look!'

'Yes.' Max looked again, then nodded. 'I think you might be right, Jane. That might explain why they never reached the posting inn. He must have taken the country road and planned to rejoin the highway at the crossroads—or, yes, there's another smaller but reasonably decent inn not far from here. They must have had an accident... Depend upon it, that's what happened.'

Jane was no longer listening. She had spurred her horse on and was trotting across to the men labouring with the broken pole.

'Excuse me...' One of the men glanced up as she spoke, and touched his forehead respectfully. 'This is my brother's carriage. Could you please tell me where he might be, sir?'

'You'll be Miss Osbourne, then?' The farmer nodded, seeming unsurprised. 'The young gentleman has mentioned you to my wife. Thinking of sending for you, he was, because of his fiancée's illness.'

'Amanda is ill?' Jane looked round at Max as he rode up to her. 'Amanda is hurt. Oh, Max! She must have been thrown when—'

'No, 'twas not that,' Bert Winters reassured her quickly. 'She got a rare soaking the night of the storm. I was on me way 'ome and found them wandering around in the dark. Took them home, I did, and my missus put the young lady to bed with a hot brick—but she woke with a fever on her. We're right worried about her.'

'Can you take me to her?' Jane asked, her heart beginning to hammer wildly. Her eyes met Max's and he could see how alarmed she was. 'I know she is susceptible to chills. Please—I must see her at once. Poor Amanda!'

'Poor John,' added Max. 'You must not quarrel with him over this, Jane. He will be out of his mind with remorse and worry. Depend upon it, he is blaming himself.'

'Yes, I know. Of course I shall not scold him. He will be wretched enough as it is.'

Jane was on thorns. None of this need have happened if she had not been so unkind to Amanda. If anything happened to the girl she would always blame herself.

'I'll take you there,' the farmer offered. 'My lads have about finished here. They can bring the carriage back to the farm when they've done.'

The farmhouse was at the end of a very long lane that seemed to wind on for ever, but was well kept and substantial, much more wholesome than the inn Jane and Massingham had stayed at the previous night.

'Oh, how fortunate that you found them,' Jane said as the farmer invited her to step into his home. 'What a lovely house this is—so clean and fresh.' It smelled of lavender and roses, and baking.

'Mrs Winters is a good housewife,' her husband said proudly. 'She do keep everything proper.'

'Yes, indeed she does…' Jane was hailed by a startled cry as a very worried-looking John came rushing out of the parlour into the hall. He stared at her with a mixture of disbelief and dawning wonder. 'John—we have found you at last.'

'Jane!' he cried. 'Oh, Jane—thank God you are here. Amanda is so ill. She needs a doctor and I don't know what to do. Mrs Winters says there's a good man some ten miles from here but she doesn't think he would come out this far—and I couldn't leave Amanda…'

'No, of course you couldn't,' Jane said. She went to him at once, embracing him warmly. 'You must be so worried, dearest—and blaming yourself, I expect?'

'Yes.' He looked shamed. 'It was such a damned fool thing to do. To tell the truth, I wasn't thinking. If I had, I would have known that you would be reasonable. You were just shocked to see us.' He stopped, his cheeks flaming. 'I never meant it to happen, Janey. It was just one of those things. I love her so much…' His voice broke on a sob. 'Now you are here I can go for this doctor…'

'Leave that to me.' Max had been watching from the doorway and now spoke for the first time. 'You're needed here—and I can engage for it that the doctor will come out for me.'

'Yes, I suppose he would.' John gave him a rueful look. 'You must be wishing me to the devil?'

'Several times,' Max replied grimly. 'But don't imagine you have incurred my wrath by running off with the woman I love—that was a figment of your sister's imagination. My anger is all on her behalf—for all the anguish and trouble you have caused *her*. Do you understand me?'

John stared at him and nodded. He was tempted to say that he had rather thought something of the kind himself, but in his new-found wisdom held his tongue.

'It's good of you to set things straight, sir,' he replied. 'I can only apologize to you for any trouble I've caused.'

'We'll talk about this another time,' Max said. 'The most important thing now is Miss Roberts's health. I shall waste no more time in getting the doctor for her.'

He nodded to Jane and went outside, leaving her with nothing to do but offer her hands to John, and accept the rather subdued embrace he gave her.

'Forgive me, John?' she said, gazing up at him anxiously. 'I was wrong to say those terrible things to you and Amanda. I wished them unsaid at once—and would have apologized if you had not run off with her.'

'It wasn't your fault, Janey. We should have come and told you as soon as we had reached an understanding. We both knew we must wait, at least until Amanda had had her come-out. We intended to do so—but then, after you scolded her, she was so upset and I could not bear to see her cry...'

'Yes, I know how it must have been,' Jane said. 'I do understand, John. I just hope we can brush through all this without too much harm to your reputations. Yours and Amanda's—because you will not care to be cut by your friends when you go up to town.'

'Is it as bad as that? Oh, Lord, I have made a mess of things, haven't I?' He looked chastened. 'I didn't think... I've been a dashed fool, haven't I?'

'You were very foolish,' Jane said gently, 'but perhaps we can come about. I think we must say that you took Amanda out for a drive, met with an accident to your carriage—and she was ill from a fall so you sent for me. Which is why I set out after you with Massingham...'

'That's a bit smoky, isn't it? Dashed if I would believe it myself.'

'Well, it's the best I can come up with at the moment,' Jane said, sighing. 'Take me up to Amanda now if you please. I want to see her.'

Max was thoughtful as he rode for the doctor. Jane's manner towards him had been subdued all that morning. He could not for the life of him think what he had done to offend her, but she had become less and less inclined to talk as the minutes passed, and there had been an odd expression in her eyes once or twice when she'd looked at him.

Was she blaming him for having endangered her life the previous night? It had been a very awkward situation, and many ladies of his acquaintance would have made a great deal more fuss than she, screaming and more than likely indulging in a fit of the hysterics.

Her behaviour when he'd had to fire on those rogues had increased his already considerable admiration for her, but he was puzzled by the way she seemed to have withdrawn from him since. What bee did she have in her very beautiful bonnet? He was at a loss to know what had brought those shadows to her eyes—unless she felt that he had compromised her reputation?

Surely she must know it was only a matter of time before he proposed marriage? Any rumours or gossip would cease once they were married. Unless she did not wish to be married?

Max frowned as he recalled something she had once told him. He'd asked in a teasing way whether or not she had been proposed to, and she'd answered—in fun, he had thought—that she could marry almost at once if she wished but did not care for the idea.

Could she be one of those women who did not like the idea of marriage? No, no, it would be such a waste. He thought of her sensuality, the perfume of her skin, which

made him go weak with desire, the look in her eyes sometimes that seemed to beg him to make love to her. Such
a woman was made for love, and for bearing children.
She must not be allowed to wither into a dried-up old
maid.

Nor would she if he had his way. Max's mouth set
determinedly as he increased his pace. He would settle
this other affair and waste no time in making her his own.

Amanda was sleeping when Jane first entered the room.
She exchanged a few whispered words with the farmer's
wife, then took her seat at Amanda's side, watching over
her and listening anxiously to her tortured breathing. It
was almost an hour before she stirred, opening her eyes
to look at Jane without knowing her. Jane felt a pang of
fear; the girl was quite clearly very ill.

She bent over her, laying a hand on her brow, and,
finding it hot to the touch, began to bathe it with a cloth
wrung out in cool water. Amanda moaned and caught at
her hand, her words so muddled and disjointed that she
found them difficult to decipher at first.

'Don't be cross…didn't mean to be wicked…' Amanda
muttered, flinging back the covers as she tossed restlessly.
'Sorry… Love John… Don't want to marry…'

'Nor shall you, my love,' Jane soothed, torn with guilt
at the part she had played in Amanda's illness. 'I would
never force you to do anything you didn't want. I should
never have said those wicked things to you. You must get
well, my dear—for my sake and John's.'

Amanda could not understand her, she knew that, but
the sound of her gentle voice seemed to soothe the sick
girl and she closed her eyes once more. Her hands still
moved restlessly on the covers, but she did not cry out
again and Jane thought she might be sleeping.

It was nearly another hour before the doctor arrived,
looking harassed, clearly having been bullied into coming
by Lord Massingham against his will. He felt for

Amanda's pulse, approved of the treatment Mrs Winters was giving her and shook his head over the patient.

'She is a high-spirited girl, I suppose? They are always the ones who succumb to virulent fevers of this kind…' He tutted again, reached for his bag and took out a bottle of dark liquid. 'This may help to quiet her if she is restless, but there is not much else you can do for her—except watch over her and keep her warm. Sweat the fever out; that's the thing to do.'

Jane looked at the bottle, guessing that it contained some kind of opium medicine. She had been accustomed to giving something similar to her father for his severe bouts of pain, but did not approve of its use for a girl with a raging fever.

'Well, you may send for me again if she takes a turn for the worse,' the doctor said, 'but I doubt I can do much for her—it is in the hands of God.'

Jane thanked him for coming, but railed inwardly. If only she were at home with her reliable Dr Morris and Bessie. Bessie was so good at coping with illness. It was her common sense that Jane needed now, her willingness to share all the duties of intensive nursing, which was what Amanda would need if she were to come through this.

'May I come in?' She turned as Max poked his head round the corner. 'Is she any better?'

'No, she is much the same,' Jane replied. 'I am truly concerned for her, Max. If I were at home I should feel easier, but here…' She drew a sighing breath. 'Not that Mrs Winters has not done everything she can, of course.'

He nodded understandingly. 'Naturally you would be more comfortable at home, but she is too ill to be moved. Is there anything I can do to help?'

She hesitated, feeling that he had already been put to a great deal of trouble for her and her ward. 'It would be a kindness…if you could return to Massingham and send on our things with Bessie and my carriage. She would be a great help to me.'

He nodded, regarding her gravely. 'It was in my mind to return there if you felt you had no need of my services for the moment. I must put Catherine's mind at rest and do what I can to stop any rumours.' His eyes narrowed thoughtfully. 'John told me what you suggested and I think it just may wash—if Catherine goes along with the story, I can see no reason why we should not be believed. There may still be some raised eyebrows, of course, but I think we shall brush through if we brazen it out. I admit I can think of nothing more convincing.'

'I shall be grateful if you will do what you can.' She gave him an uncertain smile. When he looked at her that way her unruly heart would not behave itself. 'I'm afraid we have caused you a deal of trouble, sir—and you have enough problems of your own.'

'I shall send Bessie to you,' he promised, taking her hand to hold it for a moment in his own, 'and return myself at the end of the week. Unless you would prefer I did not?'

Jane dropped her eyes. How could she ask him to come back again, when to do so would put him under an obligation? She had already asked too much of him.

'If... No, when Amanda is better I think I shall take her up to London,' Jane said. 'I promised her a visit— and I think it best if we face up to any rumours at once. But we shall be delighted if you will call on us if you are in town yourself any time this next month.' She raised her eyes to his, uncertain of his reaction.

'As you wish.' Max's gaze was intent as he studied her, his eyes seeming to ask a question she was afraid to answer. She flushed and looked down. 'I have something particular to say to you, Jane—but it is probably best if I wait a little longer. I have business of my own that I would like to see settled.'

'Yes, of course.' Her heart raced as something forced

her to look up and into his eyes. Why was he looking at
her like that? And what did he want to say to her? He
couldn't mean…? No, she would not allow herself to be
misled again. It was her over-active imagination which
had got them into this mess. 'Then we shall look forward
to seeing you in town.'

'Until then…' Max took her hand, pressed it briefly to
his lips, then smiled in a way that made her heart jump
like giddy spring lambs. 'Try not to think too much, Jane.
All will be made plain to you in time—until then look
after this foolish girl…' he glanced at Amanda as she
tossed feverishly on her pillows… 'and know that my
thoughts will be with you.'

Jane felt a rush of something akin to panic as she
watched him leave the room. She was tempted to call him
back, but what could she say? He was clearly not ready
to speak of whatever was in his mind, and until he was
there was nothing she could do but hope—hope that she
had not been mistaken in the meaning behind his words.

Bessie arrived the next morning about noon. Jane had
sat all night with her patient and was never more glad to
see her maid, in whom she had great faith, Bessie having
been a tower of strength in the past.

'Well, now, miss, what a coil this is,' Bessie said. 'The
young miss ill—and you looking exhausted. Go and lay
down now if you please, Miss Jane. I have slept all night,
which is what you have not and must certainly do if you
are not to be ill yourself. You know you may rely on me
to look after her—and to call you if you are needed.'

'Oh, Bessie,' Jane said thankfully. 'I'm so pleased to
have you here. I know Mrs Winters is a kind, capable
woman, but if Amanda should come to her senses she will
feel better with people she knows than strangers. And I
need you.'

'And who should be looking after her if not me?'
Bessie asked, slightly indignant. 'If you'd thought a little,

Miss Jane, you would have taken me with you in the first place instead of rushing off like a blue-tailed fly.'

'Don't scold me, Bessie, dear,' Jane said, and gave her a peck on the cheek, which made Bessie go bright pink and gave her a deal of pleasure. For she'd always said what a lovely lady Miss Jane was, hadn't she? And there she was treating her like a long-lost friend and so happy to see her. Lord Massingham had explained everything, and not one word out of place would ever leave her lips, though mad dogs should try to tear it out of her.

Bessie took her place beside the patient as Jane went out, bending over Amanda to lay a hand on her forehead. She was very warm still—and no wonder with all these covers on her! It was the fashion to try and sweat the fever out of a sick person, but not one Bessie approved of. She glanced over her shoulder. Miss Jane would probably have a fit if she saw what Bessie was about to do…but she wasn't here to see, was she? And Bessie had her own ideas of how to treat a fever. The first thing she was going to do was open that window…

Jane did not return to the sickroom until one o'clock in the afternoon. Bessie had just come downstairs as Jane was finishing the meal Mrs Winters had provided for her and told her that Miss Amanda was sleeping like a babe.

'It's my opinion the fever has broken, miss,' she said. 'If it don't come back—which it may, that being the way of fevers—we may start to see an improvement soon.'

Jane saw that the girl was sleeping peacefully, and she did seem much cooler. Now, what had Bessie done to achieve that? The heavy coverlet had been taken off… What did it matter? If Amanda was getting better she could only thank God for it and pray that the fever had truly broken.

She sat by the window, looking out at the tops of some trees in the distance. It was so kind of Mrs Winters to have taken them all in, when she was such a busy person,

forever baking and scrubbing her spotless kitchen, and
they must make a great deal more work for her. Jane
sighed. She had asked Massingham not to come back to
the farm because she felt it best, but there was no denying
she missed him…longed for the sound of his voice.

'Jane…is that you?' The whispery voice from the bed
brought Jane swiftly out of her reverie. 'Please…may I
have some water?'

Jane got up at once and went over to her. She saw
immediately that Amanda was sensible and looking very
much better. When she touched her forehead she was cool
and free of fever.

'Oh, my dear,' Jane said, holding her as she took a few
sips of water. 'Of course you may have some water. I am
so sorry, Amanda.'

Amanda looked puzzled. 'Why…what have you done?'

'Don't you remember? I was cross with you in the gardens at Massingham and you…' She stopped as she saw
the girl's face crease with remembered pain. 'I am so
sorry for saying those things to you, my love. It is all my
fault that you ran away and became ill.'

There was silence for a moment, then Amanda reached
out for her hand. Jane took it, holding it gently.

'It was my fault,' Amanda admitted. 'I was afraid to
tell you that we wanted to marry in case you were cross—
and I made John run away. You mustn't blame him, Jane.'

'I shall not blame either of you,' Jane said, bending to
kiss her cheek. 'All you have to do is get better, my love.
We shall forget all this nonsense—and as soon as you are
better we shall go up to London as I promised you.'

'You will take me to London—after what I've done?'
Tears started to Amanda's eyes.

'Yes, why not?' Jane smiled at her. 'It was not so very
bad, was it? You made a silly mistake and anyone may
do that. We shall go to London as soon as you are fit to
travel. John may go ahead of us and take a furnished

house for a week or so—and then come back to escort us there himself.'

'John...' Amanda looked at her shyly. 'Is he here?'

'And where else would he be?' Jane asked. 'He has been half out of his mind with worry—and blaming himself for your illness. Shall I brush your hair a little, my love, and wash your face? And then I shall send him up to you. If you would like that?'

'Oh, yes,' Amanda said. 'Yes, please.' She caught Jane's hand again as she would have turned away. 'You are so kind to me and I do not deserve it. I have abused your kindness.'

'Stuff and nonsense,' Jane said. 'It was all a storm in a teacup. You were out in the carriage and you had an accident—that is all it was, Amanda. And no matter what anyone else may whisper we shall not allow it to have been more than a sad ending to a pleasure jaunt.'

'So there you are, Max!' The commanding tones of his godmother stopped him in his tracks as he was crossing the hall at Massingham. 'I should like a word with you, sir.'

'Yes, of course.' Max smiled at her. 'Won't you come into the library? I have been meaning to speak to you since I returned.'

She fixed him with a stare that would have thrown terror into a lesser man. 'Have you indeed? Fiddlesticks! That won't wash with me, Max. I wasn't born yesterday. You have been avoiding me.'

'Forgive me?' He gave her one of his winning smiles. 'I fear I have been avoiding you, but only because I did not wish to worry you.'

'Where is Miss Osbourne? What's this tale I hear—of you riding off together? And where is Miss Roberts?' She raised her quizzing glass. 'Something is going on. I demand to be told the truth. What have you been up to? I hope you haven't done anything to upset Miss Osbourne.

She is the first decent woman you've ever taken up with, Max, and I've acquired a liking for her. Don't disappoint me.'

'Would I dare?' Max laughed. 'It is a long tale, ma'am, and I fear you will not be pleased with me, but if you promise not to blame Miss Osbourne I shall tell you.'

'Blame Miss Osbourne?' Her eyes homed in on his face. 'Out with it, sir! If you have got yourselves into trouble, you had best tell me the worst at once!'

Jane came downstairs after having spent an hour sitting with Amanda; she had been reading to her from one of her favourite novels, and was feeling pleased with the progress the girl was making.

Hearing the sound of a child's laughter, Jane went into the parlour and stopped, smiling at the sight that met her eyes. Mrs Winters and a very pretty young woman were sitting together, and a little girl of perhaps two or three was playing at their feet.

'Please come in, Miss Osbourne,' Mrs Winters said, getting to her feet and smiling in welcome. 'This is my daughter Angela—and this is Daisy. She is my first grandchild, and a little beauty, if I do say it myself, which I probably shouldn't.'

'Oh, but you should,' Jane said warmly, 'because she is. I have rarely seen such a lovely child.'

'And such a good-natured little thing,' said the doting grandmother, while the mother smiled indulgently and shook her head. 'Angela says we spoil her, but neither Bert nor I can help it.'

'So I should imagine,' Jane said. She sat down, holding her arms out to the child, who clambered up on her knee at once and demanded to be told a story. 'Yes, certainly I will, Daisy. What shall it be? A story of princes and princesses—or bears and a little girl who stole their breakfast?'

'She likes you,' said Mrs Winters, nodding approvingly. 'See how she has settled on your lap. You will make a good mother one day, Miss Osbourne—and I dare say it won't be long before you marry that nice gentleman who brought you here.'

Jane blushed but made no reply. The child's body was warm and yielding, and it gave her an odd, yearning feeling inside to hold her. She had never been this close to such a young child before; the offspring of ladies she knew were usually kept upstairs in the nursery whenever company was in the house. Maggie had taken her into the nursery to see her daughter on a couple of occasions, but she had never before held a child like this, never seen the trusting innocence of a child's look, or felt the tenderness children could arouse in a woman's breast.

It was indeed a revelation and it made Jane think how much she would like to have babes of her own—Max's children.

Her cheeks took fire at the thought, but she covered her blushes by kissing the child and launching into a very pretty story of princes and princesses who lived in ivory towers.

Amanda was young and healthy, and once the fever had broken made a quick recovery, perhaps because she had everything in the world to look forward to and no reason to stay in bed and pine.

Within two days she was on her feet again, sitting in a chair and looking almost as pretty as ever, and by the end of the week she was ready to travel. She thanked Mrs Winters very nicely for taking her in and Mr Winters for having found them when they were lost, which made his rather thick, bull-like neck go bright red. Jane had already begged to be allowed to pay for their stay at the farm, but had been firmly refused.

'I did no more than my Christian duty, Miss Osbourne,' Mrs Winters said. 'And very pleased I was to do it.'

'I shall never forget your kindness,' Jane said, making

a mental note to send their kind hostess a pretty shawl from town, and perhaps a jar of good snuff for Mr Winters. 'And now we must go. Thank you once again for all you did for Amanda. If you had not taken her in I really think she would have died.'

She held Amanda's hand as they sat together in her own comfortable closed carriage. John was driving his phaeton and was a little ahead of them on the road.

'I think I shall give a small dinner party when we are settled,' Jane said. 'I must discover those of my friends who are still in town and invite them to meet you.'

'I thought you had decided we should not go into society until next spring?' Amanda stared at her. 'You wondered what people might think of my wearing colours.'

'When in doubt of a fence take it straight on and don't falter,' Jane said, her face set determinedly. 'I mean to discover if there are any rumours flying about—and to squash them if there are. You must remember to say you were ill after the accident, my love. I don't mean that you must lie—but you *were* ill and no one need know that it was caused by a fever and not the accident itself.'

'Have I caused too much trouble for you?' Amanda asked, looking humble. 'Should I go away? Perhaps Lady Fairley would take me in hand until I can marry John.' She was determined to be brave but her bottom lip trembled. 'I will do whatever you say, Jane.'

'I would never condemn you to such a fate,' Jane assured her with a smile. 'Do not worry, Amanda. I do not see how anyone could know the truth…' But she was remembering the Ravenscrofts and that they had seen her with Max that first evening—and also his guests at Massingham, who would know that she and their host had ridden off very suddenly. If they were true friends they might be relied upon not to spread rumours, but Jane was very afraid that at least a part of the true story might have leaked out.

She was, however, determined to brazen it out if she

could. A bold approach was surely the best thing. If it was known that she was in town and had not issued invitations to her friends it would help to give any rumours credence—and if she had simply taken Amanda home the same thing might have happened.

No, she would not hang her head in shame. Amanda had been foolish but no real harm had come of it. Indeed, Jane had behaved in a far more shameful manner by sharing a room—and a bed—with Max at that dreadful inn.

She drew a sigh of relief. At least no one could know anything of that.

Chapter Eleven

'Why have you come to me with this story?' Countess Langdon asked of her visitor. Her green eyes narrowed in suspicion. 'Pray explain yourself, sir. What good will it do you to ruin Miss Osbourne?'

'I was merely telling you something I thought would interest you,' the man replied. He was watching her with an intentness that sent an odd shiver down her spine. 'If it does not, then you may forget it.'

'Oh, it interests me,' she said, the sparkle of malice in her eyes making them almost emerald in hue. 'And I know exactly what to do—that proud madam deserves to be taken down a peg or two. It may make Max regret the way he dismissed me.'

'Exactly so.' A satisfied smile played over the man's mouth. 'I knew I could rely on you.'

'But why?' she asked again. 'Do you hate Max so much?'

'Hate him?' The man's brows arched. 'Not at all. It just would not suit me to have him marry her, that's all.' He took a step towards her, towering over her. She felt a sense of menace, of fear, and retreated, but his hand shot out and gripped her wrist. 'If you tell anyone who gave you this information you will regret it. Do you understand me?'

'Yes.' She broke away from him, retreating to the other side of the room. What was wrong with him? They had never liked each other. Indeed, she had sensed his jealousy in the days when she was close to Max, but she had never been afraid of him before. 'I shall not mention you. I swear it. I have reasons enough for wanting to score over Miss Osbourne.' She lifted her head, smiling unpleasantly. 'Believe me, she will be sorry she dared to steal him from me before I have finished with her!'

Jane's first enquiries established that there were at least ten of her friends in town, seven of them ladies she had known through her mother and three gentlemen. A little to her surprise, she had learned that Sir Charles Pendlebury was staying at his town residence, something he seldom did; Sir Andrew Forbes had presented his card while they were out, two days after their arrival—and Captain Carter had gone out of his way to speak to John at his club.

John assured her that he had heard no rumours. 'Everyone has been just as they always are,' he said, sounding cheerful. 'I think you have been worrying for nothing, Janey. Massingham must have pulled rank with his friends and got us off free and clear.'

John obviously thought they had avoided any scandal. Jane was not as certain as he, but sent out her invitations with a hopeful heart and received eight replies in the affirmative. Only Lady Morton had refused, her message very brief and with no compliments—and, as yet, there was no reply at all from Sir Charles.

'I wonder if Lady Morton has heard something?' Jane said, frowning over the letter, which was barely civil. 'Mama always said she was a stickler for propriety and I'm sure she would not come if she had heard rumours.'

'Well, we shall know this evening, for we have been invited to a dance by Viscount Roxborough,' John said. 'I met him in the street and he said he was giving a little affair and we should be welcome if we cared to come. He asked after Amanda's health and was as sweet as you please.'

'But he is one of Max's closest friends,' Jane said. 'He has obviously decided to stand by us, but I am distressed by Lady Morton's refusal. She wrote to me most kindly after Papa's death, inviting me to stay with her in town when I felt able. She was most insistent. Why would she send me a note like this if she had not heard something that displeased her?'

She looked at the note again, feeling distinctly uneasy.

'She is an old tabby,' John said in a lordly fashion. 'Do not distress yourself, Jane. I am sure she had got—' He broke off as Bessie came in to announce that they had a visitor. 'Who is it, Bessie?'

'It's Sir Charles Pendlebury,' Bessie said, barely able to contain her indignation. 'He demanded to see Miss Osbourne.'

'Demanded?' Jane saw the way Bessie was bristling. 'Oh, dear, I wonder what he has on his mind? Please be so good as to show him in, Bessie.'

'What can that bag of wind want?' John asked as the girl left. 'I can't see why you asked him to your party, Jane. If you don't mind I'll make myself scarce.'

Jane sighed as he left the room hastily. She had invited Sir Charles because he would have been offended if she had not—and because she had hoped he could be relied upon to repeat any rumours to her in confidence. Now she was very much afraid that was exactly why he had called on her.

Bessie announced him. One look at his face told Jane that her worst fears had been realized. He had a high colour and looked as if he were about to explode with the importance of his news.

'Sir Charles,' she said, giving him her warm smile. 'How very good of you to call on me.'

'I can tell you I was in two minds about it,' he said,

his eyes narrowing suspiciously as he looked at her. 'I was never more shocked than when I heard what people are saying. Tell me it ain't true! I demand the truth, Miss Osbourne. Is this scurrilous tale going about town a lie or ain't it?'

'Which tale was that, sir?' Jane retained her calm, dignified manner. 'If you would be so kind, please tell me what people are saying.'

He glared down at her, his plump body quivering with rage. 'They tell me you ran off with Lord Massingham but were forced to return when your ward was taken ill. They say you spent the night together at an inn. I couldn't believe you would be so lost to all notion of propriety, Miss Osbourne—and so I said at the time, but it is all over town and there ain't no smoke without fire.'

The tale was so nearly right, but twisted around so that it seemed to ruin her reputation and not Amanda's. She drew a breath of relief. As long as no one knew the real truth perhaps they could still brush through it by denying it as a tale and nothing more.

'Surely you did not believe such a tale, sir?' She laughed as naturally as she could. 'I assure you it is very far from the truth. John took my ward out for a spin in his phaeton; it overturned and she was…ill. John could not move her so he sent for me. Massingham escorted me because it would not have been proper for me to go alone.'

'So there is some truth in it—you did ride off with Massingham alone and with no word to anyone?'

'It was not quite like that,' Jane said quietly. She did not enjoy being taken to task like this. Indeed, she found it highly impertinent in him. 'We both left messages for Lady Farringdon, but were in too much haste to take my maid with us. If you mean to scold me for not behaving quite as I ought, I wish you will not, sir. I was upset at the time and did not think of—of propriety. My ward could have been dying!'

'You must not think I am beyond understanding your very real anxiety,' he replied pompously. 'But it is not the behaviour I would expect of you, Miss Osbourne—and it leads me to wonder if I have not been mistaken in your character.'

'I fail to see what possible business it is of yours how I behave, sir,' Jane said, and then wished she had kept silent as she saw him puff out his chest. 'You have on occasion been kind enough to make me a flattering offer—but I have always refused.'

'As well for me that you did,' he said, his face an unhealthy plum colour. 'I have come to tell you that I shall not be attending your dinner party, Miss Osbourne—and that any idea you may have had of becoming my wife is at an end.'

'I had none, sir,' Jane snapped. 'If you choose to believe lies concerning my behaviour that is your business. And now, if you please, I must ask you to leave my house.'

'I was about to do so,' he said. 'If you can do nothing to disprove these rumours you will very soon find that no one will visit you, nor will you be received in any decent house. Good day, Miss Osbourne.'

Jane remained silent until he had left the room, then she gave a cry of rage and threw a plump velvet cushion across the room. How dared he? Oh, how dared he?

She paced about the room for several minutes in a flame of temper. How could the story have spread all over town so soon—unless someone had done it deliberately, out of spite? Who would want to harm her—and why had the story been altered to reflect badly on her? It was as if whoever had spread the tale did not know quite all of it...

'Miss Osbourne.' She turned at the sound of Bessie's voice. 'Sir Andrew Forbes has called to see you—shall I admit him?'

Jane hesitated for a moment, then inclined her head.

'Yes, I will see him, Bessie—but stay close in the hall in case I call for you.'

'Yes, Miss Jane.'

Bessie went out and Jane took another anxious turn about the room. She must squash this rumour quickly or it might grow and grow…but who was behind it and what could she do to stop whoever it was?

She turned as she heard a slight sound and saw Sir Andrew standing hesitantly in the doorway.

'I was not sure if you would receive me, but then I had your invitation…' He came towards her, looking uncertain. 'Have you forgiven me for my behaviour, Miss Osbourne? I took the liberty of writing to you—you had my letter?'

She had completely forgotten it! It was still in the pocket of the gown she had been wearing when Catherine had given it to her, unread. The news of Massingham's accident and then the elopement had put it right out of her mind.

'Yes, of course.'

'Then you know I was wretched for having upset you,' he said. 'Please forgive me. I do not know what made me behave the way I did that evening. It must have been the violence of my feelings.'

'You ought to have controlled them,' Jane said, 'but I have forgiven you. I might have been kinder if I had suspected—but you startled me, sir. I am sorry if I was harsh to you.'

'You could never be that,' he said, coming towards her, an eager light in his eyes. 'Please do forgive me, Miss Osbourne—Jane. I could not bear it if I had lost all respect in your eyes. I have cursed myself a thousand times for distressing you that night.'

'No, of course you have not,' she said, giving him a warmer reception than she might have if she had not still been smarting from Sir Charles's words. 'I was just startled by your impetuosity, and I am particularly pleased you have called on me, Sir Andrew, for I wanted to ask if you had heard a certain rumour…'

'A rumour concerning you and Max?' Sir Andrew frowned. 'It is ridiculous and so I told the wretch who dared to repeat it in my hearing. Naturally I denied it as being false. Had it been a man I should have been tempted to call him out. You must not worry, Miss Osbourne. None of your friends will believe such a tale.'

'Thank you,' she said, her cheeks flushing a little at the vehemence of his manner. He was a rather intense person and she still could not be quite easy in his presence, despite his loyalty. 'We have been invited to Viscount Roxborough's dance this evening—shall you be there?'

'Indeed I shall.' Sir Andrew smiled at her warmly. 'I would not miss it for the world now I know you will be there. I must take leave of you now, for I have an appointment elsewhere—but I shall look forward to this evening.'

'Thank you.'

Jane was thoughtful after he had left her. She was very grateful for Sir Andrew's loyalty, which was especially kind as he had known her only a short time—while Sir Charles, who had known her since she was in leading strings, had come only to lecture and insult her. So why could she not quite like Max's best friend?

Max had said they were almost as brothers. If they had been so close for so many years why—why did she feel that Sir Andrew used every chance he could to cast doubt on Max's character?

Or was that only a figment of her imagination? Because she was so partial to Lord Massingham herself that she could not bear to hear even the slightest criticism of him?

Jane pressed her hands to her warm cheeks. She must not let herself think like this, must not allow her thoughts to dwell so often on Max—but she did long to see him so very much!

She wondered whether he was in town yet and blushed

as she realized she was relying on his support. No, no, he
could not be here for he would surely have come to visit
her. She must be patient. He had made no promises. But
he would come soon. Surely he must!

'When do you go up to town?' Lady Fairley cornered
her godson in his library. 'Catherine says you have agreed
to escort her home tomorrow. But when you have seen
her safely back in Farringdon's care—where she belongs
in her delicate condition, I might say!—you may return
here and escort me to my house in London.'

Max frowned. 'Would you not rather go home, ma'am?
You told me you found all that racketing around town too
much for you these days.'

'I am not yet in my dotage, sir, and I shall thank you
to remember it. I have decided that I shall give a little
party—to introduce Miss Osbourne to my friends.'

'That is kind in you, ma'am,' Max replied, his mouth
softening. 'And I thank you for the thought. I shall not
tarry long at Ormond.'

'As to that, you may take as long as you please,' Lady
Fairley said, a sparkle in her eyes. 'Mrs Hurley has in-
formed me you are about to have your apartments refurbished, Max. I have told her everything must be packed
away carefully, and I intend to direct the whole myself.'

'I wish you will not put yourself to so much trouble,
ma'am.' Max made a mental note to apologize to his
housekeeper in advance. 'Please do not tire yourself.'

'Tire myself? Tire myself, sir? Confound your impu-
dence. I have not enjoyed myself as much in years. Not
since I found the Marquis of Rothmere *in flagrante* with
his valet! And in the middle of the day, if you please!
Now, that was a scandal, Max, if I had cared to spread it,
which of course I did not. And you may keep it to yourself, though the old rogue has been dead these past ten
years—and five years my junior, if you please. No stam-

ina, of course, never has been in that family. You are of finer stock, my dear.'

'And so are you,' Max said, and kissed her. 'The finest!'

Jane, Amanda and John were greeted warmly by Viscount Roxborough and his sister, a very pretty girl of about Amanda's age, when they arrived at their house that evening.

'Delighted you could come,' Roxborough said. 'I asked Massingham but he cried off on the excuse that he had to attend on his godmother, who has just arrived in town today.'

'Lord Massingham is in town?' Jane asked, her heart fluttering. Why hadn't he called on her? She smiled confidently, hiding her doubts. 'No doubt we shall see him very soon.' She passed on as some new arrivals came up to their host.

Roxborough's house was very fine, elegantly furnished in the Chinese style made fashionable by the Prince Regent in his house at Brighton. Jane and her party passed through the first reception room, where some twenty or thirty people were gathered in small groups drinking champagne. She saw one or two people she knew slightly and inclined her head but did not speak; she was gratified when Captain Carter came up to them and greeted them all with great kindness, begging both Jane and her ward for a dance later in the evening.

'If you can put up with an old windbag like myself, Miss Osbourne,' he said. 'I dare say your card will soon be full.'

'You were never a windbag, sir,' Jane said, 'but one of Father's best and dearest friends. I should love to dance with you.' She handed him her card and smiled as he scribbled his name in two places.

A waiter came up to them with a tray of glasses. Jane accepted, allowed Amanda to do so too, but warned her to make it last and choose lemonade for the remainder of the evening, then glanced across the room. Her blood chilled as she saw Countess Langdon staring at her, a look of hatred in her eyes. Then the countess deliberately turned her back on her, whispering something behind her fan to the lady standing next to her. When the woman looked at her with haughty disdain, Jane knew what must have been said—and suspected who was behind the rumours. Of course! It all made perfect sense now. The countess had heard something and turned it against Jane—in revenge for what had happened that night at Massingham.

'Come along, Amanda,' Jane said, steering her ward towards the ballroom. 'Let us see if we know anyone here.'

The ballroom was already crowded with young people, and it was not very long before the first gentleman approached Amanda and asked her for a dance. She was soon surrounded by a host of eager partners and looked to Jane in enquiry. Jane nodded and smiled. It was just as she had always thought: Amanda would be the latest rage. Despite the rumours about Jane and Lord Massingham the gentlemen were prepared to be kind to one of the most beautiful heiresses ever to be seen in a London drawing room.

Jane herself was approached by one or two of the gentlemen, though not as many as she might have expected. None of the ladies had so far come to speak to her and she knew that she was being given the cold shoulder…not quite cast out, because of her position as the guardian of one of the best matrimonial prizes of the season, but not quite accepted either.

She kept her smile in place, dancing with her brother, Captain Carter, Roxborough and two rather pleasant gentlemen who introduced themselves as friends of Massingham. Then Sir Andrew arrived and wrote his name in three spaces, which was the very most allowed by the rules of polite society.

'You look beautiful, Miss Osbourne,' he said as he released her after their first dance. 'I shall leave you for but one moment...'

Within five minutes he was back with two gentlemen, introducing them to Jane as his own particular friends. They naturally asked her to dance, filling two spaces on her card each, and, after that, several more gentlemen decided they would ignore the whispers of sisters, mamas and aunts and came to join the growing throng of admiring gentlemen who gathered wherever Amanda and Jane happened to be in the room.

The evening was turning into a success, despite the initial coldness towards Jane, and after an hour or two a lady she had met only once some years ago came up to her and exchanged a few pleasant words. Jane began to relax. Perhaps it would all blow over after all.

It was not until Captain Carter took her down to supper that it all started to go wrong.

'I swear I heard it from a reliable source...' Jane stiffened as she heard the loud voice behind her. 'She was tilting her cap at Massingham the whole time I was there. I dare say he has offered her carte blanche. For she could hardly expect marriage after what has happened.'

Jane turned slowly, her face drained of colour. She was so angry. How dared that woman say such vile things? And said in a manner meant to offend!

Countess Langdon smiled as she saw her dart had gone home. Jane took a step towards her, but her arm was caught by Captain Carter's hand. She looked up at him and he shook his head, warning her not to make things worse by causing a scene.

'I believe we shall go back upstairs, my dear Jane,' he said in a voice meant to carry. 'There is a stench in here that makes me sick to my stomach. I wonder what it can be? It has a sourness that comes from corked wine.'

It was a deadly insult, for it implied that the countess was herself spoiled goods.

Jane placed her hand on his arm, trying not to let it tremble. She whispered her thanks to him as he led her back upstairs to the ballroom.

'You are very kind, sir,' she said. 'I was about to say something I should no doubt have regretted.'

'That woman is a viper,' he replied. 'Pay no attention to her. Everyone knows she and Massingham finished their relationship some months ago. I expect she is jealous.'

'Do you happen to know why they parted company?'

'There was some gossip at the time.' Captain Carter frowned, his eyes mirroring his very real concern for her. 'I never pay much attention to tales, m'dear.'

'I think perhaps I should leave…'

'And let all the tabbies have a field day?' He gave her a stern look. 'I thought you made of stronger stuff, Jane. You'll stay until the last, my girl, and stare them all down—and if any man dares to insult you I'll call him out! Call the ladies out too if I could.'

His eyes twinkled at her, giving her courage.

'Oh, you are a darling,' Jane said, giving him a grateful smile. 'Yes, I shall stay—and be damned to them all!'

'That's the stuff,' he said approvingly. 'Never balk at the fences, Jane. Go over or through them. If the worst comes to the worst, m'dear, you can always marry me.'

It was said with such a look in his eye that she could not help laughing. The next moment he had swept her onto the dance floor, twirling her around in great style. Jane smiled up at him, her heart lifting. She had flouted convention but she had done nothing to be ashamed of and she was not going to be run out of town by Countess Langdon!

Max wiped the sweat from his brow. He had just finished a fast and furious contest with his fencing partner;

about to replace his foil and follow his friends to the Turkish baths, he paused as Sir Andrew came into the room.

'Andrew.' He greeted him with a smile. 'I have not seen you here before. I thought you had no love of the sport?'

'I can fence as well as the next man if I care to.' Sir Andrew gave him such a strange look that Max caught his breath. Had he been drinking? 'Just because you could always beat me when we wrestled, it does not follow you are the better swordsman.'

Max hesitated, then waved his hand towards the rapiers lying on a table nearby. 'Would you care to put me to the test?'

Andrew picked one up at random, then turned, that odd smile on his mouth. 'Why not?' he asked, and lunged at Max without preamble. 'Now we shall see…'

Max was at a disadvantage, but he managed to side-step Sir Andrew's first thrust, and brought his own blade up to meet the next. For a few seconds they crossed swords furiously, feinting and parrying, evenly matched in skill. Yet so fierce was Sir Andrew's attack that Max found himself being driven back. He felt a tingling sensation in the nape of his neck, sensing that this was not just a test of skill. Andrew was desperate to best him.

Max came back at him, forcing him to retreat; thrust, feint, parry: advance. Thrust, feint, parry: advance. His skill was beginning to tell. He was driving Andrew back, slowly but surely. The wall was at Andrew's back; he could retreat no further. Max lowered his sword, looking into the other man's eyes, then he stepped back, returning to the centre of the floor.

'The best of three?' he asked, a smile on his lips.

'No, to hell with it, Max,' Sir Andrew cried, and laughed. 'You've bested me as usual. I came only to ask if you were going to your club this evening. And you force a fight on me. What ails you, Max? You know I've never cared for fencing.'

Max felt the chill begin at the base of his spine and spread throughout his body. How could Andrew's manner change so swiftly? At one moment he had seemed to hate Max, and now it was the way it had always been between them.

Could it be that Andrew was ill?

'What are you looking at me like that for?'

Andrew's voice broke the spell. Max gave himself a mental shake. He must have imagined that look. Andrew didn't hate him. They had always been as brothers.

Chapter Twelve

Jane sat in bed the morning after Roxborough's dance, drinking the hot chocolate Bessie had brought in for her and reading her messages. There were just three of them, two from ladies who had accepted invitations for her dinner party and had unfortunately discovered that they had a prior engagement—and the third was from Lady Fairley, inviting her to a small card party that very evening.

Jane would normally have expected to receive a flood of invitations for both her and Amanda by this time, and she could not quite shake off her feeling of despondency. If she had ruined Amanda's hopes of being the toast of London... She sighed and tossed the two refusals aside. If they chose to believe ill of her they were not worth bothering with.

She felt a sudden surge of anger. This was all because of Countess Langdon's spite! How could she have learned the story? Max's friends would not have told her—or would she? Could it have been Max himself? If so, it was most unwise of him, after he had promised to do all in his power to squash the story—and why had he not called on her as soon as he reached town?

Jane experienced an irritation of the nerves. If Massingham had been there last evening they could have squashed the rumours before they had hardly started—but by now Countess Langdon's spiteful whispers must have spread all over town.

Jane did not care so very much for herself—after all, she seldom went into society—but even so it was not pleasant to be cut by ladies who would normally have gone out of their way to speak to her—and if she were to be ostracized by society she could not even take a house in Bath for she would have no friends to speak of, or none that she really wanted.

Why hadn't Massingham called? If she could have talked to him... She would talk to him!

She would call on him this very morning. Oh, dear, what was she thinking of? Was she so lost to propriety as to flout the very strict rule which said no unmarried lady could call at a gentleman's house, unless invited and accompanied by a member of her family—an older lady preferably? Jane had no female relatives in town. Her aunts all lived in the country and never set foot in London if they could help it.

She would write to him and ask him to call on her urgently, Jane decided, flinging back the covers and calling to Bessie as she took paper and pen from the drawer of her desk. She would ask him to call this very morning!

'You wanted to see me, ma'am?' Countess Langdon met the cold stare of the other woman's eyes and felt distinctly uncomfortable. 'It is really most inconvenient. I have a prior appointment.'

'My business will not long delay you,' Lady Fairley said, raising her quizzing glass. 'We have never liked each other, madam, but while Max seemed to have a fondness for you I was not your enemy, though you may have thought it.'

'It matters not either way.'

'No, for your arrangement is at an end, as it must be in the circumstances.' Lady Fairley's mouth thinned. 'I believe you may guess why I am here this afternoon?'

'Why should I?' The countess dropped her eyes before the other's piercing gaze.

'It has come to my ears that you have been spreading rumours about Miss Jane Osbourne. No, do not trouble yourself to deny it. I have come to tell you that you will stop at once. You will tell your friends that you were mistaken. Max was merely escorting a lady of unblemished reputation to her ward, who had been involved in a carriage accident. There was no impropriety, and any other version of this story is untrue.'

'And why should I oblige you?' Countess Langdon said. 'I see that you wish to hush up the scandal, but why should I help you?'

'Because you know very well that I could finish you in society if I so wished,' Lady Fairley replied. 'I have only to say that I would not accept an invitation to a house in which you had been recently entertained, and you would find that suddenly no one wished to know you.'

'You old witch!' cried the countess. 'You would not dare!'

She knew that Lady Fairley could carry out her threat. There was a small core of hostesses who ruled London society, and Max's godmother was one of them. She could ruin any aspiring lady or gentleman with a look—and she was quite capable of doing it.

'I shall do whatever I have to do.' Lady Fairley gave her a hard stare. 'Please do not force me to do something I should find distasteful.'

Countess Langdon knew she was beaten. 'Very well,' she said. 'I shall do as you ask.'

'I was sure that you would.' A grim smile touched the older woman's mouth. 'Perhaps you would be good enough to tell me where you had your information from, madam?'

'That I cannot—will not—say!'

'And why is that, pray?'

'Because he would kill me.'

Lady Fairley saw the fear in her eyes and nodded. 'Very well, I shall say no more. Providing you recant the scurrilous tales you have been spreading you will hear nothing more from me.' She stood up and inclined her head. 'Good day, madam.'

Countess Langdon scowled as she left the room. She had lost everything on the throw of the dice, but she had already known her case was hopeless. Max would never take her back. She still wanted him, loved him in her way, but it was over.

Anger flared in her as she thought of the woman he intended to marry. There was nothing she could do…and yet it might all come to nothing. For Max had an enemy, a man more dangerous, more ruthless than he could possibly guess.

Massingham frowned over Jane's note. He was well aware of the rumours flying round town, and of their likely source. Helena Langdon had already received a visit from him, but he feared the outcome of a rather stormy interview would do nothing to persuade her to give up her vendetta against Jane.

He had ended their affair some months previously, and since then she had lost no chance of trying to win him back, throwing herself at him at every opportunity. He had done his best to end it kindly, but she had refused to accept their relationship was finally over.

'You know I love you, Max,' she had cried when he'd told her he knew she had betrayed him with another man. '*That* was…just a fling. Please forgive me. I promise it will never happen again.'

'Our relationship was almost over anyway, Helena,' Max had told her. 'We both knew that. Besides, you no longer need me. You are free—to take lovers or a husband as you choose.'

That conversation had taken place just after her husband's death, but Helena had continued to follow him to

Massingham to plead for his forgiveness. He knew she hoped for marriage, and at one time he might have considered it, but that was before she had betrayed him, before he fell in love.

Max had never expected to feel like this about any woman. He wanted to protect and cherish her, to sweep her up in his arms and run off with her to his home. He had been on the verge of speaking several times, but something, some instinct, had made him hesitate. If he were to endanger her by speaking too soon... But no, surely his enemy would not stoop so low?

Yet he could not be sure. He had begun to think that he had been foolish—careless. For years he had known that something was not right, that someone close to him was not all he appeared to be. But he had always dismissed the occasional flare-ups as mere temperament, believing that his own friendship exercised control over a slightly unbalanced nature.

Max frowned, putting the troublesome thoughts from his mind. He was not yet certain of his facts and until he had proof his hands were tied. There was one sure way to squash the rumours about himself and Jane, but if he took that route he might push his enemy into making a strike at him through her.

It was a damned coil and one that had him at a stand, which was not something that often happened to him. Should he risk Jane's displeasure—or speak out and...? No, her safety was more important than damned convention. To hell with all the tabbies! They would be eating out of her hand soon enough.

Jane jumped up eagerly as Massingham was announced that afternoon. She smiled as he came in, holding her hands out to him in welcome.

'Oh, Max,' she cried, unconsciously betraying her feelings. 'I have been longing for you to come. Have you heard the terrible things they are saying?'

He took her outstretched hands, looking down at her, seeing the hurt she was trying to hide and inwardly cursing the man who had caused all this. If it had not been for a certain jealous heart none of it need ever have happened.

'Surely you are not going to let a few old tabbies upset you?' he asked, frowning at her. 'That is not like you, Jane. You have faced cut-throats and rogues, remember?'

'Oh, pray do not remind me,' she said with a little shiver. 'Have you discovered who is trying to kill you, Max? Is that why you have been so long in coming...?' She blushed as she realized what her words implied. 'Not that it is so very long, of course.'

'A few days?' He gave her a mocking smile. 'I did not think you would miss me, Jane. You sent me packing, remember?'

'Yes, I know.'

She looked so wistful that he was tempted to speak out and to hell with the rest of it, but caution held him back.

'Well, I am here now,' he said. 'Why did you want to see me?'

'You must speak to Countess Langdon,' she said. 'Make her stop spreading these rumours, Max. I have received almost no invitations and Amanda's pleasure will all be ruined if—'

'To hell with Amanda's pleasure!' Max exclaimed, his eyes flashing with impatience. 'That wretched girl is the cause of all this, if you remember.'

'That is most unkind in you,' Jane said. 'You promised you would help hush it all up and now look what has happened—that woman has ruined everything.'

'Helena Langdon has a spiteful tongue,' Max admitted. 'But we must just put up with it for the moment. Most people will know what a shrew she can be and take what she says with a pinch of salt.'

'I have already been cut by three ladies who were friends of my mother,' Jane said, bristling at his careless attitude. 'You may not have a care for my reputation but…'

'I did ask you to remain at Massingham and let me go alone—if you remember?'

His very reasonable manner was the last straw. How dared he remind her that it was all her own fault? A gentleman would at least sympathise, or better still accept the blame himself.

'I can see it is of no use to apply for help to you,' she cried, eyes darting flames at him. 'You are beyond anything, Max! Why I ever imagined you a suitable husband for Amanda I don't know—you are not fit to be husband to any woman!'

Fortunately for his peace of mind, Massingham was endowed with a very particular sense of humour and did not give much credence to her outburst. His own sister had been known to accuse him in a similar way on occasion, but, as he well knew, she loved him very dearly, second only to her beloved Farringdon.

'I fear you are very right,' he said, smiling in the slightly mocking way that could be so very infuriating. 'But I have hopes of being reclaimed in due course by the right woman—for she, *you* should know, is so far above me that I am bound to be saved.' As she gave him what could only be termed an old-fashioned look, he laughed softly and took her hand, kissing it briefly before comforting her with these words. 'Forgive me, dearest Jane. I do understand your distress but I believe you will discover that the case is not as bad as you fear. Lady Fairley has a great deal of influence with the ladies who matter in London society and she is very much on your side—as you will discover this evening.'

'Is she?' Jane looked at him doubtfully. She had been wondering what sort of reception she might expect that evening from Massingham's godmother but his words reassured her. 'I thought she might have summoned me to give me a scold.'

She looked so downcast that he was tempted to take her into his arms and kiss away her fears. But the thought of what that might lead to held him back.

'You wrong her. She was much amused by the story. Do not be deceived by the person she appears to be, Jane. In her youth she was known as a flirt and had several…adventures…I believe.' His smile made her feel so much better that, despite herself, she felt her spirits lifting. 'And now I must leave you. I shall be much occupied for the next few days, so you must forgive me if I do not call on you as often as I would like.'

'We shall be here for another few days,' Jane said. 'Then we must go home to prepare for Catherine's dance. Perhaps you would care to attend my dinner on Thursday night? I did not invite you because I was not aware you were in town, but…'

'I shall be delighted to come,' he assured her. He took her hand, holding it for a moment, a smile in his eyes. 'But if something should happen—if I were forced to cry off—I trust you would find it in your heart to forgive me?'

'Oh, Max!' she cried in sudden dismay. She had not forgotten in the midst of all this that his life was in constant danger. 'I wish you would speak more plainly.'

'I wish that I could,' he replied, his expression serious now. 'Forgive me, Jane. I must leave you. Trust in Lady Fairley to bring you about and do not worry so.'

Jane caught her breath on a sob as he left her. Her emotions were all of a jumble. He was such an impossible man! His looks, his voice, his smile: all seemed to promise so much and still he said nothing. What was she to think? Was it all in her imagination? It must be for she was aware that she had betrayed her own feelings more than once.

If he truly cared for her surely he would have spoken?

'You won't mind if Amanda and I go to Heatherington's dance this evening, will you?' John asked

when he came in just after Max had left. 'She would much
rather attend a dance than be lectured by Lady Fairley—
and Heatherington's sister was very kind to Amanda last
night. I told Lady Heatherington that you had a prior engagement, and she has asked Amanda to go there to dress
and to stay with them overnight—so you need not worry
that it won't look proper, because Amanda will be chap-
eroned by Lady Heatherington. I can still take you to your
party and come for you afterwards, if you like?'

Jane tried not to feel hurt at his desertion. She was
pleased that Amanda had been invited to a dance, but it
was a small affair given by one of John's personal friends,
and could not rank as an important occasion. It was much
more important to please the leaders of society, some of
whom would undoubtedly be at Lady Fairley's card
party—but perhaps it would be best if Jane went alone.
At least Amanda would not have to bear the brunt of their
displeasure.

'I dare say Captain Carter will escort me,' Jane said.
'Lady Fairley said I was welcome to bring a guest of my
choosing. I shall send a note to his lodgings immediately.
You will not want to come away from your party early,
dearest.'

'You're the best of sports, Janey,' John said, and kissed
her cheek. 'I rather thought Massingham might be there?
He would look after you, no doubt.'

'I think Lord Massingham has other engagements,' Jane
replied, frowning. 'No, no, I shall ask Captain Carter. He
promised to escort me wherever I wished to go.'

'You're not thinking of marrying Carter, Jane?' Her
brother stared at her when she did not immediately answer. He hesitated, then moved his feet awkwardly. 'I'd
imagined Massingham might have come up to scratch before this but…'

'John!' She stared at him in dismay. 'What are you
suggesting?'

'Why else did he invite us to Massingham?' John asked

with a lift of his eyebrows. 'It wasn't because he was interested in Amanda; we all know that now. Amanda is certain he is in love with you. Besides, he has rather compromised you, hasn't he? He ought as a gentleman to make you an offer. It's the decent thing to do in the circumstances. Should I have a quiet word in his ear?'

'Please do not!' Jane was horrified. She frowned at her brother. 'You have no right to suggest that Max… No, no, it was entirely my fault. Pray do not say any more. I am most distressed that you should think he would have done anything to harm me.'

'Forgive me, Janey,' he said, at once contrite. 'I thought you quite liked him—and it would be a way out of this mess, wouldn't it? I know it's my fault this has happened. I'm really the one to blame, and it's unfair that you should suffer. I suppose I just hoped Massingham liked you enough to make you an offer.'

'If he made me an offer for the reasons you suggest I should refuse it,' Jane said, her cheeks flushed. 'I can think of nothing I should hate more. No, no, John. I wish you will not think of such a thing again. It is quite out of the question.'

John apologized once again, kissed her cheek and went out to tell Amanda to get ready to leave for the Heatheringtons' house.

Jane was left alone to wonder and sigh.

'It was very kind of you to invite me,' Jane said as she was greeted by her hostess that evening. 'May I present Captain Carter—a neighbour and friend of my father— who has been very kind to me these past several months?'

'Captain Carter and I are already acquainted,' Lady Fairley said, giving him an approving nod, then, turning her quizzing glass on Jane, asked, 'Well, miss—what have you to say for yourself?' She frowned as Jane flushed and looked awkward. 'No, no, none of that. I have it on the best authority that this muddle was none of your making.

If it were not for the spite of a certain person it need not have happened, but it has and we must make the best of it.' Her bright gaze fixed on Captain Carter. 'Leave Jane with me, if you please. She is to remain with me while I greet my guests, sir—and you may take a drink or gossip with the gentlemen you will find at the card tables. We shall send for you when you are needed.'

The gentleman knew himself dismissed and wandered off, quite content to have a comfortable coze with friends he discovered in the further salon. If he knew anything, and he prided himself that he did, his young friend was in good hands, and he need have no further worries on her behalf.

Jane remained at Lady Fairley's side to receive the remainder of her guests for the evening. One or two of the ladies looked surprised to find Jane so obviously favoured by a hostess who was known for her outspoken ways— and her lectures!—but because Lady Fairley was a leader of society and beyond reproach they greeted her protégée kindly enough and decided that they had known the rumours were false all the time. One could immediately see that Miss Osbourne was quality, and Countess Langdon was known for her spite—besides which, the circumstance of Miss Osbourne being favoured in this way by Massingham's godmother led one to an inevitable conclusion—and that put quite a different complexion on the matter. For if there were a secret understanding between Miss Osbourne and Lord Massingham then there was no more to be said, except to smile to oneself and count the months until their first child was born.

It was as well for Jane's peace of mind that she had no idea why all the ladies were so amazingly kind to her, several of them mentioning a little affair they were giving and begging Miss Osbourne to favour them with her company.

Jane said that she would be leaving town in a few days to attend Lady Farringdon's costume ball—a cause for

more nods and winks as the suspicion of an understanding
became a certainty in the minds of several ladies—but
would be happy to accept their invitations to take tea and
was herself giving a dinner on Thursday evening. Two of
her new acquaintances accepted her kind invitation, and
the others were forced to decline only because of prior
engagements.

Jane was feeling very much better by the end of the
evening, and inclined to believe she had made too much
of the slight coolness shown her by some ladies at
Roxborough's dance. It seemed that very few people had
chosen to believe the countess's spite after all, and she
knew who she had to thank for that. She was very grateful
to her hostess for sponsoring her and kissed her cheek
before she took her leave a little before ten o'clock.

'You have been very kind to me,' Jane said. 'Thank
you for coming to my rescue.'

'I would have done so even if Massingham had not
explained,' Lady Fairley said, giving her a look of approval. 'I told you at Massingham you had my blessing
and I meant it.'

It was not until Jane was on her way home in the carriage that she suddenly realized what her hostess had
meant by that last remark—and why everyone had been
so amazingly civil to her. They all believed she had a
private understanding with Massingham!

Jane felt a rush of heat to her cheeks. This was terrible!
It would be all over town in a few days—and that would
almost certainly cause Lord Massingham to feel that he
was obliged to make her an offer. Just as John had already
suggested...

'Oh, no, no,' she muttered. It was the very last thing
she wanted. 'How foolish...'

Captain Carter turned to look at her as she moaned
aloud. 'Something wrong, m'dear? I thought the evening
went very well. I told you we should brush through. No

one with an ounce of sense would believe a word Countess Langdon says.'

'No.' Jane smothered a sigh. 'Nothing wrong…just a little headache.'

'Then I shan't come in,' her kind escort said as the carriage stopped and a groom came to open the door for her. 'You get to your bed, m'dear. I dare say you did not sleep well last evening but you'll be able to rest now that everything is right and tight.'

He left her with a smile and a sigh of regret. He was going to miss Jane when she married, for her company had filled many a lonely hour for him. Still, there were ladies enough in London, and perhaps one of them might take pity on him. Indeed, a handsome widow had rather caught his eye that evening, and she had smiled at him several times.

Setting his hat at a rakish angle, he walked briskly towards his club. There was always another day, and another adventure waiting round the corner.

Jane was grateful for his kindness in escorting her that evening, but very relieved when she reached the privacy of her own room. She felt tired and sent Bessie off to her bed as soon as she had unfastened the hooks at the back of her gown. Alone, she sat brushing her long hair before the mirror, her face pale in the candlelight.

It seemed she had recovered her reputation but at a heavy price. If Max made her an offer now—and Lady Fairley obviously believed it was certain he would—Jane would never be sure that it had not been done merely out of kindness, because he was a gentleman.

The next morning Jane received a very civil note from Lady Morton saying that she had mixed her dates, and was free to attend Jane's dinner party the following evening after all.

Although gratified that a woman she had counted as one of her mother's best friends had clearly reviewed her opinion of Jane's character, she was unable to be easy in her mind. And when she received a note from Max apologizing for not being able to attend her party but promising to call on her without fail before she left town she was thrown into a panic.

What would she do if he proposed to her? It was what she wanted above all things, but only if he truly loved her. If he married her simply because he believed he had compromised her good name— The thought was so painful that Jane instantly dismissed it, but it lingered at the back of her mind throughout a restless night.

The next morning she was gratified to see that there were at least twenty messages for her, most of them inviting her to little supper dances or card parties. Many of them were for dates after her planned return to the country, but what mattered was that Countess Langdon's campaign of spite had not ended in Jane being cast out of polite society. She would be able to bring Amanda back to town in the spring.

But by then everyone would know she was not engaged to Massingham, because she had decided she must refuse him if he were to offer… At least, she had almost decided.

Jane's dinner party was a success that evening. She was asked several times if she expected to see Massingham at her table and managed, without blushing, to reply that he was detained elsewhere on urgent matters.

'He had expected to be here,' she told Lady Morton, 'but was forced to cry off because of business.'

'It is the way of all men,' Lady Morton said, giving her an arch smile, 'but I dare say you have forgiven him?'

'Oh, yes…' Now Jane could not hide the betraying flush that stained her cheeks. It was quite clear that her mother's friend believed her already secretly engaged. 'I think…we are good friends…'

'Ah, yes.' The elderly lady nodded wisely. 'Selina Fairley has confided in me, my dear. I hope you will not take offence if I presume on an old friendship to wish you happy?'

Jane smiled and looked shy, which did her an inestimable amount of good in Lady Morton's eyes, for there was nothing so pretty as modesty in a gel—especially a gel with Jane Osbourne's looks!

'You—you are very kind, ma'am.'

'I was fond of your mother,' Lady Morton said, and touched her hand. 'I know she would be happy to see you so well suited.'

Jane could think of nothing to say, but was not pressed to reply. Glancing up at that moment, she noticed Sir Andrew watching them from across the room. He was not close enough to overhear what they were saying, and Captain Carter was regaling him with a rousing hunting tale, but his eyes had narrowed in suspicion and she had a feeling that he knew what was being whispered in the best circles—and that he was angry! So angry that he was finding it difficult to control his feelings.

No, surely not? Why should he be angry? And yet perhaps it was not so surprising given his own passionate declaration.

Her nerves were a little on edge as she noticed him staring at her several times during the evening, but he said nothing to distress her, and when he took his leave pressed her hand and thanked her warmly for a delightful evening.

'I have to go out of town for a few days,' he told her. 'But I know we shall meet at the Farringdons' dance—if not before.'

Jane was not sure why she felt chilled by his words. It was foolish of her to feel this distrust towards Max's childhood friend, but something about him was beginning to cause her increasing anxiety. She could not have said what it was—just that he made her feel nervous.

How silly she was! He had declared his love for her with a passion that was overwhelming and unnerving, but that was surely not a reason to feel that he might be dangerous?

Ridiculous! Where had that thought come from? She must put it out of her mind at once. Max would be hurt if he thought that she had taken an aversion to his special friend.

All at once Jane was overcome with a rush of emotion. She was so very fond of her dearest Max. She had hoped that he might care for her but he had not spoken. She really could not bear it if he made her an offer merely out of a sense of obligation.

After another two days of torturing herself as she waited for Max to pay his promised visit, Jane decided she would leave for the country a day earlier than she had planned. Amanda's fittings were finished and the girl had made several new friends, who had invited her to visit them at their country homes later that year. She was quite ready to go back to Cornwall. She and John were in a great excitement over their costumes, which had been delivered and tried on in secrecy.

'Oh, yes, dearest Jane,' she said when Jane asked her if she was ready to leave. 'It will not be long before we come back. Besides, at home John and I can spend so much more time together.'

'I think we might announce your engagement at Christmas,' Jane told her. 'And then perhaps next spring…'

'We shall be married in the summer,' Amanda told her, brimming with bright confidence. 'After I've had my season. John is quite determined I should and I must do as he says, mustn't I?'

Jane smiled. Amanda could twist John around her little finger and well she knew it, but it was a sensible arrangement.

It seemed that her ward and brother had all their plans well in hand. Jane only wished that she had more confidence in her own future.

Chapter Thirteen

'I've missed you, dearest Jane.' Maggie got up to embrace her rather clumsily. She laughed at herself. 'Oh, dear, I am not a pretty sight at the moment.'

'I think you look beautiful,' Jane said. 'You are so lucky, Maggie—to be married to a man who worships the ground you tread, to have your darling little Sarah, and be carrying your second child.'

Maggie was surprised by the wistful note in her friend's voice. She had not thought Jane much interested in children until now. But perhaps that was because she had been so preoccupied with running the estate, which was, to Maggie's mind, more properly a man's work. Perhaps it was not so surprising that Jane should become a little broody now that she had more time on her hands.

'Would you like to come up to the nursery?' she asked, her mouth curving in a smile of maternal pride. 'She has just started to walk. And only just thirteen months this very week. Can you believe it? Mrs Howard was telling me her son was fifteen months before he took a step.'

'May I really see her?' Jane asked. 'I have never liked to ask before, in case it disturbed her routine. But when we stayed at the farm there was such a pretty child, Maggie—oh, no prettier than your own Sarah, but she climbed on my knee and I confess I lost my heart to her.'

'It is time you had your own nursery,' Maggie said. 'Was there no one at Massingham you liked? No one at all?'

'Oh, Maggie,' Jane cried. 'I must tell you. You will think me very foolish...but I have fallen in love with someone. I think he is about to make me an offer, but I am not sure what I ought to do.'

'First of all, you must tell me everything,' Maggie said, slipping her arm through Jane's. 'Though I think I may have guessed...'

'Will you ride down to Ormond with me, Andrew?' Max asked, laying a casual arm about his friend's shoulders. 'It seems an age since we spent any time alone together.'

'You have had other things on your mind,' Sir Andrew replied. 'All this business with Richard. It must have caused you a great deal of trouble.'

'Yes...some,' Max agreed, his expression bland, giving nothing away. 'But I am not so sure it was Richard, you know. I do not see that he has much to gain by killing me. Suspicion would be bound to fall on him, you know—and that might prohibit him from inheriting.'

Sir Andrew gave him a long, hard look. 'So you have decided it was someone else—who?'

'I have no idea,' Max replied. 'I have cudgelled my brains in an effort to discover my enemy, if indeed I have one. Can you think of anyone I have ridden over roughshod, Andrew? Anyone who might hate me enough to want me dead?'

'You won a fortune from Barchester a couple of months ago.'

'And lost another to him this week,' Max said, grimacing. 'He was never ruined, Andrew. Indeed, he has more money than he rightly knows how to spend.'

'Then I do not know who your enemy might be.'

'No, nor do I,' Max said, and smiled at him. 'I am

inclined to think it was all made out to be more than it was; what say you?'

'Perhaps, though I think you would do well to keep a close eye on that cousin of yours.'

'And so I shall—a very close eye,' Max said, and there was a hint of warning in his voice. 'Come, Andrew, you have not given me an answer. Will you ride down to Ormond with me? I am convinced that I shall be perfectly safe with you to bear me company.'

'If you put it like that,' Sir Andrew said, 'you leave me with no choice. Yes, I shall ride with you, Max.'

'Then I know I shall be perfectly safe,' Max said. 'For you have always been as a brother to me—and who better than a brother to watch my back?'

Jane galloped her mare across the moors. It was a cool day and there was a hint of rain in the air, a threat that autumn might be coming sooner than it ought, but Jane relished the chance to be alone with the elements—and her thoughts.

She had been at home for almost a week now and there was no word from Massingham. Oh, why did he not come? She was half inclined to regret her hasty departure from town, because he had promised to visit her there the very next day. She had run from him because she was afraid of what he might say to her—and now she was pining for a sight of him. How very foolish she was!

Jane tried to dismiss her unhappy thoughts. She had come to the painful conclusion that it would be better to remain unwed than marry a man who did not love her, who would marry only because he thought it his duty, and perhaps for the sake of an heir—and yet her whole being cried out for the man she loved.

The hard ride did her good and she was feeling a little better as she dismounted and went into the house. Bessie met her in the hall.

'You've a visitor, Miss Jane,' she said. 'I told him I

was not sure when you would be back but he insisted on waiting for you.'

'Is it Lord Massingham?' Jane's heart took a dizzying leap, but her hopes were soon dashed.

'No, miss. It's Sir Andrew Forbes.'

'Oh…' Jane stopped in her tracks, then took a deep breath. 'I see… Thank you, Bessie. Stay close in case I should ring for you. Better still, bring in a tray of wine and biscuits in a few minutes—and then stay near.'

'Yes, miss.'

Bessie went away and Jane walked into her little parlour. Sir Andrew was looking at a portrait of the late Mrs Osbourne, staring up at it with a frowning concentration. He turned as Jane entered and she was shocked by the very odd expression in his eyes. Anger? Grief? She could not be certain, but it was a very deeply felt emotion. What could he be thinking of—his mother or sister?

Remembering his personal tragedy, Jane was ashamed of her unkind thoughts concerning him. It was no wonder that he sometimes seemed a little odd. Any man who had suffered as he had might be forgiven a few odd moments.

'Sir Andrew,' she said, giving him her hand. 'How very good of you to call on me. When did you come down?'

'Max and I arrived last night,' he said. 'We are staying with the Farringdons until after their dance. He had some business of his own but I came at once to call on you.'

'Oh…' The news that Max was here, staying with his sister, gave her a little shock. Why had he not come to her at once? Or perhaps it was better that he did not. Oh, why could she not be easy in her mind? 'It was kind of you to call. ' She smiled politely at her visitor, hoping that he would not be offended by her distracted manner.

'I came because I wished to speak to you,' he said, a note of suppressed passion in his voice. 'I heard certain worrying rumours in town…that you might have a secret understanding with Massingham.' Jane was silent, her hands clasped before her, face pale. 'Please tell me it is not true? That you have not deceived me?'

'Deceived you?' Jane's brows rose. What was he implying? 'I fear I do not understand you, sir. I have made you no promises…given you no reason to hope that… your feelings were returned.' She held her breath, praying that he was not about to renew his advances to her.

'But you do like me, Jane?' he asked, moving towards her eagerly. 'You did say that…'

He was interrupted by the arrival of Bessie; she was carrying a tray and the news that Jane had another visitor.

'Lord Massingham is here, Miss Osbourne,' she said. 'Shall I show him in?'

Jane hesitated, catching her breath as she saw the look in Sir Andrew's eyes. He was furious! His manner was very odd, very odd indeed. She had a sudden terrible suspicion and her reaction was instinctive.

'Please tell Lord Massingham that I cannot see him, Bessie. Ask him to call another time.'

'Are you sure, miss? He seemed to think it was urgent.'

'I am perfectly sure. Please do as I ask, Bessie. *All* that I have asked.'

Bessie went out, looking puzzled.

'I am gratified that you have sent him away.' Andrew took a step towards her, his eyes bright with excitement. 'It gives me hope…hope that you may care for me a little, that in time you may return my love for you. Oh, Jane, I know you do not care for excess passion but…'

She thought that he was about to seize her and would have moved away, but before she could do or say anything the door was flung open and Max strode in, looking angry.

'Jane…' he began, then stopped, eyes narrowing in suspicion as he sensed the atmosphere between her and Andrew. 'I thought… What are you doing here, Andrew?'

'I came to call on Miss Osbourne, of course,' Sir

Andrew replied with a careless shrug of his shoulders. The brilliance had gone from his eyes and he was once more the normal, polite gentleman Jane had first met at Massingham and rather liked. 'If you had told me you were coming, Max, we might have ridden over together. I thought you had business in the village?'

Jane held her breath. Surely Max would see something was very wrong here? She was almost sure she was right, but she dared not speak. Not now, not at this moment, though she must do so soon.

'I had several errands, but they took less time than I thought so I rode on here to bring a message for Miss Osbourne from my sister.' His eyes were thoughtful as he looked at her. 'Catherine says she will call on you later this afternoon—if that is convenient?'

'Yes, of course.' Jane blushed under his fierce stare. He was annoyed with her—why? 'Catherine knows she is always welcome here.' She glanced at the tray of wine and biscuits. 'May I invite you both to take some refreshment?'

'I came only to deliver the message,' Max said, glaring at her. What had she done to upset him? 'I shall not intrude…'

'I was just about to leave,' Sir Andrew said. 'Shall we ride back together?'

'Of course, if you wish.' Massingham's expression was impossible to read. 'Miss Osbourne, your servant.' He turned, about to leave, when John and Amanda came rushing in. 'Miss Roberts. John.'

'Bessie said you were here,' Amanda cried, giving him one of her enchanting smiles. 'I do not believe I have thanked you for helping Jane when I was ill, sir.'

'There was no need,' he said, relaxing a little. 'Please do not put me to the trouble again, minx, for next time you shall not escape so easily. Remember, you have been warned.'

Amanda laughed at his teasing, at ease again. 'Oh,

you!' She pouted. 'I know you are funning. Have you a splendid costume for the ball, sir? I am expecting something clever from you.'

'I must try not to disappoint you,' he said, then glanced at Jane. Was he trying to pass a message to her? She could not be sure. 'Forgive me, I must go. Andrew…do you come or stay?'

'What a bear he is,' Sir Andrew said, seeming to smile in his old way. 'It is small wonder no woman has ever married him. No sensible woman would think of it—what say you, Miss Osbourne?'

Jane felt chilled. She did not answer, merely shaking her head. How could Sir Andrew's personality change so suddenly? At one moment he was passionate, angry—and the next so completely at ease, so calm: the friend Max loved as a brother. She was shocked by the terrible idea that had just come to her mind—an idea so unacceptable to her that she now dismissed it.

No, no, she must be wrong! It was unthinkable. She was wicked and unjust to have entertained it for a moment.

Amanda noticed she was looking pale after the gentlemen had departed together, Andrew relaxed and smiling, Massingham looking black and unlike himself.

'Is something wrong, Jane?' she asked. 'Are you upset?'

'No…it is nothing at all.' Jane gave herself a little shake. 'Just foolishness, that's all.'

'You are trembling,' Amanda said, all concern. 'Are you ill?'

Jane made an effort to control her thoughts. She was quite mistaken. She had to be.

'No, I am not ill,' she replied. 'If you and John will excuse me, I think I shall walk down the lane and speak to Maggie Graham…'

'You can't mean it?' Maggie said some twenty minutes or so later after Jane had unburdened her heart to her.

'You think that Sir Andrew... Oh, surely not? You must be mistaken.'

'Yes, perhaps I am. Oh, I don't know,' cried Jane, taking an agitated turn about the room. 'It seems so unlikely, doesn't it? After all, they have been friends for years. Surely Max would know if his friend were... And yet he was so odd, Maggie. I believe there is something very wrong with him. I think he is...'

'Insane?' Maggie asked with a lift of her brows. 'That is what you are suggesting, isn't it, Jane? If you believe that he might be behind these attacks on Lord Massingham, he must indeed be out of his mind. It is the only explanation.'

'No... Oh, no,' Jane said, horrified at what she had been suggesting. 'It was just an idea—a wicked, wicked thought of mine. Sir Andrew could not possibly be... He is so charming most of the time. When we first met I really liked him but... I do not know what to believe, Maggie.'

'But you think there is something unnatural about his behaviour at times? What makes you suspect he might have tried to kill Massingham? What possible reason could he have—unless he truly is insane?'

'He couldn't...' Jane said, pacing about the room in a fever of worry. 'Of course he couldn't. I am wicked even to suspect him—but I never thought Richard a likely murderer, you know. He might sulk and fly up into the boughs when Max tries to control his gambling, but...I actually think he is rather fond of Max in his own way.'

'The mind is a very strange thing,' Maggie said, placing her hands over her bulging stomach. 'It plays tricks on one, especially when one is in an emotional state.'

'Yes, I expect you are right,' Jane said, relieved. 'I have been very foolish even to think of it for one moment.'

'I did not mean you,' her friend said. 'I would trust your judgement above anyone's. I was thinking of Sir

Andrew. You say he has been Max's friend for years—
there could be some imagined slight in his mind, something that has grown out of proportion. Something that
could lead an unbalanced mind to seek revenge.'

'Oh, Maggie!' Jane looked at her in dismay, her stomach churning. 'Then you think I could be right to suspect
him? What should I do, Maggie? Ought I to tell Max?
Ought I to warn him against his friend?'

Maggie hesitated, looking thoughtful.

'I think, my dear, my very dearest Jane, that you should
be on your guard. It would be best to stay away from Sir
Andrew as much as you can. If he is jealous of
Massingham and means him harm there is no telling what
he might do! And if he thought you suspected him he
might very well take it into his head to murder you, too!'

'I hope you don't mind me calling on you like this?'
Catherine asked as she sat with Jane in her parlour that
afternoon. 'But I felt I had to come. Lady Fairley told me
there was an understanding between you and Max, but he
will tell me nothing and is in such a mood...'

'Lady Fairley thought—that is...' Jane stared at her.
'What do you mean? Why is Max in a mood?'

'I had hoped you might be able to tell me,' Catherine
said. 'I know he has a great deal on his mind, and he was
quiet when he first came down from London, but after his
visit to you this morning... I have never known him like
it. He is usually so good-humoured, able to see the amusing side of any situation—but he was barely civil to poor
Andrew, and Richard was given a terrible tongue-lashing
when he arrived just after nuncheon. I am worried about
him, Jane. It is just so unlike him to behave in this way.'

'He must have something on his mind,' Jane said, not
quite able to meet her eyes. 'I must admit he did seem a
little put out this morning when he arrived.'

'Jane...' Catherine looked at her oddly. 'Is there any
truth in the rumour that you and Max have an understand-

ing? I know that Andrew asked you to marry him but I thought you had refused him?'

'I have.' Jane barely repressed a shudder. 'I am sorry, Catherine, but I do not like him. He makes me nervous.'

She knew that she could never confide her thoughts to Max's sister in the way she had to her friend. Maggie was able to give an unbiased view but Catherine might be offended. She had known Sir Andrew all her life, and like Max was fond of him.

'Only, I wondered…' Catherine looked awkward. 'There has always been a certain rivalry between Max and Andrew, even when they were boys, and…' She took a deep breath. 'I think Andrew might try to take you from Max if he thought Max really cared for you. That sounds awful, I know, but it is the way things have always been with them. I believe brothers are often rivals, and they grew up together, sharing everything. Andrew was always at our home, for he lived not more than a mile or so from us. So, you see, it might be that he wanted you because he believed Max intended to ask you to be his wife.'

'Yes, I believe you might be right.' Jane was struck by this, not having considered it before. 'It would explain why Sir Andrew spoke to me at Massingham, before we had hardly met. He thought that…' She stopped and blushed.

'That Max had invited you to Massingham in order to get to know you before making an offer. Of course he did, Jane. We all knew that. Max asked me if I thought he had a chance of engaging your affections and I said I was not sure. I expected him to make you an offer weeks ago, and was surprised that he did not do so. He has not spoken to you, has he?'

'No.' Jane could not look at her. Her heart was racing so wildly that she could scarcely breathe. 'I thought once—after he helped me find Amanda— But if he had wanted to speak he must have done so before now, surely?'

'Unless he had a reason to keep silent,' Catherine said, looking anxious. 'I think he may be worried about Richard's reaction. If Max marries you Richard cannot hope to inherit and he has been allowed to believe that he is Max's heir—' She broke off as a little cry escaped Jane's lips, and, seeing the sheen of tears in her eyes, pressed her hand. 'I should not have upset you.'

'No, no, you have not,' Jane said, blinking bravely. 'It was just something you said about...'

'About Richard?'

'Yes.' Jane nodded thoughtfully. 'I cannot explain what I mean, Catherine—but I think you have misjudged Richard. If Max has an enemy, I do not believe it is his cousin.'

'What can you mean?' Catherine was puzzled. 'Pray tell me, Jane.'

Jane was silent for a moment, then gave her friend a look of regret. 'Forgive me, I may not—for Max's sake. If I told you you might betray your feelings. And I believe we must all be very, very careful for the time being. Very careful indeed.'

Max could not remember ever having felt this angry in his life. What on earth was Jane about, encouraging Andrew's attentions? He was smarting beneath an emotion he had never had cause to feel before and disliked. Damn it! He could not be jealous. He wasn't a jealous man...but the sight of Andrew and Jane together, obviously in some sort of highly emotional scene, had made him want to tear the other man limb from limb. Only with the greatest self-control had he managed to keep silent on the return journey to his sister's house.

Surely Jane could not be considering accepting an offer from Andrew? She must be aware of his own feelings for her—that he had been on the verge of speaking several times, keeping silent only because it might endanger her own life. She must know that he loved her! He was certain she could not still be unaware of his feelings for her.

He had believed she cared for him. In his mind he still believed it, but the heart was vulnerable. Max laughed at himself. What a fool he was! For the first time in his life he had fallen deeply in love, and was feeling all the uncertainty suffered by any green youth.

Jane could not care for Andrew. She loved *him*. He had seen it in her eyes, sensed how close she was to giving herself to him that night they had spent together at that disreputable inn, lying so close together and yet not touching—because one touch would have been too much for them both. Oh, how he had wanted her that night, the scent of her body torturing him as he kept his distance, suppressing his desire to make her his own.

Max's smile disappeared as he remembered the reasons he had held back when he'd longed to take her in his arms, to make love to her, possess her…know every inch of her tantalisingly lovely self.

If Jane had refused an offer from Andrew—and that might well have been the reason for her unease when he'd arrived unexpectedly that morning—then it made it all the more likely that Andrew might choose to strike at him through her.

Damn him! Max knew a moment of intense frustration. He had almost decided to speak that morning, but finding Andrew there before him had thrown him and now he was torn by indecision again.

He could not continue like this. He must break the stalemate or he would be in limbo for the rest of his days…waiting for his enemy to strike, unable to claim the woman he loved. A situation that was causing him a great deal of grief.

It was so difficult to believe that Andrew could have plotted to have him murdered…had hired an assassin to do just that. But Max was almost certain of it now. That rogue at the inn had denied all knowledge of Andrew, and of making the attempts on Max's life, but the truth had been there in the fear in his eyes.

The rogue had expected Max to turn him over to the authorities, but after questioning him for some time Max had pretended to believe him and let him go with a warning to stay out of his way, in the belief that it was better to recognize your enemy. At least he would be on his guard if he saw the man following him again—and he was obviously a poor shot, since he had twice failed to kill Max. Unless that was Andrew himself? Andrew had never been a decent shot, unlike Richard.

That was really what had made Max begin to suspect that his cousin was not behind the attempts on his life. Richard would not have needed a second shot.

'Why would he do it?' Max asked himself the question that had plagued him for weeks. He had won most of their sporting bets—and when they were children Max had always been the winner when they wrestled—but murder? 'A man does not kill for a lost bet.'

Was Andrew of unstable mind? Max had sometimes wondered at his sudden rages, his strange moods—but then, when they were over, he was always calm again, the friend he had known and loved for so many years. A little touchy at times, volatile—but still a friend.

There had been one incident when they were boys— when for a moment Andrew had held a knife to his throat and he had believed he meant to kill him—but then they had laughed together. Besides, they *were* friends. Max had won countless wagers, but he was generous, selling Andrew horses at much less than their true worth, giving him the freedom of his home, paying off a gambling debt when his friend was temporarily without funds.

The man who had attacked him at the fencing school was not that friend, but a stranger Max had not recognized. For a few short moments it had seemed as if another person had taken over Andrew's mind, and that person had hated him.

If Andrew hated him enough to want him dead there must be something else, something that had festered and grown in his mind like a canker, taking over a mind that was beginning to fail. But what? Andrew had always been volatile, but this was something new…something that had become much worse over the past year or so.

Oh, no! Not that! Surely it could not be that—and yet it made sense of all the rest. The death of Andrew's sister had affected him deeply and Max had done his best to comfort him. It had never once occurred to him that Andrew might blame him for her decline into illness.

It was true that Marion Forbes had had a childish crush on Max, that he had been forced to tell her very gently that he was not in love with her and did not wish to marry her—but he had never once given her cause to hope. Any small attention he had shown her had been merely kindness towards a rather silly, delicate girl.

Andrew could not blame him for her death? And yet it would make sense of all this—would explain the gradual deterioration of Andrew's mental state. And Max was beginning to realize that his friend must indeed be ill. Which made him very dangerous.

If Andrew held him responsible for his sister's death…might he not choose to strike at Max through the woman he loved? Was that why there had been no further attempts on his life?

He had given Andrew every opportunity to attack him on their way down to Cornwall, choosing quiet country lanes and riding ahead of him, offering his back as an easy target, but nothing had happened.

Max knew that he could bear his own death more easily than the loss of the woman he loved. Andrew, who knew him better than anyone, would be aware of that.

He must be constantly on his guard, must have a watch kept over her whenever she went out riding alone as she so often did. And he must do nothing to push Andrew over the edge.

Chapter Fourteen

Jane walked into her parlour on the night of Lady Farringdon's ball to find Amanda and John waiting for her. She clapped her hands and laughed as she saw their costumes for the first time, immediately recognizing where the inspiration had come from. John had dressed as Massingham's privateer ancestor right down to the last detail of the portrait in the gallery, and Amanda was Queen Bess.

'Oh, my dears,' Jane said, kissing both of them in turn. 'What a wonderful idea. You both look quite splendid.'

'We did it to amuse Max,' Amanda said. 'It was so wicked of him to tell us all those tales.' She looked at Jane, taking note of the simple grey tunic with a low-slung girdle of gold threads and a cap of gold mesh set at the back of her head, her lovely hair allowed to fall loosely down her back for once. 'You look wonderful—that's medieval, isn't it?'

'How clever of you to see it,' Jane said. 'I took it from a picture I once saw of a medieval martyr. She was burnt as a witch for helping the sick—but really because her enemies were afraid of her.'

'Oh, Jane…' Amanda gave a little gasp of admiration. 'I should never have thought of such a thing—it is so simple and yet so effective. You do look as if you might have an aura of saintliness in that costume.'

'Please do not say so!' begged Jane, laughing. 'I chose it because it looked comfortable to wear and was easy to copy.'

'I think it makes you look rather regal,' John said with a thoughtful look. 'You might as well be Queen Elenore as a martyr. It suits you, Janey.'

'As long as it will do,' Jane said. 'And now, if you are ready, I think we should be leaving, for you will not want to be late.'

'Oh, no,' Amanda cried, eyes sparkling like precious jewels. 'I cannot wait to see what Max is wearing!'

Jane saw him at once. They were not the first to arrive by any means and the Farringdons' elegant salons held a fair assortment of Cavaliers, Roundheads, sultans in glittering turbans, queens, princesses, Puritan maidens, and colourful jesters with bells on their pointed shoes. Max was dressed as a Roman in a purple tunic with a gold cloak draped over his shoulder. It suited him perfectly, and she knew that nothing else could have looked half so well on him. He looked every inch the noble patrician of the great Roman Empire.

Jane smiled as she looked about her. So many of her friends and neighbours were at the ball, just as she had expected. Everyone looked forward to Lady Farringdon's special occasions.

Captain Carter was one of several Cavaliers. He gave her a rueful smile as she congratulated him on his costume.

'Not very original, I fear,' he said. 'Massingham has outshone us all—except for you, Jane. I'm not perfectly sure what you're meant to be, but it is very fetching. You make every other woman here look over-dressed.'

'No, no, of course I don't,' Jane denied with a smile. 'It was so easy, you see—and comfortable. Amanda is far more splendid, but I fear she will become rather hot as the evening wears on.'

'By Jove, yes, you're right,' her friend agreed, running a finger inside his elaborate lace falling band. 'I'm already beginning to feel warm… Ah, here comes Massingham.'

'Jane.' Max's eyes were warm and teasing as he studied her. 'Let me guess—certainly medieval. Not Queen Elenore. Perhaps a saint or a martyr on her way to the stake?'

'Oh, you guessed, shame on you!' she cried, pouting with a disappointment she did not feel. It was pleasing that their minds met like this. 'Or did someone tell you?'

'I believe I may have seen the picture—or one very like it,' Max said, a quiver of amusement at the corner of his mouth. 'We have several in the library at Massingham.' His eyes mocked and provoked her, as if daring her to remember that night: the night she had sensed he was very close to making love to her. 'Yes, I like it—it becomes you—but somehow I don't see you in the role. A witch, yes, but not a martyr.'

'Her name was Bertha and she was burnt as a witch for making sick people well again.'

'Ah…' Max nodded. 'Then that air of innocence is meant to deceive. Now I understand—and it suits you very well.'

'Wretch!' cried Jane, smothering the desire to laugh. 'I am no deceiver, sir. Shame on you!'

'Nor are you a saint,' he said with a smile. 'Pray do not fly into the boughs, dearest Jane. Come and dance with me while we have the chance.'

He took her hand very firmly in his own, leading her into the ballroom, where a few couples had started to waltz. At public dances or élite gatherings of the *ton* permission would be needed from a leading lady of society before an unmarried girl might accept an invitation to waltz, but there was no difficulty at a private dance in the country.

Jane allowed Massingham to place his hand at her waist. His touch was light but sent a quiver of pleasure through her, making her pulses race. Then they were twirling gracefully round and round to the music, their bodies so close as to be almost touching but not quite. It was an exquisite sensation, and Jane knew a longing so fierce and overwhelming that she was shocked.

Were ladies of quality expected to feel like this: an eager, urgent desire to feel Max's body touching every bit of hers in the most intimate way? She rather thought not. Ladies were meant to be delicate, fragile creatures who consented to their husband's demands with obedience but took no pleasure from the act of submission, except that of being dutiful. Jane found it hard to keep the delightful feelings under control and knew that she would have cast herself into his arms had they not happened to be on a dance floor. It was extremely wanton of her. But she could not regret her lack of modesty on this occasion. Indeed, she wished their dance might go on for ever.

Alas, it could not. Max released her immediately the music ceased. It was all she could do to hold back her sigh of regret, but retained enough composure to smile and thank him as he escorted her back to Amanda.

'The pleasure was mine, believe me,' he said, such a wicked gleam in his eye that she laughed, her disappointment vanishing like mist on a hot summer's day. When he looked at her like that she could believe anything. 'A pleasure I intend to have more often in future.'

Jane's eyes lifted to meet his intense gaze. That wicked, wicked sense of humour! Had he sensed the longing in her? Did he know that she was lost to any balance, any measure of propriety when in his arms, that he had only to say one word and she would fall into them, counting the world and propriety as nothing against the joy of being his?

'Jane. You look wonderful!' Sir Andrew's greeting cut across her thoughts. 'May I claim this dance?'

He was wearing the restrained costume of a Puritan gentleman with black doublet and hose and a large white falling band at his neck. Jane thought it suited him. If he had lived in those troubled times he would undoubtedly have fought for Parliament, while Max… Yes, Max would have held for the king. As would Jane herself.

She recalled her wandering thoughts and smiled. She had come this evening determined to be polite to Max's friend. Her thoughts concerning him were no more resolved than they had been the previous day, but she would give him no reason to think himself slighted. Say nothing that might offend or anger him.

'You are very kind to me, sir,' she said. 'And well dressed—that costume becomes you.'

'I felt it more dignified than some.' Sir Andrew glanced at Massingham, who was dancing with his sister. 'I am not given to ostentation.'

'No, of course not,' Jane replied. It was clear to her who he was meaning to slight and it made her angry, but she hid her feelings beneath a society manner. 'But this is a party, after all. Do you not think Amanda makes a splendid Queen Bess?'

'You would have made a better,' he said, gazing down at her with an intensity that made her uncomfortable. 'But you are still a queen for all your modesty. This is something I have always seen in you, Jane. Your good taste, your sense of what is proper. I admire decency and order.'

Jane barely repressed a shiver of revulsion. For him to speak in such a way when he was capable of such ungovernable passion…but perhaps he did not realize it? He was always so calm after one of his outbursts—almost too calm, changing from one mood to the next in the fraction of a second.

Jane could not pretend to understand. She was not a doctor, nor would it have helped much to consult one about such an illness, for she was beginning to believe Andrew must be ill. No one truly understood the poor wretches who succumbed to fevers of the brain—which was why they were so often cruelly treated, chained to their cots in hospitals unworthy of the name, despised, mocked and neglected.

Not that she would ever suggest Andrew was one of them or needed to be so confined. No, no, it was merely that he was suffering under the strain of grief—his sudden passions an aberration of a troubled mind. He could not have tried to kill Max; that was all in her imagination.

But she would be very careful just the same.

Jane was dancing with Andrew for the fourth time that evening! Max watched, his stupid jealousy gnawing at him like a toothache. And the way she smiled at him! So warm and open...almost inviting.

He was tempted to snatch her away, take her somewhere private and make her admit her love for him. His chosen method of persuasion was so pleasing to his heated emotions that he relaxed slightly. He was a fool! Jane was merely being polite—but he could not quite squash his feelings of jealousy.

Why watch? It was his own fault if Jane had grown tired of waiting for him to speak. And if his suspicions were all wrong...if it *was* Richard and not Andrew who wanted him dead, what then? The devil of it was that he could not be sure.

Max left the ballroom, going out onto the terraces for a breath of air. He paused for a moment, then walked across the lawns towards the shrubbery. He could not allow this situation to continue. He must do something to force the issue, bring it to a head.

He stiffened as he saw a furtive movement in the bushes. What was that? Someone lurking—but who? Friend or foe? Was it possible that his enemy had set a trap for this evening, perhaps hoping to take him off his guard at his sister's party?

A gleam of satisfaction entered his eyes. If that were

the case he might as well make it easier for whoever it
was. The situation was intolerable and could not go on.
He must draw his enemy out. Far better to bring the
rogue's attention on himself than risk it falling on Jane.

Max began to walk purposefully, away from the lights
and noise of the ball. He knew exactly where he was
going and what he planned to do. He had had this moment
in mind for far too long. The sooner it was done and over
the better.

It was much, much later that evening when Jane realized she had not seen Max for hours. Where was he? It
was odd of him to have deserted his sister's guests. He
was usually so attentive, so considerate of others. She saw
Catherine enter the ballroom alone and went up to her.
Perhaps Catherine knew something.

'Jane—have you seen Max recently?' his anxious sister
asked before she could speak. 'I've had the house
searched but cannot find him anywhere.'

'I think…' Jane cast her mind back. When was it she
had seen him last? 'I was dancing with Sir Andrew. I
think Max went outside to the terraces. Yes, I'm sure he
did. I supposed he must have returned to the house before
this, but thought he must be bored with the dancing. Are
you sure he is not in the card room?'

'Max loves to dance,' Catherine said, clearly upset.
'This is not like him, Jane. He never abandons guests. He
would consider it rude.'

'I had wondered where he had got to.' Jane was begin-
ning to feel uneasy herself. Why had Max gone outside?
Was he tempting fate again? It would be so like him.
'What do you suppose can have happened?'

'I don't know. I am tempted to send the grooms out to
search the grounds but…' She sighed deeply. 'Farringdon
says I'm making too much of it. He believes Max has
simply gone for a walk to think things over, and he may
be right. As I told you yesterday, my brother has been in

an odd mood of late. I haven't seen him like this—oh, not since our father died.'

'You are probably worrying for nothing,' Jane said, knowing that it would not do for Catherine to get herself into a state in her delicate condition. 'I'm sure Max can take care of himself.'

'He is so like Father.' Catherine suppressed a sob. 'But he died in a fall from his horse: an accident. I am so very fond of Max. I could not bear it if…'

Nor could she, thought Jane. But it would not do to say so to his worried sister.

'I'm sure he will be all right,' she said comfortingly. 'In the morning he will look at you in astonishment and wonder what all the fuss was about.' She squeezed Catherine's arm. 'You must not worry, truly you mustn't. Max knows what he is about.'

'Yes, that's what Farringdon says.' Catherine gave her a rueful smile. 'He seems to think Max has it all under control—though how that can be I fail to see. If someone is trying to kill him, how can he be in control of the situation?'

Jane thought she could see a way. Massingham was no fool. He had been caught off guard at the start, but he would surely have taken certain measures as a safety precaution?

'Your guests are leaving,' Jane said, 'and I think we should be going too.'

'Will you not stay the night? All of you?' Catherine looked at her pleadingly. 'We have more than enough room and I should feel so much better if you were here, Jane.'

Jane hesitated, then agreed. A message could be sent to her home—besides, she could not rest easy until she was certain Max was safe.

'I'll speak to John and Amanda,' Jane said. 'We must let Bessie know or she will worry—but I think I should like to stay, Catherine. I could not rest, wondering whether or not Max had come home.'

'Of course.' Catherine smiled her relief. 'You are always so brave and calm—but I know you must be as worried as I am. You may try not to show your feelings, Jane—but I know you care for Max. I have seen the way you look at him when you think no one is looking. And I am convinced the foolish man worships you. I cannot understand why he has not spoken long before this.'

Jane smiled. She had felt the same until a few hours earlier when she had noticed Max watching her with Andrew. A certain suspicion had begun to dawn in her mind. Perhaps Max was keeping silent for the same reason that she had gone out of her way to be pleasant to a man she did not truly like.

Jane went up to the guest chamber her hostess had provided. Most of the other guests had either left for their homes or retired to bed. There was still no sign of Max. Catherine had resisted the temptation to set up a search for him outside the house, but spoke of doing so if he did not return by the morning.

Lord Farringdon had insisted that she go to bed, promising that he would ask the servants to make sure her brother was not in the house and to wait up himself for another hour or so. He had advised Jane to get some rest, and promised she would be called if necessary. Because she knew he was concerned for his wife, she helped persuade Catherine to retire and accompanied her upstairs herself.

Alone in her room, Jane lay down on the bed but did not undress. Indeed, her costume felt as comfortable as any nightgown and she wanted to be ready if anyone came to rouse her.

'Oh, Max, where are you?' she whispered. 'You wretched, tiresome man! Why must you worry us so?'

She closed her eyes, slept fitfully for perhaps an hour,

dreaming of a headless Cavalier haunting the passages at Massingham, then woke with a start. Why had she dreamed of such a thing? It was because of Max's sto-ries…the day they had taken a picnic to the Abbey ruins.

Jane jumped up in a sudden irritation of the nerves and began to pace about the room. Why did her mind keep running on that day—on the discovery of a secret passage ending in the cellar under Ormond House?

It was the very place to hide a body! Jane's blood ran cold. Surely she was losing her wits? Yet it was as if Max was speaking to her…telling her where he was…or was that her imagination?

She knew she was probably worrying for nothing. Max might even be here, asleep in his own bed.

Her body felt as if it were on fire. Burning needles were pricking her skin. Max was in danger. In the cellar be-neath this very house. She could sense his presence—feel him close to her—thinking of her.

She could bear it no longer. She must tell someone! If only to be reassured. Leaving her own room, she went out into the hall. Candles were still burning in their sconces at intervals, lighting her way as she walked softly down the stairs; she went carefully, not wanting to rouse the house and give everyone a fright.

A sleepy porter was dozing in his chair in the main hall. He woke as she approached, but shook his head when she enquired if Lord Massingham had returned.

'No, Miss Osbourne. Lord Farringdon desired me to wake him if the gentleman came in, but he has not—and he must have passed me, for all the other doors are bolted from the inside as always.'

Jane thanked him. She hesitated, then walked up the stairs, turning away from her own bedchamber and mak-ing her way down the long passage to the east wing where John's room was situated.

She thought he was probably sleeping and was loath to wake him, but she could not bear her thoughts alone another moment. She knocked once and then again a little louder. John answered her second knock, wearing a long velvet dressing robe and yawning sleepily, as though she had roused him.

'Good grief!' he cried. 'Have they found him? Is something wrong, Janey?'

'The porter says he hasn't come in,' Jane said. 'I couldn't sleep. I'm so worried about him, John. I keep thinking… I know it's foolish, but I keep thinking he's here—in the cellar. The one you and he discovered together.'

'The one that can only be entered from the Abbey ruins?' John stared at her, his manner suddenly alert and interested. She saw that the idea appealed to him. He was not dismissing her fears as mere irritation of the nerves. 'It is the perfect place to hide a body.'

'John!' He had given voice to her worst nightmare.

He saw her face and cursed himself. 'Or to keep someone a prisoner,' he amended swiftly. 'Yes, I think you might be right. Farringdon had a search made of the grounds after you went up. They found the cloak Max was wearing.'

'Oh, John!' Her hand flew to her mouth to prevent a scream. 'You think that he…?'

'Something made him cast it off.' John frowned. 'It was not torn or damaged so he may simply have dropped it—but he may have had a reason.'

'What are you saying?' Jane stared at him, her heart racing.

'Max ain't a fool,' her brother said. 'He wouldn't walk blindly into a trap—but he might try to lure this fellow into following him.'

'Yes,' agreed Jane, looking thoughtful. 'I had thought something similar. He may have done just that—but I'm afraid for him, John. Supposing he was set upon by more than one? It's foolish, but I just cannot stop thinking about that cellar.'

'Do you want to go and look for him? Just you and me?' She nodded and he grinned, obviously thinking it an adventure. 'Go and get your cloak, Jane. I'll dress and meet you downstairs in ten minutes.'

Max had a smile of grim satisfaction on his lips as he looked at the man lying on the ground in front of him. He had been aware that he was being followed from the beginning and had waited until he was almost at the ruins to spring his own trap. Taking advantage of sudden darkness as a cloud covered the moon, he had stepped behind a crumbling wall and jumped out on his victim, felling him with a sharp blow to the neck.

The man had then been carried to the cellar beneath Ormond House. Max's foresight in leaving candles and a tinder box just inside the entrance to the passage had come in very useful. He wished he'd had something more substantial with which to bind the wretch, but the cord from his Roman cloak was fragile and sufficient only to secure his wrists. The rogue had been unceremoniously dumped on the floor of the cellar and Max had been waiting patiently for him to recover his senses these past several hours, but so far he had given no sign of life.

Damn it! He had not used sufficient force to kill the rogue, had he? He stirred the body with his foot and heard a slight moan. Not dead, then. Shamming it, perhaps. Afraid to move in case Max set on him again?

'Wake up, damn you,' Max said in a tone of command. 'I am not fooled by this silence of yours. I warned you what would happen if you crossed my path again. You had your chance, man—now I intend that you shall answer my questions or it will be the worse for you.'

'Go to hell!' came the snarled reply. 'I'll hang sooner or later—for this or another crime, it makes little difference.'

'Not if you tell me what I want to know.' Max watched as the would-be assassin pulled himself up into a sitting position against the wall, his eyes hooded and wary. 'Do as I ask and by the morning you could be on a ship for France with a purse full of guineas.'

'He would kill me if I told…' There was fear in the man's eyes. 'He's mad. Got the devil in him. I've met his kind afore. You think they're all right and tight at first and then… He'd see us both dead sooner than spit.'

'But you would be safe in France. A rich man…' Max smiled, his manner deceptively pleasant, almost confiding. 'And I shall see you hang if you will not speak.'

There was silence as the man digested this, then he lifted his head, staring at Max, eyes sullen, disbelieving.

'How can I be sure you won't just turn me over to the reelers after I've told? I'll be gallows bait for sure.'

'You must take my word.'

'I dare say a man of your jib sets some store by his word?'

'You have my word as a gentleman,' Max said. 'Give me the name of the man who employed you and where you met, what he paid you, your instructions. I want nothing more of you. Your death will give me no satisfaction.'

'And my gold?' His eyes gleamed with sudden greed. 'When do I get that?'

'I will meet you at the ruins in an hour. You may be gone before morning—before anyone—' Max broke off as he heard voices. A light was coming down the passage towards the cellar. He turned, uttering a startled oath as he saw Jane and her brother. Jane was carrying a lanthorn and John was sporting a fearsome pistol. 'Good grief! What the hell are you two doing here?'

'So that's the worth of a gentleman's word!'

Events moved so quickly in the next few seconds that Jane could not have said afterwards exactly what had happened. While Max's attention was diverted by the arrival of her and her brother, the assassin had somehow managed to free his hands. With a great snarl of rage he leapt to his feet and hurled himself at Max from behind. Jane screamed. Max turned to meet his attacker. There was a short, sharp tussle as the two men struggled. John was pointing his pistol, trying to get a clear shot but unable to do so for fear of hitting Max.

Max threw the man off and managed to get one hard punch at his head; he staggered back, seemed to realize he was outnumbered, snatched up an empty wooden cask and threw it at John who was blocking the only way of escape. As John reeled from the force of the blow, the wretch pushed past him and made a dash for freedom. Max did nothing, but John recovered quickly and fired a shot off after him. A muffled shout told them the ball must have found its mark, but when John would have gone after him Max suddenly swung into action, barring his way.

'I might get another shot at the scoundrel!' John protested, the light of battle in his eyes.

'I would have preferred it if you had not fired at all,' Max said in a tone that revealed the depth of his fury. 'You damned fool! What do you mean by exposing your sister to danger? You had no right to interfere in my affairs.'

'We thought you might be in danger,' Jane cried, coming to her brother's defence. 'Catherine was worried. You seemed to have disappeared.'

'Good grief!' Max cried, exasperated. 'May I not go off alone for a few hours without a search party being sent out after me? Am I to have no privacy?'

'We thought...' Jane was trembling inwardly, her face white with shock. It *had* seemed that Max was in control when they arrived, but the assassin had managed to free himself. 'Several attempts have been made on your life, Max. You cannot deny that. What were we to think? I could not sleep for worrying. It was my idea to come here.' She choked back a sob. He was so very angry! 'I kept thinking you might be hurt...lying here...bleeding to death...'

'Do you really think me such a fool?' Max cried, incensed. 'Do you imagine I have given no thought to my own safety?' He turned towards a pile of broken wood and old sacks. 'Come out if you please, Thompson.'

A man emerged reluctantly. It was immediately obvious from his neat dress and clean appearance that he was a professional person of some kind. John slapped his thigh and gave a shout of mirth as he suddenly realized who he must be.

'Well, I'll be damned! You've hired an agent—one of those fly fellows, up to all kinds of larks. What do they call themselves—a nark or a nose, some such thing?'

'Now, young sir,' Mr Thompson said in a dignified manner. 'There ain't no call for you to use such cant terms in the presence of a lady. I ain't quite any of them things, for them terms mean an informer what lives on the wrong side of the law and rats on his friends. What I am is a professional man his lordship has hired to investigate this unpleasant business. And, I might add, we was doing very nicely until you turned up.' He turned to Max with rather more respect than he had shown John. 'My men have their orders, my lord. I take it they remain the same?'

'Yes, of course—though this will have set the cat among the pigeons, no doubt. However, that may be all to the good. I had hoped we might finish this business tonight, Thompson—but that will unfortunately not now be the case. Carry on as usual and report anything necessary to me immediately.'

'As your lordship wishes.' He tipped his tall hat to Jane. 'I am sorry if you were upset, ma'am. The young gentleman had no business bringing you here. His lordship was in no danger. It ain't often I've met with a gentleman more up to snuff and able to fend for himself and...' He was quelled by a look from Massingham. 'Well, I'll be on my way, sir. You may rest assured that your orders will be carried out to the letter.'

After he had gone there was a strained silence, then Jane looked at Max. 'It really was my fault,' she said in a low voice. She was close to tears and wished she had never started this mad venture. 'I wish you will not blame John.'

'I blame the pair of you,' Max replied wrathfully. 'I almost had the name. It was on the tip of that rogue's tongue…'

'But surely…' Jane trembled inwardly as she met his angry stare. 'You must know who it is? You must be aware that he—that he is not what he appears? Those sudden rages—then so calm afterwards. It is unnatural, Max.'

'Are we speaking of the same man?' Max asked with a lift of his brows. 'You do not mean my cousin, I take it?'

'No,' she said. 'I am speaking of your…'

'Do not say it,' Max ordered, his brow furrowed. 'I forbid you to speak one word of this to anyone. Do you understand me, Jane? You have caused enough trouble as it is. Remember my words and take heed. I shall not hear one more word of this!'

He was so angry with her. Jane nodded, dropping her gaze and feeling miserable. It was just as she had always feared. He was not prepared to listen to a word against his friend.

Chapter Fifteen

Alone in her own room half an hour or so later, Jane gave way to tears. It really was most unkind of Max to blame her and John for what had happened; by going in search of him they had intended only his good, and could not have known they were about to ruin his own plans. Max ought to have known that—but he had shown himself to have a temper beyond what was bearable and his manner had hurt her.

It was clear that he cared more for his long-standing friendship with Sir Andrew than for her, thought Jane, now thoroughly miserable. In her heart, she believed he had considered making her an offer when he'd first invited her to Massingham, but Amanda's elopement and her own behaviour—which was really very improper!—had made him think twice, and now he was angry with her.

He had thought her a suitable wife, but was not particularly in love with her; it was the only explanation she could think of in her distressed state. Recalling the look in his eyes when she had gone down to the library at Massingham did not help. *That* was desire and men might feel that for any number of women, or so she imagined.

She spent a restless night, turning from side to side as she tried in vain to sleep, unable to put a certain look on Max's face from her mind. There had been such horror in his eyes when she had tried to tell him it was Sir Andrew who was behind the attempts on his life, and of course she had no proof.

She must have been mistaken. Max knew his friend so much better than she, and if he had seen nothing untoward she was wrong. She ought not to have spoken—and Max had every right to be angry with her. But it had hurt her.

Worn out with an excess of emotion, Jane finally fell into an uneasy slumber, though she moaned and cried out several times, her cheeks stained with tears. She woke to find the sun streaming in at the window and Bessie bringing in her breakfast tray.

She yawned and sat up, feeling heavy-eyed. 'Have I slept late?' she asked. 'What time is it, Bessie?'

'Half past twelve,' Bessie said. 'Lady Farringdon said you were to sleep for the rest of the day, but when I looked in a few minutes back I thought you looked as if you were stirring—so I took the liberty of bringing up your tray. I thought that was what you would want?'

'Thank you,' Jane said as the maid placed the tray across her lap. 'If you will bring me some hot water I shall get up very soon.'

'Yes, miss…' Bessie looked at her, seemed about to say something, then held her silence. The house was all at sixes and sevens this morning, but it wasn't for her to pass comment. 'I brought your riding things in case you wanted them—and there's your green muslin should you need it.'

'Thank you.'

Jane was reflective as she sipped her chocolate and ate a small, lightly buttered muffin. She rather thought that she might like to ride this morning. A good, hard gallop over the moors was just what was needed to blow away the cobwebs—and it might help to ease the ache inside her. Oh, why had she made such an unfortunate remark last evening? Why had she dragged her poor brother on such a stupid venture, bringing Max's wrath down on both their heads?

Half an hour or so later she was dressed and ready. Bessie had thoughtfully arranged for a groom to lead Jane's mare over for her first thing that morning, and he had Dainty Miss waiting for her when she went down to the courtyard. He also had his own horse saddled and ready.

The air had a clean bright sparkle that morning, the sun warmer than it had been for several days. Jane breathed deeply, suddenly eager for a good hard ride. Her headache was clearing. She would feel much better in a little while, and then perhaps she could think clearly.

'Would you like me to accompany you, miss?' her groom asked hopefully.

'No, thank you, Jed,' she said, giving him a smile that was a shadow of its former self. 'Just help me up, if you please. I am in the mood for a gallop across the moors and I fear your horse will not keep up with me.'

The groom watched her ride off at a brisk trot. Now what was he to do? Lord Massingham had given strict orders earlier that day that Miss Osbourne was to be accompanied whenever she went out, but the gentleman was not his master—and *he* did not know that Miss Osbourne had a way with her. She was always polite to her servants, but made it very clear she wanted her orders obeyed. And he wasn't the man to go against her—no, not him.

Jed scratched his head. Maybe he ought to speak to the head groom of the Farringdons' stables. Jed would not feel it right to enter the house himself—he knew his place—but someone ought to tell Lord Massingham that Miss Osbourne had gone off alone.

'There is no sign of him.' Farringdon looked at his brother-in-law anxiously as they met in his study at about the same moment as Jane rode out of the stable yard. 'You may depend upon it he took fright and made a bolt for it.

Damn it, Max! I wish you had confided in me earlier. It gives one the shivers to know that a madman has been sharing one's house. He might have murdered us all in our beds.'

'Andrew does not hate you,' Max said, 'but you do have the right to be angry, Harry. I apologize. I should have finished this long ago but I could not be sure.'

'Or did not want to be,' Farringdon suggested, knowing the nature of his brother-in-law. 'I do understand what it must have meant to you to suspect that he... And after you have been so decent to the fellow. Why, you were almost as brothers.'

'Yes...' Max nodded, looked thoughtful. 'I am going to tell you something in confidence. Something I wish you will not disclose to another person. I must have your word on it, Harry.'

'Of course.' Farringdon stared at him. 'You know I would not breathe a word—besides, I think I may have an idea of what you're going to say, Max—and I must tell you I do not believe the story.'

'How could you? No one knew...' Max stared in disbelief. He had thought no one else could possibly have heard the tale.

'My father mentioned something years ago,' Farringdon said apologetically. 'But he swore he gave the rumour no credence.'

Max was about to question him further when there was a commotion at the door and a groom entered, looking awkward, the butler following behind, apologizing, indignant at this unworthy person thrusting his way into his lordship's private study.

'This man demanded to see you, Lord Massingham. I tried to keep him out but he would have it that you must be told at once.'

'Begging your pardon, my lord,' said the unfortunate groom. 'I've come to tell you Miss Osbourne has gone riding alone. Her groom was ready to go with her but she wouldn't have him—said she was going for a good gallop on the moors and he wouldn't be able to keep up with her.'

'Damn!' Max jumped to his feet in alarm. 'This is something I have feared for a long time. I should have warned her to stay close myself—but Catherine thought she was sleeping and…' He looked at the groom. 'Have my horse saddled immediately—and your own. In fact I shall want as many of you as possible. We have to find her. We have to find her before he does!'

Jane was beginning to feel better already. Her headache was clearing and she was enjoying her ride in the Farringdons' beautiful grounds. She was thinking with her head now, not her heart. Max had been angry with her, but perhaps if she apologized? Asked him to forgive her? No, no, she would not beg. Her head went up. If Max cared for her so little he was not ready to listen to her opinions…well, perhaps it was for the best that she had discovered it now instead of later.

She realized that she was riding in the direction of the ruins. She had decided not to go out onto the moors, because that might not be wise—if she was right in her suspicions. And despite Max's angry denials she still thought she might be. Which meant she must not tempt fate and cause more trouble for Max. No, she would remain on the Farringdons' estate and then she would be quite safe.

Approaching the ruins, she slowed her horse to a trot, then reined in. It was such a lovely morning. Perhaps she would just sit for a while in the sunshine and think. She was almost certain Max did love her. Surely he could not be so blind to Sir Andrew's strange moods that he saw nothing? So had there been another reason for his anger? Perhaps that he had been worried for her sake?

The thought eased the ache inside her a little, bringing a smile to her face. She had always known Max had a temper, but it had not stopped her falling in love with him. Indeed, she could not have loved him so well if he had been a man she could too easily dominate. If they married—her heart skipped a beat—if they married there would no doubt be many a battle royal between them.

Dismounting, she secured her horse's reins to a bush and wandered into the ruins, where it was a little cooler. They had had such a happy time that day they had brought a picnic here—and she had already begun to fall in love with Max, though she hadn't realized it. She loved him so much! She did not know how she would endure her life if anything happened to him.

'Why so pensive, Jane?' The familiar voice sent a chill through her. She whirled round, her heart racing wildly. Sir Andrew! And looking so strange…almost wild. He did not appear to have shaved that morning and his cravat was anyhow, his coat creased, his shirt stained. But it was his eyes that frightened her. Such a terrible staring look! 'Are you dreaming of me? Or was it of someone else?' He laughed, a shrill, spiteful, unnerving sound. 'Of Max, I dare say? Oh, I know you love him. I've seen it in your eyes. You are so transparent, Jane. Did you know that?'

'Am I?' She stood quite still, feeling the sickness swirl inside her. There was something different about him to-day. She had seen him in a passion before, but this was not the same; it was as if something inside him had finally snapped…as if the evil creature that had lived inside his head for a long time had at last gained the upper hand. 'I'm sorry if it offends you, sir. I did not mean…'

He moved towards her, his eyes glittering with the madness that now had him securely in its grip. She tried not to flinch as he caught her wrist, knowing instinctively that she must be calm. She must give no sign of fear, nor must she resist him too forcefully. If she defied him he might kill her.

'You are always so correct,' he said, sneering at her. 'At least, that is the way you like to appear—but you were not so correct when you spent the night in Massingham's arms at that inn…' A trickle of saliva came from the corner of his mouth. 'Oh, yes, I knew about that. Who do you imagine supplied Helena Langdon with her information? Who told her to come down to Massingham when he first brought you there?'

'Why did you do that, sir?'

'To turn you against him, of course. But you would not listen to me. No one does what I tell them.' He frowned, seeming angry. 'The wretch I had paid to kill Max failed again. I should have shot him when he came crawling back to me, found a better marksman…or done the deed myself. But a brother cannot kill his brother, can he, Miss Osbourne?'

He looked at her, triumph in his eyes.

'A brother…' She felt faint. Her head was whirling. She was so frightened. 'I do not understand you, sir.'

'Did Max not tell you I was his half-brother?' He nodded as she gasped. 'Yes, it is perfectly true. My mother told me when I was a child. She had a brief affair with Max's father. It was not her first or her last. No wonder then that her husband eventually drank himself to death. She was a slut. And he could never resist a pretty woman—my father and Max's, I mean.' Sir Andrew laughed. 'It is not so very shocking after all…' His smile faded suddenly as he remembered something. 'What is shocking is his refusal to admit I was his son. I begged him to, you know. Begged him to tell me that he had cared for her—that he cared for me. But he refused. Do you not think that shocking, Jane?'

'Perhaps he was ashamed of what he had done?' Jane watched the changing expressions on Sir Andrew's face. There were tears in his eyes, tears of self-pity.

'He was so rich. He could have afforded to settle a small estate on me,' he went on, his mind caught up in the past as he dwelt on some slight, real or imagined. 'He could have shown me some affection—a father should love his son, shouldn't he, Jane?'

'Perhaps he did not know how to show affection—to anyone.'

'Yes, perhaps that was so…' Andrew nodded, his eyes narrowing in thought. 'Max loved his father—but they quarrelled. I believe he knows that I am his brother. If he died I would inherit Massingham.'

'No, of course you wouldn't,' Jane blurted out without thinking. 'Even if Max's father had acknowledged you you could not inherit. You were not his son by marriage. Bastards do not inherit. Richard is Max's heir.'

'How clever you are,' he said, a crafty, sly expression coming to his eyes. 'Richard is the heir—but just think what might happen if he were to hang for murder. I have proof, you see—a letter written to my mother from my father. He promised to put things right for her one day…said that his wife was a cold woman and that he should never have married her.'

Jane could hardly believe her ears. Did he really imagine that he could destroy everyone who stood between him and the Massingham fortune without detection? If Catherine had a son her child would be the next male in line after Richard. A shiver went down Jane's spine as she realized that this man would not have stopped in his quest to right a wrong he believed had been done him. Neither Catherine nor her child would have been safe— just as Max's bride-to-be was not safe. If Andrew believed that Max meant to marry her he would kill her.

He was quite, quite mad!

His mind must have been cracking under the strain for a long time. Just as Maggie had suggested—imagined slights, small injuries, building up until finally he had plotted against his friend's life. A man he believed his own brother. And yet he had not been able to bring himself to do the deed personally. Why? Because he feared he was not strong enough—or because he had once loved

Max? Perhaps still did with the part of him that had remained sane for so long, defying the gradual encroachment of his illness.

'I know you are not feeling quite yourself,' Jane said. 'Your sister's death and...'

'Max killed her, you know,' he said, his eyes narrowing to slits of cold, unfeeling menace. 'She loved him, believed he would make her an offer...and he told her she was just a silly child, that he had merely been kind to her. It sent her into a decline from which she never recovered. He encouraged her to believe he meant to marry her, then jilted her.'

'I do not believe Max would have been so cruel,' Jane said. 'He might have told her he was sorry he did not want...'

'He killed her!' Andrew's grip tightened on Jane's wrist, twisting her flesh so painfully that she could hardly restrain her cry of pain. 'He betrayed her—just as my father betrayed my mother. Marion was the only person who ever really loved me. I've been planning Max's death ever since.' He smiled strangely. 'At first I wanted to just go out and kill him with my bare hands. But then, when that urn almost fell on him—that was an accident, you know—I pushed him out of the way. I saved his life— and so his life is mine, to take as I please: that's an unwritten law, you know.'

He sounded like a judge pronouncing sentence, convinced of his divine right to take or grant life.

'Perhaps you saved him because you don't really want to kill him,' Jane said persuasively. 'You are angry because your father would not acknowledge you—and hurt because your sister died—but you don't hate Max. He is your brother. You can't kill your own brother. Surely you must see that?'

'I see you know me, Jane. You know my love of order and right. I too thought that way at first,' Andrew replied, nodding his head. 'But then the voices told me. Max has to die, because that is the only way I can take my proper place in the world. If my father had not married that cold woman who gave birth to Max he would have married my mother—I should have been his only son. I should be Lord Massingham. It is my right, don't you see that?'

She could see he had come to believe in his right to take Max's place, that, in his madness, he felt it was his due. It was useless to argue with him, for it would only make him angry.

Jane swallowed. Her mouth was dry. She was so very frightened, but she must try to keep calm.

'Perhaps Max will share his fortune with you,' she suggested cautiously. 'If you explained it to him—made him see the right of your cause.'

'You are trying to fool me.' Andrew's eyes were suddenly very bright, suspicious. 'You want me to let you go—but I have a better plan. I'm going to keep you safe. I shan't hurt you, Jane, though I shall have to tie you up. I know Max. He will come looking for you and when he does...' A sly smile played about his mouth. He reached out to touch her face. 'Pretty Jane. You want to be Lady Massingham, don't you? When I am Lord Massingham I may marry you...if you are good to me. You will be good to me, won't you, Jane?' He grabbed her by the back of the neck and held her face close to his. His breath had a sourness that made her want to gag. 'You will be good to me, won't you? You'll let me do all the things you did with Max that night, won't you?'

She could not bear this another moment!

'I would rather die!' Jane gathered what moisture she had left in her mouth and spat in his face.

'You little slut!' His hand tightened at the back of her head as he forced his mouth over hers. 'I've wanted you for a long time and now I am going to have you...'

Jane moaned. She tried to push him away but she was feeling very odd. Her head was going round and round as the dizziness washed over her—and then, for the first time in her life, she fainted.

Jane came to herself to discover she was alone, her wrists bound behind her back and her ankles fastened with a thick rope. The rope was cutting into her flesh and felt uncomfortable.

It was gloomy but not quite dark; she was able to make out her surroundings, which told her she was in the cellar beneath Ormond House. She twisted her head around but could see no sign of her kidnapper. A wave of revulsion and fear went through her as she remembered. Had he carried out his threat to ravish her body? She could feel no pain or soreness apart from that caused by the rope and she thought—prayed!—that her faint had saved her. Sir Andrew had wanted to humiliate her. He needed her to be aware of what was happening to her. Faced with her unconscious body, he had probably seized his chance to bind her and bring her here.

Why here? she wondered. Why not take her somewhere Max would not be able to find her?

She pondered the thought for a while and then realized that he wanted Max to find her. He had seized her for that very purpose. He knew about this place, knew that Max had captured the assassin he had hired, and he wanted to draw Max here…to kill him.

He might even kill Jane, too. Who knew what was going on in that tortured mind of his? A man who believed that an unacknowledged bastard could hope to inherit his father's title when there were at least three legitimate heirs before him—even if he could prove the connection!—could convince himself of anything.

Andrew was lost to all reason. No sane man would ever have come up with such a plan. Revenge? Yes, she could understand his desire for revenge if he believed Massingham had destroyed his sister…but all the rest was nonsense. Andrew could not really believe it, not in the part of him that remained sane…if there was any sanity left in him?

No, of course there was not. For a long time he had retained some kind of control, his lapses brief and soon hidden beneath a studied calm, but now he had toppled over the edge into madness, perhaps when he'd discovered that his plans to kill Max had failed yet again. After Max returned to the house, having shown his hand by outwitting the rogue Andrew had hired to kill him, he must have believed that he could no longer hide behind Richard—or perhaps he had gone too far to think at all, was acting with a kind of animal cunning?

Oh, Max, Jane cried inwardly. Don't let him trap you. Don't let me be the cause of your death… But in her heart she knew he would come once he realized she was missing. How long would that be? How long before Max fell into the trap that had been set for him?

She heard a scuffling sound and froze. What was that? Was it Sir Andrew returning? She closed her eyes. Let him believe she had not recovered from her faint. Oh, don't let him touch her…don't let him do the things he had threatened!

She heard the noise again, much closer, and opened her eyes despite her determination to keep them shut—then she saw the creature staring at her, sitting up on its hind quarters, rubbing its whiskers with tiny paws. A rat! Jane had seen them before, dead in a trap, but not alive and free. A shiver of horror went through her. She was afraid of the rat, especially as she could do nothing to scare it away, but she held onto her nerves, stifling the scream that was there waiting to come out if she let it.

'Oh, please come soon, someone!' she whispered. 'But don't come alone, Max. Please don't be so foolish as to come alone…'

'I must go alone,' Max said as he stared at the note, which had been delivered at the kitchen door some ten minutes before, by a labourer from one of Farringdon's own farms. The letters were ill formed and almost childish, a fact which sent a chill down Max's spine. If Andrew had written this scrawl he must have lost all reason—all balance. He read it to his sister's husband, his face white and strained.

'If you want to see her again come alone and unarmed. Come tonight. If you delay she will die by dawn. If you love her do not let her suffer. You know where she will be.'

'He means the cellar. I am sure of it. He was probably watching the day I explored it with John.' Max groaned aloud. 'You see what he says, Harry. He will kill Jane if I do not go alone. God knows what he has done to her already…'

'And he will kill the pair of you if you are fool enough to do as he demands,' Farringdon said. 'It's madness, Max. You can't go alone. It's exactly what he wants.'

'Yes, of course—but if there is a chance of saving her I must take it,' Max said. 'It is what I have feared all along—that's why I did not speak, why I did not ask her to do me the honour of becoming my wife.' He took a turn about the room, his manner so agitated that Farringdon feared for him. 'I was afraid it might push him over the edge if he believed I was about to marry.'

'What I fail to see is why it should affect him,' Farringdon said. 'Surely Richard is the only one who would gain by your death?'

'Unless…' Max frowned. 'I think…I'm not sure, but I think Andrew believes he is my half-brother.'

Farringdon nodded. 'I heard something once. I believe your father did have a brief affair with his mother.'

'Yes, that much is true—though Father denied absolutely that Andrew was his son. Mother believed it at

once—or said she did. She told me on the day of the
costume ball. I asked him about it a few days later. We
quarrelled. I told him I did not believe him when he swore
it was not true…called him a liar…' Max's face was white
with remembered grief. 'It was the morning he was
thrown from his horse…'

'Oh, Max!' Lady Farringdon had appeared on the
threshold. 'No wonder you were so strange when Father
died. You blamed yourself for his fall—didn't you?'

Max was silent for a moment, then inclined his head in
assent, his expression one of sadness and regret. 'Yes. He
was upset when he left, swearing to disown me, calling
me an ungrateful pup. He had taken that fence a thousand
times…would have done so again if I had not so distressed him.' Max clenched his fists at his sides. 'And all
for nothing. Just before she died Mama told me she knew
it wasn't true. She had said it only to hurt him through
me. She had known of the affair and waited for her chance
to strike back.'

'Oh, Max, dearest,' his sister said. 'And you have carried the pain with you all this time. My poor brother.'

'It hurt me to believe that I had caused my father's
death,' Max said. 'I was a fool to believe her. I knew that
she hated him.'

'She was a cold woman,' Catherine said. 'She was to
blame, not you. You could not have known what would
happen.'

'No, but…I have always wished that we had been given
a chance to make up our quarrel.' Max shrugged it off.
'It is not important. Not now. I did not think anyone else
knew of it. But if Andrew believes we are brothers—and
I am sure he holds me responsible for Marion's death…'

'He cannot!' Catherine cried. 'You were never more
than kind to her—and she was such a silly girl.
Although—' She broke off and looked thoughtful for a
moment. 'I have often wondered…but perhaps I should
not say it.' She nodded to herself, deciding to speak out,

though what she had to say was shocking. 'Marion once told me she was afraid of Andrew—she said his love for her was too intense—more like a lover than a brother.'

Farringdon frowned. 'My God, what a family!' he said. 'I heard there was an uncle of Forbes' mother's locked away in Bedlam but I do not know how true it may be.'

'I have never heard it, but it may well be true,' Max said. 'Both Mrs Forbes and Marion were nervous, timid women. I have wondered if there was some instability in the family.'

'Oh, dear, this is all so horrible.' Catherine gave a little shudder, asking innocently, 'Where is Jane? I came to enquire if anyone had seen her. She is not in her room. I was told she went riding—but that was some time ago.'

'Oh, did I not mention it?' Farringdon gave her brother a speaking look. His own heir might be at risk here. 'She begged me to tell you she was going home,' he said. 'Forgive me, dearest, I had forgot in all the excitement.'

'Without saying goodbye to me?' Catherine looked hurt. 'Well, that is unlike her—but it's your fault, Max. She was so upset when you disappeared like that last night. No wonder she has gone off without a word.'

'Yes,' Max said, turning to look out of the window, his back towards her. 'I am afraid it is very much my fault.' He stopped speaking and glanced towards the door as a newcomer entered the room. 'Richard…what are you doing here? I thought you had gone back to Massingham?'

'I decided to stay. If that's all right with you, Catherine?' He glared at no one in particular, obviously in a huff. 'If I'm not welcome I can leave…'

'For God's sake don't talk rubbish,' Max snapped. 'Stay or go as you please. It is all the same to me.'

He walked from the room, scowling.

'What the devil is the matter with him?' Richard kicked at the fender moodily. 'I wish someone would tell me what I'm supposed to have done,' he said. 'All of you

have been treating me as if I were some kind of a murderer for months...'

'Oh, Richard,' Catherine said apologetically. 'I'm
afraid that's just what we have done. I'm so sorry, my
dear. So very sorry.'

'And so I should think,' said Richard, in high dudgeon.
'Did none of you think to ask? As it happens I am rather
fond of him.' He scowled at no one in particular. 'And
I'm damned well going to have it out with him!'

With that he strode from the room in Max's wake before Lord Farringdon could stop him.

Max left the house immediately. His nerves felt as if
they were on fire. He knew he should not have lost his
temper with Richard like that—it was very wrong of him.
Poor Richard had done nothing to deserve such treatment
from him. He knew now that his suspicions of his cousin
had been completely unfounded. Suspicions that had been
planted in the first place by Andrew.

Max cursed himself. He was a damned fool! He should
have seen what was happening to his friend; if the truth
were told he had—but although he did not believe there
was a blood tie between them he had loved Andrew like
a brother. It still hurt to believe that his friend could have
plotted against him for so long. And now he had
Jane...was holding her a prisoner in the cellar.

What was he going to do? The note had said he must
wait until dark but he could not bear to think of her in
danger, at the mercy of that mad brute. There was no
telling what he might do to her—might have already done
to her.

Max groaned aloud as the terrible thoughts tortured
him. His sweet, lovely Jane in danger. It was his fault,
his alone. He should have had someone watching her, but
he had believed her safe in her own bedchamber.

He had left instructions that she should be accompanied

always…and yet in spite of all his precautions Andrew had managed to snatch her from under their noses.

He should have warned her to stay close to the house, made sure she understood him the previous night, when he had forbidden her to speak of her suspicions. He had meant only that it might be dangerous for her if Andrew guessed she suspected him—but her unexpected arrival in the cellar had thrown him. He had been angry—with her. He had said such things to her! Curse his wicked temper! The look in her eyes had told him he had hurt her. And now—if anything should harm her—he would never be able to forgive himself.

Chapter Sixteen

Jane watched the rat. It was sniffing at her feet; she wondered if it was considering her as its next meal. Somehow she was no longer afraid of the creature; indeed it had helped her through her lonely ordeal—and it seemed to mean her no harm, was merely curious.

Her legs were beginning to feel numb and she thought she must have been here for some time, but there was no way of telling because the light in here was not like daylight, but a kind of murky gloom that came through a crack in the roof above her head. Andrew had not left her a lighted candle and she dreaded to think what it would be like when even that faint light began to fade.

Supposing he simply left her here to die? He was mad; he might forget all about her. She might lie here for days or weeks…if she didn't die of starvation she would go mad herself. She was not sure how much longer she could bear this, but knew that if she once gave way to her feelings she would be lost.

The rat stiffened suddenly, lifting its head, sniffing the air…listening. It had heard something and suddenly ran off into a dark corner to hide. Jane wished that she could hide too. Someone was coming down the passage…that someone was not carrying a lanthorn and he was being careful not to make a noise. If the rat had not heard him she would not have known he was coming. She tensed, her heart beginning to beat madly. Was it Sir Andrew— and what would he do to her if he found her awake?

She felt the scream building inside her. Oh, please God, don't let him hurt her! Don't let him try to kiss her again!

'Jane…' The soft whisper stopped her heart for one moment. 'Are you there, my dearest? Are you hurt? Can you hear me?'

'Oh, Max!' Tears rushed to her eyes. 'You shouldn't have come. He wants to kill you. He is mad; insane…' Her tears spilled out as she saw the bulk of Max's body come out of the narrow passage and into the cellar, and then in a moment he was beside her, lighting a candle, looking down at her. And there was such a look in his eyes, a look she would never forget if she lived to be a hundred. 'He will kill you—both of us. He blames you for his sister's death—and says he is your half-brother. He thinks if he murders you everyone will blame Richard and he will inherit everything.' Her words came tumbling out on a strangled sob.

'Hush now, my darling,' Max said as he knelt beside her, taking a knife from his pocket to sever the rope binding her ankles. He rubbed gently at the red marks to restore the circulation, then cut the thinner rope from her wrists. She gave a sob of relief and he caught her up in his arms, holding her tenderly, kissing her hair. 'I know, my love. I know about Andrew. I've suspected it for a long time, but I kept hoping it wasn't true. I should have told you last night, warned you not to ride out alone— but I didn't want Catherine to be upset or frightened because of her condition. And I thought you would be quite safe.'

'You had given orders for me to be accompanied, hadn't you? And he wouldn't have come after me if I had not been alone—because he wants everyone to think it was Richard who made those attacks on you.' She looked up at him as he stroked the hair from her face. 'Oh, Max,

I didn't think. I was so upset because you didn't seem to believe me about Andrew and I thought you cared for his friendship more than—'

'Foolish, foolish woman,' Max said, and silenced her with a kiss that drove all the doubts from her mind for ever. 'I have loved you almost from the first moment I saw you.'

'Oh, Max, have you really?' Jane was struck by his confession. 'I believe it was a little longer before I realized what my own feelings were for you.'

'I know,' he said with a rueful smile. 'You imagined I was in love with that child—and you would not allow yourself to love me. Was that not the whole of it?'

'Yes,' she agreed, and leaned her head against his shoulder. It was so very comforting to be held in those strong arms. 'I was so foolish, Max. Will you forgive me?'

'Of course,' he said, and kissed her again. 'I shall always love you, Jane. You are the woman I have looked for all my life…'

'How touching!' a drawling voice said behind them. 'Such a pity that neither of you will live long enough to enjoy your happiness. I had thought I might let you live, Jane—but now I see it will not be possible.'

'Andrew…' Max rose, helping Jane to her feet and holding her as she swayed unsteadily for a moment. 'You are angry with me. I understand your anger. My father should have left some provision for you—if only in memory of his relationship with Mrs Forbes. This is all a mistake. I am sure we can sort something out.'

'You knew I was your brother,' Andrew said, not listening, 'and yet you did nothing. If you had told me, Max—acknowledged it openly—I might have spared you, forgiven you. I loved you once.'

'Who told you?' Max asked, one hand keeping Jane behind him, shielding her with his body. 'Was it Mrs Forbes?'

'She showed me his letters,' Andrew said, eyes glittering in the light of the candle Max had lit. 'He broke his promises to her and then he lied to me…denied it when I asked him…when I begged him to care for me…'

'You spoke to my father about this?' Max's eyes narrowed sharply. 'When?'

'Our father!' Andrew cried. 'He was there on his horse, looking down at me—that proud, impatient look in his eyes—the look you have sometimes, Max. He told me to let go of his reins but I wouldn't…so he struck me with his whip. He told me my mother was mad and that he had finished his affair with her long before I was conceived. But he lied. You know he did, Max.'

'Yes…' Max's voice was deceptively soft and soothing. 'Yes, he lied, Andrew. I know you are my brother and I'm going to share my inheritance with you. But tell me—when did you have this conversation with our father? Was it on the morning he died?'

A high-pitched giggle left Andrew's lips, his eyes bright with madness. 'When he hit me I stuck a pin in the horse's rump…it was one of Mother's hat pins.' He laughed again, sending a shiver down Jane's spine. 'A fitting weapon for justice, don't you think?'

'Did you plan to kill him, Andrew? Was it always your intention?' Max asked in a casual tone, almost as if he were discussing the weather. 'Did you go there with it in your mind to kill him that morning?'

'Oh, no,' Andrew replied carelessly. 'I thought he would be pleased I knew the truth. I had picked the pin up without thinking from her dressing table. I'm not sure why.' He frowned as if trying to remember, as if it might be important for some reason. 'It must have been meant, I suppose. I never expected he would die, Max. I just wanted to punish him a little—to make him sorry he had lied to me. '

'You devil!' Max forgot caution in his anger. 'You murdered my father. My father, Andrew, never yours. Do you hear me? He told me the truth. He was not your father.'

Andrew gave a cry of rage and sprang at him, his hands going to Max's throat. Max threw them off and they wrestled once more, falling to the floor of the cellar as they fought, rolling over and over on the ground in a fierce struggle.

Jane watched fearfully, afraid to move. She ought to run and find someone to help them, but her feet were glued to the floor and she could not move. A scream escaped her as Andrew seemed to gain the advantage, sitting astride Max, his hands around his throat. She came to life then and looked around for a weapon, but before she could find anything Max had thrown him off and the two men were on their feet again. Then she saw that Andrew had a pistol in his hand and froze.

'Put that down,' Max commanded. 'You're sick, Andrew. I'll help you. I'll put things right…'

'I don't want you to,' Andrew said; then, as he heard a sound behind him, he swung round. 'What the devil are you doing here?' he asked, clearly surprised.

'I came to find Max and sort it out with him,' Richard said, a sulky look on his face. 'I'm damned if I can put up with this a moment…' His words died away as he suddenly saw the pistol Andrew was pointing at Max and immediately realized what was going on. 'You devil! It was you all the time. All those damned insinuations of yours! Suggesting that I had tried to kill Max by pushing an urn off that ledge—and you were behind it all. Well, if that isn't the outside of enough!' He sounded so indignant that Jane would have laughed if it had not been so terrifying.

'And now you have conveniently turned up just where I want you,' Andrew said, a look of triumph in his mad eyes. 'I couldn't have arranged it better. When they find you both dead they will imagine you fought and the gun went off, killing Max—and then of course you were frightened and killed yourself. Perfect. A perfect solution…'

'You damned scoundrel!' Richard cried, incensed that he was to take the blame for his cousin's death. 'I've had enough of this.'

Perhaps it was his fury that made him act as he did, springing at Andrew with a great roar of rage and taking him down to the ground. They struggled for a few seconds and then the gun went off…and both men lay still.

'Richard!' Jane cried as she saw he was spattered in blood. 'Is he dead? What has happened? Oh, Max…'

Max was kneeling on the ground beside them. As he turned Andrew over onto his back they saw the bloody wound where the ball had entered his chest. He was not yet dead, though it could not be long—no one could survive such a terrible injury for more than a few minutes.

'He has done for me,' Andrew whispered as Max bent over him. 'Never thought he had it in him… Sorry, Max. Forgive me.'

For a moment before they closed for the last time his eyes were clear and calm, free of the madness that had finally claimed him.

'Max,' Richard moaned, and stared up at Jane as she touched his forehead. 'I think—tell Max I think I've broken my shoulder…' And then he fainted from the pain.

'Oh, poor Richard,' Catherine said when they all sat together in her parlour the following morning, Jane having been placed in the care of her faithful maid and sent straight to bed when Massingham had brought her home the previous afternoon. 'To think that we have been imagining him the villain all this time and he has turned out to be a hero. For I think he saved your life, Max. If he had not followed you—who knows what might have happened?'

'I dare say Thompson would have arrived in the nick of time,' Max said. 'I told him to wait for five minutes after he saw Andrew come in, but once he saw Richard he held back. You see, he knew that I had at first suspected my cousin and wanted to be sure we got the right man.'

'You must not let Richard hear you say that again,' Catherine said, a smile hovering about her mouth. 'He was so indignant because we had all been treating him as if he were a murderer. And it really was too bad of us, Max. But I confess I did think it might be him, because he was so resentful of you.'

'He is just a sulky boy,' Max said. 'I ought to have known it at the beginning—but I did not want to believe the alternative.' He turned and smiled at Jane. 'Of course Jane knew at once, as soon as they met, that he was not the culprit. It was something she said, together with the poor aim of that wretch Andrew hired to shoot me. By the way, Thompson tells me the man has John's ball in his nether regions, and is at the moment on a ship for France.'

'You mean you have not had him arrested? After he tried to kill you at least twice?'

'I think his heart was not in it,' Max said, and shrugged carelessly. 'And his other crimes are not of my concern. I thought we should all sleep better for knowing he wasn't lurking about the place.'

'He should hang,' Catherine said, 'but I suppose it does not matter now. It is all over, isn't it?'

'Yes—apart from Richard's broken shoulder, which I think is causing him a deal of pain. Poor fellow, I must go up and thank him later.'

'He will recover,' Catherine said, a look of relief in her eyes. It was so good to have her brother back to his normal self. She did not know what had been said between him and Jane, but whatever it was the shadows had lifted. 'By the time everyone has finished spoiling him he will be beyond bearing.'

'I think I shall settle the estate in Hampshire on him

immediately,' Max said. 'He did act very bravely, though unwisely as usual—and I believe the cares of an estate will steady him down a little.'

Catherine nodded her approval. 'Then we can all be easy again,' she said, and looked at her brother. 'So, Max—when do you intend to ask Jane to marry you? You have kept us all waiting quite long enough.'

'Indeed?' Max gave her a hard stare. 'I think that is my business—and you need not think I mean to do it with you watching, my dear sister. I have been waiting for this moment for a long time—and I intend to be quite alone with Jane.'

Max turned his mocking gaze on Jane, bringing a flush to her face. She was in no doubt of what was in his mind and her heart took a dizzying leap as she rose to her feet.

'And it must keep for another day,' she said. 'I must go home. John will be anxious until he knows all this is settled—and Amanda will be wondering where I am. I promised her I would take her to Maggie's for tea this afternoon.'

'Damn Amanda,' Max said, taking her arm. 'For once that minx can wait her turn. I have something particular to say to you, Miss Osbourne. And if you will not stay to hear it I shall ride back with you to your home...'

Chapter Seventeen

They had tethered their horses to a scrubby bush and were strolling on the moors, quite alone, away from all those interested persons who might have wished to know the outcome of the very important question Max was about to ask his beloved.

'Max…' Jane sighed as he released her from a very satisfying embrace. 'Oh, my dearest love—I can hardly believe it is all over, that you are no longer in danger.'

'I was never really in danger after those first two attempts,' Max said. 'When I was in London I hired Mr Thompson and his men and from then on there was always someone watching my back. You were my one real worry. I tried to have you watched, but it was not easy. I was afraid of frightening you—and I knew you were safe enough until Andrew came down to Ormond House. I insisted that we travel together, thinking he might take the chance to attack me himself…but he never did.'

'I think he cared for you in his own way,' Jane said. 'I know that sounds foolish after what he did…but that was the madness, the illness that had grown like a canker in his mind. You must try to forgive him, dearest—for your own sake.'

'How wise you are,' Max said, touching her cheek. 'My

brave, beautiful Jane. How much I love you. You will marry me, won't you?'

'Should I?' Jane tipped her head on one side, looking up at him with mischief in her eyes. 'I must tell you I have had more romantic proposals, sir.'

'From the Trio?' Max asked, giving a husky laugh. 'Trying to make me jealous, Jane? Oh, yes, John told me about your devoted admirers before I sent him and Amanda home—which I did as soon as I had you safely back beneath Farringdon's roof. That pair have a habit of intruding at the wrong moment and I wanted to be sure of getting you alone.'

'Poor Max.' Jane pouted at him teasingly. 'What a terrible time we have given you, to be sure. I wonder that you wish to continue the association.'

'Witch!' he said, and reached out for her, drawing her close. As he heard her indrawn breath and saw the look of desire in her lovely eyes, he smiled. 'Shall I tell you why, my darling—or shall I wait and show you on our wedding night?'

'Oh, Max,' Jane breathed. 'I hope you mean to marry me very soon, because I have been having some very improper thoughts...'

He chuckled deep in his throat. 'I confess I should be very disappointed if I thought you had not, Jane. One of the things that instantly attracted me to you was the fact that you are no milk and water miss, but, I believe, a very warm and passionate woman. A woman I cannot wait to claim as my wife. I think we could be married within two weeks by special licence...if that does not seem indecent haste to you?'

Jane gazed up at him, her eyes teasing and full of love. 'As it happens, I did buy myself a rather pretty gown when we were in town—just in case you should ask me.'

'Wicked woman,' he said. 'I dare say it will give the old tabbies something to gossip about. They will count the months to the birth of our first child, Jane—but I doubt

if one of them will turn down an invitation to one of Lady
Massingham's very elegant parties—and you do mean to
give elegant parties, don't you, my love?'

'Oh, yes, when we are in town,' she said, 'but I think
we shall spend most of our time at Massingham, if you
would not find that too dull?'

'With you?' he asked. 'It is what I should like above
all things.'

'Of course I am happy for you, dearest Jane,' Amanda
said when told the news a little later that day. 'Only what
shall I do? It would not be proper for me to stay here,
would it? And if I came to stay with you...I should hardly
ever see John.'

There was a hint of mutiny about her pretty face and
Jane laughed. 'We have thought of that,' she said. 'Lady
Fairley is to stay with Catherine during the months of her
confinement, and we think it would solve the problem if
you were to visit with the Farringdons, too. Catherine will
not be able to go out once her condition becomes...more
visible...but Lady Fairley would be happy to oblige. And
there is always Molly Wainwright; she might stay with
you if you asked her.'

Jane had wondered if her suggestion might meet with
resistance, but in the circumstances it was the very best
she could do—unless she made Max wait until after
Amanda's season. She had suggested it once, but his reaction had been so positive that she dared not do so again.

Amanda was nodding, beginning to see the advantages
of being so close to John.

'He would be able to ride over and see me every day,'
she said, and smiled at Jane. 'Oh, yes, I believe it will do
very well. You are so kind to think of me, dearest Jane.'

'As it happens it was Max who thought of it,' Jane said
wryly. There was no need to tell her ward exactly what
Max had said or threatened. 'So you must thank him when
he calls.'

'Yes, I shall do so,' Amanda promised. 'And I am to be one of your bridesmaids, aren't I? Please say I may.'

'Of course you may. There is no one else I would prefer.' Jane kissed her cheek. 'And of course I shall take you to London in the spring just as I promised. Max and I will be back from our honeymoon trip long before then.'

He was taking her to Italy, but Jane had made him promise that they would not be too long away. She was looking forward to becoming the mistress at Massingham—but first there was all the excitement of the wedding, which Max had declared was to be a grand affair.

'We shall invite everyone who is anyone,' he'd said with a gleam in his eyes when she'd protested. 'I suppose that must include Prinny—which is unfortunate, but must be done if he is not to feel put out...'

'That is hardly the way to speak of the Prince Regent, my love,' Jane chided, then laughed as he pulled a face. 'You do not want to be banished for calling him a fat fool as Brummel did.'

'Fat, perhaps, but no fool,' her husband countered. 'We have been on terms for too long for me to think him that.'

Jane nodded. The fact that her husband-to-be was on intimate terms with the highest in the land might have been daunting, for much would be expected of Massingham's bride—but she did not think it beyond her. Indeed, she was looking forward to the challenge. Her life had often been boring in the past, but that was all at an end. The future would be very different, because Max would always be at her side.

'You look very pretty, Jane,' said Lady Fairley, giving her a naughty look through the quizzing glass. They were in one of the many salons at Massingham, from where she and Max were to be married, since Jane's home would never have held all the guests who had accepted his very flattering invitations to see him marry the lady he had

chosen to share his life. 'My godson ain't one to let the
grass grow under his feet when he makes up his mind,
but the moment I saw you I knew you would do for him.
I'm very fond of the wretch, you know, and I thought he
might never find happiness. His mother was a cold
woman—and a man like Max needs a loving woman in
his bed.'

Jane's cheeks went pink. 'I love him very much,
ma'am, and I shall do my best to make him happy.'

'You don't need my advice,' the elderly lady said and
chuckled. 'I don't know if Max has told you, but I was a
bit of a flirt in my day. I wouldn't have been if my marriage had been a love match, but it wasn't. I was married
for my money and took what pleasure I could from life.
You are luckier, Jane. Massingham is a fine man. None
better.'

'I know.' Jane bent to kiss her. 'I am very lucky.'

'As to that, he is fortunate to have found a gel like
you.' She pushed a small wrapped gift into Jane's hands.
'That's for you, to show my approval. Take it and enjoy
it. It was given to me by my lover—the only one I ever
cared for.'

Jane opened the box and looked at the magnificent ba-
roque pearl hanging from a choker of perfectly matched
pearls.

'It's beautiful, ma'am—but don't you want to keep it?'

'It belongs about the neck of a young woman,' Lady
Fairley said. 'Well, I shall go down now and wait with
the others until we leave for church.'

Captain Carter had begged for the honour of giving
Jane to her husband. For, as he said, she had no father to
do it for her and he was the next best thing, and if John
had no objection it would make him very proud. So it was
on his arm that she walked down the aisle to stand beside
Max in the old church, with the autumn sun shining

through the windows and all her dearest friends gathered to watch her take her vows.

Richard was Max's best man. His arm was still in a sling, but if he was in any pain he bore up bravely and basked in the admiration of his family and friends as be-fitted a hero.

'For you know if I hadn't gone after Max,' he had told his friends—so many times that they were tired of hearing it—'he might have been killed and then there would have been no wedding.'

Richard had shrugged off his sulks, and looked fair to becoming a sensible man. He had declared his fondness for his cousin's bride and vowed to visit them at least twice a year, but was looking forward to taking up resi-dence in his *own* house and meant to set out immediately the wedding breakfast was over.

Max turned to look at his bride as she walked down the aisle to his side, demure in a gown of straw satin and a bonnet that framed her lovely face with silk flowers. She looked so fragile and lovely that his heart stopped, then, as she met his eyes, her mischievous spirit shining through, raced on wildly and he began to think of the moment when at last he would make her his own.

To have and to hold for all time forth...

Jane sat at the dressing table in her silk nightgown, brushing her hair. As the door connecting her husband's room to hers opened, her heart began to beat madly, her pulses racing as Max came towards her. He was wearing a dark blue velvet dressing robe similar to the one she had once seen lying abandoned in his room and looked so handsome that she felt a sharp, searing pang of desire.

'My darling Jane,' he said, and handed her a large vel-vet box. 'This is a little gift for your wedding day...'

'But you have already given me so much,' she said, gasping as she opened the box and saw the necklace of huge diamonds. 'Oh...these are wonderful.'

'The Massingham diamonds,' he said with a smile. 'I had them reset for you. One day I will show you the rest of the collection and you can decide which of the other trinkets you want altered to your own taste.'

'Thank you.' Jane laid the box down on the dressing table and stood up, turning to face him. 'But it is you I want, Max. You I love—so very much, my dearest dear.'

He reached out to touch her face, stroking it tenderly with his fingertips, then took her hand and led her to the bed.

'I want you, Jane,' he said, 'in every way a man can want a woman. I love you, respect you, adore you—but this feeling I have now cannot wait. Will you trust me, my love, even if what I do hurts just a little at first? It will not always do so, I promise. This thing between a man and a woman can be glorious... Let me show you how lovely it can be and do not fear me?'

'Fear you?' Her eyes were bright, her mouth parting a little in anticipation as she went to his arms willingly and without reserve. 'I only fear that you will think me a wanton wretch—for I have been dreaming of this for...much longer than I ought. Indeed, if you had not been a gentleman you might have had your way with me long since.'

'Oh, Jane!' Max threw back his head and laughed with delight. 'What a terrible wanton you are—and how very glad I am I met you!'

And then, without more ado, Lord Massingham swept up his eager wife and laid her on the bed. With lips and tongue he lavished tender caresses on her willing flesh, kissing first her lips, then her fluttering eyelids, her sweet, full breasts, then on down the length of her quivering body, until he sought out the most secret places of her inner self.

Jane moaned with pleasure, her body quivering at his touch. Her arms slipped up around his neck, her mouth soft and warm beneath his; she opened to him as he gathered her closer so that their flesh became one. One being, one heart, one soul. He took her so gently, so sweetly, initiating her into the joy of physical love with such tenderness that she followed him joyfully, allowing him to lead her on and on, to an enchanted place that only true lovers ever find...

* * * * *

MILLS & BOON®

Historical Romance™

Coming next month

THE PASSIONATE FRIENDS
by Meg Alexander

Book 3 of this exciting Regency trilogy: Dan's story

Dan was back. Judith hadn't seen him since she had
refused his proposal and now she was betrothed to
someone else. Dan clearly couldn't forget the past but
then, neither could Judith.

THE WAYWARD HEART
by Paula Marshall

Book 5 in Paula Marshall's Schuyler Family Chronicles

Nicholas had forsaken his family name and fortune to
pursue a career as an author and had fallen in love with
Verena Marlowe. But how could he convince her family
that he was good enough to marry without relying on
his family name?

On sale from 9th October 1998

Available from WH Smith, John Menzies and Volume One

JASMINE CRESSWELL

THE DAUGHTER

Maggie Slade's been on the run for seven years now.
Seven years of living without a life or a future because
she's a woman with a past. And then she meets Sean
McLeod. Maggie has two choices. She can either run,
or learn to trust again and prove her innocence.

"Romantic suspense at its finest."

—Affaire de Coeur

1-55166-425-9
**AVAILABLE IN PAPERBACK
FROM SEPTEMBER, 1998**

CHRISTIANE HEGGAN

SUSPICION

Kate Logan's gut instincts told her that neither of her
clients was guilty of murder, and homicide detective
Mitch Calhoon wanted to help her prove it. What neither suspected was how dangerous the truth would be.

*"Christiane Heggan delivers a tale that will leave you
breathless."*

—Literary Times

1-55166-305-8
AVAILABLE IN PAPERBACK
FROM SEPTEMBER, 1998

4 FREE

books and a surprise gift!

We would like to take this opportunity to thank you for reading this Mills & Boon® book by offering you the chance to take FOUR more specially selected titles from the Historical Romance™ series absolutely FREE! We're also making this offer to introduce you to the benefits of the Reader Service™—

- ★ FREE home delivery
- ★ FREE gifts and competitions
- ★ FREE monthly newsletter
- ★ Books available before they're in the shops
- ★ Exclusive Reader Service discounts

Accepting these FREE books and gift places you under no obligation to buy, you may cancel at any time, even after receiving your free shipment. Simply complete your details below and return the entire page to the address below. ***You don't even need a stamp!***

YES! Please send me 4 free Historical Romance books and a surprise gift. I understand that unless you hear from me, I will receive 4 superb new titles every month for just £2.99 each, postage and packing free. I am under no obligation to purchase any books and may cancel my subscription at any time. The free books and gift will be mine to keep in any case.

H8YE

Ms/Mrs/Miss/Mr.................................Initials ....
BLOCK CAPITALS PLEASE

Surname ....

Address ....

....

....Postcode...................................

Send this whole page to:
THE READER SERVICE, FREEPOST, CROYDON, CR9 3WZ
(Eire readers please send coupon to: P.O. BOX 4546, DUBLIN 24.)

SHANNON OCORK

SECRETS OF THE
TITANIC

**The voyage of the century
—where secrets, love and destiny collide.**

They were the richest of the rich, Rhode Island's
elite, their glittering jewels and polished manners
hiding tarnished secrets on a voyage that would
change their lives forever.

They had it all and everything to lose.

"Miss OCork is a natural writer and storyteller."
—New York Times Book Review

1-55166-401-1
MIRA Available from October 1998 in paperback